The Pixie
Effect

By
Allen (Pud) Deters

PROLOGUE

"Sounds like fun", laughed the pixie. "Count us in!"

"Your troubles will soon be over!" promised another.

They smiled beatifically, half a dozen of them, without a hint of mischief. But there was more than enough exuberance.

"This is no frivolous task", warned the Lord of Light. "The Unnaturals I speak of - trolls, witches, goblins, and others - may be in service to the Darkness. They are dangerous. Not for you to deal with! Leave that to your older kin, the larger fairies. You are asked only to spy them out, nothing more. No mischief!"

"Does that mean we're not allowed to enjoy our work?"

The pixies looked crestfallen, but the Lord pressed the point home: "That's for later. You will take joy and satisfaction from a job well done".

"But what if the doing is joyful?"

"Don't get carried away, pixies. Do you hear?"

They smiled beatifically again, for the thought of doing was already making them joyful. The Lord sent them down to earth and wondered how many more to send. Obviously they were the mischief, but quite a few would be needed. The earth was a big place.

In the event He brought forth quite a multitude of pixies out of the same leftover stardust from which He had created larger fairy folk before them. Pixies belong to that family, but with several traits of their very own: They are *all girls*, they are *smaller*, and they are *much less serious* compared to full-grown fairies. He put comet dust on their wings, giving them more natural light than larger fairies. They would need it where they were expected to go.

Results were mixed. The Lord's suspicions were confirmed about the *Unnaturals* who are indeed sponsored by the Darkness - that part of the Universe which will not accept the Light. To their credit, pixies exposed them exactly as the Lord wished. But they didn't stop there. They didn't stop at anything. They teased the creatures and turned it into a game of bravado. Unfortunately, many were caught and eaten. The flocks of pixies that once frolicked the earth dwindled into history. When the Age of Mankind arrived the last pixies removed themselves to the Night Sky with their fairy sisters seeking a quiet place of their own.

That's their tumultuous story. The comet-tail dressing was a bit much, perhaps. Comets are the show-offs of the heavens with their spectacular tails, and pixies lived up to their example in every way.

In the larger picture, vigilance faltered after their departure and Unnaturals reappeared in strength. But the Lord declined to send more pixies, leaving it to fairy folk themselves to meet the threat while their Age of the World lasted. That presented problems. The boys still dwelt on earth, whereabouts unknown, and couldn't be counted on, while the girls in the Night Sky had their own troubles. The duty lingered.

"Somehow, you must meet this challenge", the Lord reminded them not long ago. "It is part of your birthright in this world to resist the Darkness".

TABLE OF CONTENTS

PROLOGUE iii

Chapter 1 – THE STONE TROLLS 3

Chapter 2 – PIXIE TORTE 58

Chapter 3 – ISHI & COMPANY 71

Chapter 4 – THE DOORWARDS 103

Chapter 5 – THE STORM CROW 123

Chapter 6 – FOX AND KITS 158

Chapter 7 – THE WATER WITCH 186

Chapter 8 – THE JACKPOT 206

PART ONE

THE PIXIE EFFECT

CHAPTER

1

THE STONE TROLLS

Winter ended all in one day and spring came to the hill. Atel the hummingbird arrived with it in a rush of wind so warm and so early in the season that her chosen task did not seem farfetched.

She began her work immediately, collecting dust particles from under the brown grass. *There* was one she needed, and one more. There was a third. She gathered them and flew off to the pine thicket near the top of the hill. The trees were young, not as tall as she might wish for her purpose, but otherwise perfect: Open to both east and west, to sunrise and sunset. She placed the dust particles temporarily on a pinecone that hung in a sheltered nook. To her practiced eye they glowed faintly there, but so faintly that no one should notice. Then she went for more and kept on well into the evening.

The dust particles she searched for - the luminous ones - were easier to find at this hour and she found many, but hummingbirds cannot work forever on empty stomachs. It was time to visit a few lonely flowers of the early spring, brave stepchildren of the South Wind, before they closed for the night.

Later, when the world was asleep, she caught gossamer - the will-o-wisp strands that appear in the air where moonlight mixes with shadow - and began to weave the dust into a chrysalis. Days and nights were consumed in this labor until three were finished. They were fairy chrysalises, or would be when the time came, and the dust was fairy dust from one who had perished there. Nothing else will do, as the hummingbird well knew, and she meant to bring pixies back home to the Green Earth.

The chrysalises were all but invisible even at night, suspended from their branch, and only during a good breeze could they be seen at all. Then a soft sheen might flicker where the branch moved, and the moonlight caught them. Yet if anyone approached in daylight they appeared as ordinary pinecones, such was the craft of the weaver.

Only then did she tend seriously to her own needs, working the anemones, marsh marigolds and snowdrops while they lasted. She would need it in the days to come but she put something of the toughness and nourishment of the nectar into the chrysalises themselves, especially the snowdrops which are known to be a sign of renewal.

Then the weather turned. Rain and sleet came on a biting wind, and then snow and more snow. Yesterday's flowers were covered over and crushed under the drifts. There would be no more for a while and the hummingbird retreated to a perch near her planned nursery to wait it out; but as winter regained its grip her metabolism and active mind slowed down. There was no other way to survive.

Between fitful naps she worried about days being wasted. Summers were short anyway, this far north. Even if her task proved fruitful it would be nearly autumn before the chrysalises hatched. Time was fleeting. But the North Wind cared nothing for life of any kind and howled until she succumbed to stark dreams of swirling snow.

In her dreams tiny spirits came and shielded her heart against the deathly weather. It was the impinima, the heartwarmers, who adopted her. Lost spirits themselves, they are drawn to others who are lost, or nearly so, and thereby the hummingbird survived until the weather changed once more.

All in one night it changed for the better. The North Wind faltered and failed. The South Wind returned with a vengeance. By morning the snow was melting, and a fragile scent of spring returned to the air; but more was coming, much more. Atel waited.

All day the South Wind blew mightily. By evening the air felt almost balmy but Atel never stirred, waiting and watching the chrysalises until fresh clouds covered over the moon. Then she slept.

In the morning the Storm Crow passed overhead with his warning. It rained, the first warm rain of spring, and it thundered. As the rolling thunder reached new crescendos it lifted her spirits and drove winter away for good. She closed her eyes against the lightning and luxuriated in the change of seasons.

When the storm moved on she knew something had happened in the nursery. It felt different. She hovered near the chrysalises most of the afternoon reflecting warm sunlight onto them with her 'mirror', her metallic breast feathers, and was rewarded by faint stirrings within.

<hr>

That was then.

Now, at the end of summer, the pixie babes would soon hatch. Atel knew them well already - Airy, Lolly and Poo - from a long season of nanny duty. Babes in the chrysalis will not grow without nectar, naturally; nor learn anything sensible without a teacher; nor live long enough to hatch at all, maybe, without a nanny. There are many ordinary perils for pixies in the chrysalis, not to mention extraordinary ones.

The babes had survived two ordinary perils already: A woodpecker had pecked holes in the chrysalises one fine spring day trying to get at the 'bugs' inside; and just now - during the night - a lightning bolt had struck the nearby knob of the hill, the highest open ground. Fortunately, it missed their tree and only scared the babes speechless.

The hummingbird had not been so lucky and sprawled senseless in the grass near the strike, thrown violently down by the bolt. She lay motionless there, her addled brain unable to focus, until the storm moved on. Finally quietude returned. Fragments of thought tried to organize in her mind but were interrupted by heavy footsteps and rude voices.

"Looky here! That's where it hit".

"Be careful there, Laddie".

"Yeah... Ooo! Still hot!"

Two huge creatures stood framed against the full moon. The lightning bolt had blasted a shallow pit on the rocky knob. It still smoked and 'Laddie', the larger of the two, couldn't resist testing it with a finger. He licked it now and the other laughed at him.

"You'll learn! Do what I say".

"Yeah - hey! Let's have a fire".

"No. She'll want a look-about when she wakes up. We can't have smoke up our nose".

"A drink then. At least that".

"One won't hurt. Here now, hold the rock".

He tossed a stone about the size and shape of his big nose. The other quickly dropped a burlap bag and caught the stone with his unburnt hand. "Can't I set it down?"

"If you don't forget where you set it. Mustn't step on it, Laddie. She wouldn't like that at all!" He laughed again. This was 'Jag', known mostly as 'the Juggler'. That was for the flagon that usually hung from his forefinger, as it did now. Or maybe it was for habitually tossing it back and forth, from one hand to the other. He was a foot or two shorter than 'Laddie' and not as massive, but clearly the boss. Jag had a droopy nose and droopy ears that constantly twisted in all directions, listening.

The other had wide, almost goblinish ears, and loose flakes of skin on his head and arms that laid flat or stood up like the hair on your neck when he was nervous. They stood up now. The Juggler treated him as a juvenile, but old enough to drink. All trolls drink, even 2-year-olds like Laddie. That's what they were: Trolls. And that's when they're most troublesome: Drunk. Jag uncorked the jug and they both had a pull at it.

Yes, they were trolls. Even the hummingbird could see that with her addled brain. Trolls of the worst kind, too. These were the great stone trolls who come out of their holes when the sun goes down. Seeing them now, a memory at nagged her. She felt an instinctive fear of them. Trolls were bad. But why? Something beyond their awful smell and bad manners troubled her.

"Another snort to sharpen the senses?" suggested the young troll. He didn't have to ask twice. Jag passed the jug, and while he had both hands free laid a finger alongside his nose and blew it out onto the ground like a lout. He wiped his nose on his arm and accepted the jug back politely, as a gentleman might accept a goblet of wine, swirling the brew slowly and lovingly. Then he drained it all in one quaff and sniffed the night air.

"Pixies", he whispered. "I smell 'em".

It all came rushing back to the hummingbird: The babes, the storm, everything! Trolls of any kind are horribly dangerous to fairy folk. Boy fairies - miners and treasure hunters by trade - are held for ransom, sometimes for centuries. That's rough, but at least they aren't eaten. It's worse for the girls who are considered a delicacy, the sweetest of treats. Pixies, the smallest ones, are preferred, being just the right size to stubbornly stick to the palate and prolong the delicious taste before they are swallowed. And pixies in the chrysalis are doubly preferred, having consumed the very sweetest nectars. Only one treat could top it: Fairy wing frosting! But that was off-limits to ordinary trolls. The Troll-Mother wanted the wings, and she didn't use them for frosting.

Mind you, fairies are not easily captured. They are very elusive. But they're also rash and daring - especially the *pixies* who tease the big trolls every chance they get. So trouble is common - or used to be when pixie lasses were plentiful on earth. In those days, trolls learned a simple trick. They watched for the lightning during storms. Fairy girls often frequent the highest ground for a better view of the stars, and that's where the lightning strikes. So, whenever lightning bolts favored one hill more than others, the trolls guessed: *Fairies! An*d they paid a visit after dark, like these ruffians were doing now.

The young troll sniffed and shook his head. "Don't smell anything".

"You don't know what they smell like. You've never smelled any - or et any! Maybe we can fix that tonight".

"But Mum gets the wings, hey? After *we* do all the work?"

"We ain't done any work yet, Laddie. Anyhow, she's the best tracker".

"Could you sniff 'em out?"

"Probably".

Moonlight bounced off the young troll's eyes like fire. He licked his lips. Jag put a quick finger to his own.

"Leave it there, Kiddo. She might hear you".

"She can't hear nuthin'. How could she? That's her nose!"

As if to prove him wrong, the stone he had set down began to make popping noises and break open, growing larger and turning itself inside-out. A black boot popped free attached to a skinny, hairy leg, and kicked at the young troll. A buttocks cheek was next, followed by a pause. Obviously, the stone was giving birth to something and having a bit of trouble with breech delivery. There was a muffled oath, a loud 'pop', and the rest came: A pint-sized witch rolled out wearing a black dress and squashed, pointy hat. One hand still gripped the stone tightly, and the stone turned out to be the nose on her face.

She ignored the trolls while she straightened the hat and adjusted her dress. Then she stretched luxuriously and blew a bit of fresh air under each arm. That made her feel like a Lady. She smiled and turned to the trolls, but her eyes went to the empty jug and the smile vanished. She shook an angry finger at the Juggler.

"...And never saved a drop for your dear Mum? That's not what you've been taught!"

"Didn't think you'd want any, Mum. Turns out we've got trackin' to do".

Mum paused and sniffed the breeze, her huge nose bobbing and weaving. The smile returned, half-hidden underneath it. Her proboscis was bigger even than the Juggler's but appeared now to have softened somewhat with her mood. It stuck out on a short stem, then bulged into the shape of a huge potato with several warts, drooping almost to her chin when at rest.

It wasn't at rest now. Atel, still sprawled in the grass nearby, felt a twinge of alarm. She shook her head to clear it and tried moving her free wing. It hurt but wasn't broken. The other wing moved also when she rolled off it, but dizziness returned. She closed her eyes, and it went away, but alarm bells rang again. She had seen that nose before, hadn't she? Oh, yes! On Ishi, the Troll- Mother.

9

Ishi was meant to be the 13th witch in a Coven of 12, invited by the Great Witches to fill a lesser role back in an earlier Age. She had refused and gone on to become greater than any of them by spawning the race of stone trolls. It was her grand triumph but also a source of headaches and exasperation. They didn't mind their 'Mum' very well.

"Yes, something's in the air", she whispered presently. "Good boys! Have you found a trail?"

"No, Mum. Been waiting for you".

Mum scowled again at the empty jug and without a word put her nose to the ground. The nose, being larger than the brain, took over from that point, snuffling in different directions, searching for a clear trail to follow. Usually this works. Fairies do leave a faint scent and trolls quickly find it. Tonight, it didn't work. No fairies had lately been about the immediate grounds, but the nose did pull Ishi toward the pine woods. The trolls followed in the same manner, noses nearly on the ground, rumps wiggling high in the air as if bidding farewell to the hummingbird.

Atel looked away, but at least the wiggling rumps posed no danger. The other end was the worrisome one. Their noses suspected something and would undoubtedly smell fairy dust in the open grass below the pines. She hadn't collected it all. That would lead them nowhere, but the chrysalises weren't far away. They were high up, perhaps higher than the trolls could reach, but would surely have a trace of scent about them unless the wind took it away. Tonight there was some breeze.

She took to the air and found that she could fly. Dizziness returned but when she closed one eye it gave a clearer picture. Good! She must have a chat with Ishi, her first in several years. The Troll Mother was an infrequent visitor and an unpleasant one.

"Good evening madam", she offered in greeting. "May I be of help?" Ishi didn't even bother to look.

"Scram!"

"Hunting fairies again, I presume? Sorry. The scent is old, but I'm sure you know that".

Ishi ignored her.

"They were here a few weeks ago", Atel lied. "The usual fellows. Would you like me to take a message?"

Ishi slowly straightened up, putting a hand behind her back for leverage as her nose struggled to stay down in the grass. The nose finally gave up and pouted, sagging onto her chin. Ishi talked around it.

"Still here, 'little boss'? I'm surprised. How long do hummingbirds live?"

"It depends, madam. My relatives are very long-lived".

"Mine too, but we don't follow the same rules. What's your secret?"

"Oh, just live a clean life. Be nice to strangers. Share advice sparingly".

"Yeah. So here you still are, full of it".

"The hill is my summer home. I feel obliged to help visitors".

"You're a pest".

"If you say so, but we still have to deal with each other".

That wasn't easy. Their differences were fundamental. Atel (A fairy once, in another Age) came from the bright stardust originally; Ishi (and all witches) were spit out from an unclean layer of our own atmosphere. There was no love lost between them.

Ishi looked away and grunted something at the trolls who were still traipsing after their noses. They grunted in reply and moved up to the pines where they began shaking the trees. Ishi watched Atel's reaction. It was casual.

"Birds are nesting in those trees", she commented. "Doves and others. They poop when disturbed. Your boys will learn".

"Won't care. They're big boys".

That's where Mum was wrong. They quit the rough stuff when the doves splattered them, but searched on through the pines anyway, paying attention even to the high branches. That was unsettling. Atel pretended not to notice and made chit-chat with their Mum.

"I've met the one with the jug, but not the other", she said. "Is he new around here?"

"My youngest". Ishi couldn't conceal her pride. "Handsome, that one!"

"If you say so. Does he have a name?"

"No. I don't name any of them. They pick up nicknames".

"Okay. I'll call them *half-wits*, then. They'll never sneak up on a fairy-lad with those loud snuffling noses. Fairies can hear it a mile away".

"Tell it to the boys. Here they come".

The Juggler was less pleased even than his Mum to see the hummingbird. Trolls never forgive and never forget. The bird brought back irritating memories.

"You should leave the body-painting to your mother", laughed Atel in greeting. "It runs when you do it. Look at each other!"

The trolls did look, reactively, and that made them angrier. Not even trolls enjoy unclean dribbles down their foreheads - or having it pointed out. That was the idea. Atel had bugged them in the past until they got mad and went away. The big lunks couldn't catch her and it infuriated them. They were furious now, but Ishi grunted sharply and held up a bony finger of authority. No one else in the world could restrain them, but she could – in person. The trolls held their tongues. Atel smiled at their Mum.

"Will you be staying long?" she asked sweetly. She expected an unpleasant answer and got one.

"A while. We're taking a holiday. The boys are going to brew some beer".

They broke up a fallen tree and built a huge fire over the pit where the bolt had struck, then roasted a whole hog over the coals. Beer was missing from the occasion, but trolls enjoy gluttony almost as much, and other vices too. If there's any kind of wrongdoing they haven't enjoyed, well, they just haven't thought of it yet.

Atel watched for a while from the edge of the pines, thinking the boys had overdone the fire (or *would,* some night), and certainly the noise. They were ungodly loud. The hill was isolated and remote but there were farms and humans not many miles away. Some farmer would be missing a large hog come morning, and probably several more before the 'boys' finished brewing their beer. Good home brew takes time. Her nerves would be frayed and others in the neighborhood might be up in arms before the troll's holiday came to an end.

She counted her blessings out of habit: First, trolls are creatures of the night - not counting Ishi who was a problem at any hour - and secondly, the pixie babes were just the opposite. That would help. The babes were noisemakers too, for their size, but the trolls would be gone during the day. Thirdly, of the two trolls only the Juggler was really dangerous. And fourthly, the babes might hatch any day. As soon as their wings dried they would fly and be safe. Things could be worse.

When the sun came up in the morning the trolls were gone. Ishi seemed to be gone too, although that was hard to be sure of. Atel knew her habits and the hill was littered with rocks. She might have folded herself into any of them or gone underground with her 'Boys'. The little witch was unpredictable, but her trolls could not survive in the sunlight.

All that remained of their camp was trampled grass on a rocky knob where the grass was poor anyway, and a few scattered bones that coyotes would soon run off with. The coals were burned out and covered over. No one would find anything unusual even if they had

been curious about a strange fire during the night. That's a troll's life nowadays. Most of the world belongs to humans, but the night still belongs to them.

Atel searched for clues to where they had disappeared but found nothing. A number of sinkholes dotted the surrounding area and the trolls likely used one of them. Sinkholes are their front doors and lead to places a hummingbird wouldn't want to go.

Her search ate into the morning a little, but the babes weren't early risers anyway. They needed their sleep and usually got it because the hill was out-of-the-way and quiet. Atel expected to find them in good moods but was met with the opposite.

Troll noise was to blame. The three had slept through the racket but it upset their dreams and they were crabby. Just now as their Nanny arrived with morning nectar an argument turned into tears. Poo, the redhead, had freckles. Airy (the blond) and dark-haired Lolly were laughing about the freckles this fine morning. Atel knew it would happen one day, and this was the day. She swallowed the nectar herself - none of the girls wanted to eat anyway - and seized their attention.

"Freckles are *beauty spots*", she informed them, and began a story.

The Ugly Girl

There was a handsome prince in a kingdom by the sea who rode his horse each day along the shore. He was a fine lad (if anyone cared) but mainly he was heir to the throne. That's what drew the girls, especially the rich ones. All the daughters of all the richest families plotted to marry him and become queen.

The rich girls had no work to do so they spent their days lolling on the beach working on their tans, hoping to catch his eye as he rode past. But the prince was shy and galloped by.

One day the king, a spendthrift who had depleted the Royal Treasury, called his son before the throne.

"It's time you married!" he decreed. "Choose a wife from among the girls on the beach, for they are the prettiest in the land!" ("...and the *richest*, too!" he thought pleasantly, but said nothing about that.)

Even a prince must take orders from the crown, so he looked closer the next day, but it only confused him.

"I can't decide", he told his father. "They are all very pretty, but also very much alike".

The king smiled and quietly spread the gossip, so the girls all set out to be different. It caused trouble at the beauty parlors, but no two girls looked alike afterward; and to keep it that way they hired the stylists and beauticians to attend them right at the beach, putting the parlors out of business.

On a tip from the king, the richest girl of all ordered ice fetched down from the mountains for lemonade, the prince's favorite treat, and veiled an ugly peasant girl to serve it in her tent. But the prince didn't stop the first day, nor the second.

On the third day, the ugly girl was put to work out front fanning her mistress under the hot sun. When the prince came galloping the mistress said, "Girl, run quick and bring him a cool drink, compliments of your Lady".

Knowing she would be whipped if she failed, the girl ran swiftly and stopped the prince by leaping recklessly in front of his horse.

"Girl, you were lucky not to be killed!" exclaimed the prince when he had gotten the horse under control.

"I'm lucky to be alive at all", she laughed. "That's what they all say".

"Why do they say that?"

"Because I'm the ugliest girl in the kingdom", laughed the peasant girl, and offered the cool drink, un-spilled, because she moved more gracefully than one would expect from such a loathsome thing; and the prince accepted the drink, being charmed by the laughing blue eyes.

"It's very warm today", he replied curiously. "Why do you wear such heavy clothing?"

"I must!" said the girl. "It's but a small price to pay so others can be happy".

"I don't understand", said the prince.

"It's my ugliness, Your Highness. The sight of me would make others *un*happy, so it's best if I cover up". But she laughed, and her eyes were shining, and they talked on, and the ice melted before he finished the drink, which was not lost on her mistress who watched from the pavilion.

Next morning early the mistress took her seat in front of the mirror, and while the stylists and beauticians worked their magic she summoned the peasant girl. "Invite the prince inside today", she ordered crossly. "I shall serve the drink myself!"

So the girl did, and the prince accepted. The peasant girl quickly took her place with a fan while her mistress curtsied and welcomed the prince. Another servant poured lemonade but the mistress herself added the rare ice. Unfortunately, she wasn't used to such a menial job, and it splashed spectacularly up into the prince's face.

"Oh!" was all she could say or do, and every servant but one stood stiff as their mistress; but the ugly girl, laughing at the silly mishap, offered a towel which the prince gladly accepted, and the awkward moment passed.

The mistress regained her composure and entertained the prince with music, hors d'ourves and polite conversation, but his eyes strayed often to the peasant girl, and this was obvious to everyone. The following day the girl was gone, sent off to the mountains with the ice detail, but the prince asked about her.

"Sent on an errand with other servants", replied the mistress shortly. "They'll be gone for days".

When the prince looked disappointed she pouted. "Why ask about her? Am *I* not beautiful?"

16

"You are", he replied, for indeed she was. "But I wish to speak with that one again".

"Then you must stop each day and see about her!" said the mistress, confident she could turn his eye.

The prince did stop regularly, but only to inquire about the ugly servant girl and then leave again, commenting, "You are lucky to have her".

"She is lucky to be alive at all!" the mistress exploded one day. "She is the ugliest girl in the kingdom! Didn't you know?"

But when she saw the prince was offended she ordered the girl fetched (for she had been stashed at a nearby villa since returning days earlier), and the prince asked questions in the meanwhile about her unsightliness. Had there been an accident? Had she been burned, or scalded? Or taken a bad fall? What was the nature of her disfigurement?

"No accident", replied the rich mistress in her coolest tones. "Nor any tragedy at all except her birth. She was born with the abnormality".

But how is it she smiles and laughs, even so?"

"Who can say?" the mistress shrugged irritably. "Dogs are just the same. They don't know any better".

Finally, the ugly one was brought forth. She bowed quickly, then stood proudly as always, and the prince knew it was her by her merry eyes. But the mistress in a fit of petulance ordered servants to tear away the veil - and lo! The girl was not deformed as such, but thoroughly plastered with brown spots. The mistress quickly averted her eyes.

"See then, Highness!" she wailed. "The girl is *freckled!* I would have spared you the sight!"

"I find her to be...not ugly at all!" said the prince, amazed.

"First time anyone said *that!*" laughed the girl.

"Then I will say more", the prince went on. "I find you beautiful inside and out, which is rare in this kingdom".

Atel finished the tale and Poo was smiling, but the others were puzzled.

"Where do freckles come from?" asked Airy.

"They happen when there's so much beauty inside there isn't room for it all. Some must come out and freckles are the beauty marks".

"An' will Poo grow up to marry a handsome prince - *but we won't?*" asked Lolly.

"I have no idea, but it's been said that girls with freckles are lucky in love".

"Can we get them too?"

"I doubt it. Poo has red hair like the servant girl, and redheads often get freckles. But who knows? If you're nice to others and it builds up inside you, it could come out as freckles one day".

She left them with that thought and went for nectar. The babes needed a lot now, and wild roses were beginning to bloom. The nectar is very tangy, but fairy lasses need this. Atel hoped they would swallow it, but they didn't. They made faces and spit it out.

"You *do* want to marry princes, don't you?" said Atel angrily. "Nectar of the rose will give you *radiance,* which boys can't resist.

You'll meet boys someday and there will only be one chance to make a great first impression. Rose will give you that chance, but not if you spit it out!"

She went for more and on inspiration gathered several ripe strawberries too, the tiny ones that like sandy ground near the edge of a wood. She put drops of rose nectar on them and it almost solved the problem. The babes loved the strawberries! But then they tasted the rose and spit everything out.

What more could a nanny do? "Somehow you must swallow it", she insisted. "It's your best chance at true radiance".

"Does that mean we're *not* beautiful now?" asked Airy.

"No, of course you are. All babies are beautiful. But some lose it as they grow older".

"An' what is strawberry for?"

"It is said to give foresight. A glimpse of things to come".

"All I can see is Poo with her handsome prince", grumbled Lolly.

What more can a nanny say? She dropped the subject and went for more strawberries. But when she returned to the nursery only Poo showed her face in her window, so she got the strawberries. What of the others? Were they asleep?

"No", explained Poo. "They are covering their faces because th'don't have freckles. Th'say they are the ugliest girls in the kingdom".

On that note the hummingbird decided to take the rest of the morning off from nanny duty, and part of the afternoon also, to serve herself. First on her list was breakfast, and then lunch. She chose bee balm, as much as she could drink of it, because it was the most tenacious flower on the hill during hot weather and the quality came through in the nectar. Tenacity would be much needed in the days ahead. A late summer heat wave was settling in, hot and dry. New flowers wouldn't last long and competition for them was heating up with the weather. Bees are always numerous late in summer, and they were everywhere, staking their claims to the blossoms. She was bigger than they, but as everyone knows, that means nothing to a bee. By mid-afternoon it was a battle out there and way past time to feed the babes anyway (exactly as she intended). She brought bee balm, which they were beginning to tire of, but there wasn't much else on a hot afternoon in late summer. They would have to put up with it. The nectar itself was supposed to encourage 'putting up with it', but that wasn't working.

"Think of it as a blessing", Atel advised them. "There's nothing else. You would have to go hungry without it".

There were frowns but no bad behavior. Atel went for more in better spirits. The problem today wasn't really their fault anyway, just bad dreams and lack of sleep. Those problems might become common now and the hummingbird was unsure how much to tell them about their new neighbors, or if she should say anything at all. But they brought it up themselves. It didn't surprise her. Fairies and trolls have been natural enemies for ages. Even in slumber, troll noise would leave an impression.

"There are monsters in th'woods", confided Airy. "We thought you should know".

"You have seen them?"

"We dreamed of them last night. Th'stink!". The babes could still smell it and so could Atel. It's a lot like skunk and hangs around a while, just like skunk.

"What did they look like?"

The pixies all pitched in, describing the Juggler and the young troll perfectly, and wanted to know more. There was no use beating around the bush.

"Yes, they were here", confirmed Atel. "They were looking for fairies. They may be back tonight".

"Why?"

"They *eat* fairies. They especially crave small pixies like you".

The faces disappeared from their windows.

"Not me", came Airy's voice. "Th'won't catch me".

"Why not? You can't fly. Your wings aren't ready".

"Th'feel strong!"

"Try to bust out, then".

She couldn't. None of them could. Call it magic, or call it nature's way, but a chrysalis knows. It will not yield until the occupant is strong enough to be out in the world.

"You're stuck here yet for a while", said Atel. "So you must not attract their attention! They are excellent hunters and will take notice of noise or movement, no matter how small. But their noses are the worst danger. They've already smelled fairies in this area - not you, but others who come here sometimes - and the scent will keep them here for a while. I don't think they suspect *you* just yet. Your chrysalises are hard to see and will help to contain your scent. Just be warned".

"The one thing in our favor is, your schedules are different. You are for the daytime and the big trolls come out at night, so our days can be normal. You can eat and grow, and probably even hatch and be safe before they find you! Isn't that nice?" The babes were thinking it over, so Atel went on.

"That still leaves their Mum, however. Did the Troll-Mother get into your dreams? Think very carefully. Ishi is smaller than her 'boys' and wears clothes".

She hadn't, and Atel breathed a sigh of relief. It meant they were likely safe for now. Big trolls have no magic about them. Their racket can get into anyone's dreams, and that's all there is to it. But Ishi is a witch of sorts. If *she* comes into your dreams it means she's become aware of your thought, that she knows who you are and where you are, and her boys will come for you. She is very clever, very low key about it. If you realize she's in your dream you can kick her out. But many victims don't remember her when they wake up in the morning.

Atel brought fresh sprigs of yarrow and wove them into the pine needles about the nursery, replacing the dry ones from yesterday. The plant afforded some protection against witchery, according to folklore. It had long been used to shield young children in their beds, so maybe there was some truth to it.

After that until near sundown she fetched bee balm nectar and heard no complaints about it. It was a race now against the trolls, and against the frost too. Free fairies don't mind cold at all, but a frost in September could still hurt babes in the chrysalis. By sundown they were stuffed with warm nectar, trolls were forgotten, and by all appearances the three had drifted into happy dreams. Darkness spread over the hill from east to west. The first fireflies appeared. It was troll time.

———————◆◆◆◆———————

Atel waited at the nursery for the inevitable bonfire to flare up signaling their arrival. Trolls are known primarily for three things, she reminded herself: Felonies, misdemeanors, and bonfires, in no particular order. And they are careless with the fire. If there was any saving grace to the lightning bolt it's that it struck where it did, on a rocky knob with little grass. Even a big bonfire wasn't likely to spread from there. Now she heard heavy footsteps from beyond the knob, from the direction of the sinkholes. They certainly weren't trying to sneak up on anyone tonight. But the bonfire wasn't their very first order of business. Firewood was. They needed a bunch of it and looked no further than the pines.

A dead pine stood at the near edge of the woods and the young troll busied himself breaking off branches while the Juggler watched, idly tossing his jug back and forth. Atel decided to say hello.

"Good evening, noisy ones. You are keeping me awake".

"Get used to it", replied the Juggler.

"Only a troll could get used to it. Where's 'Mum' tonight?"

"Here & there. Mostly 'there' by the looks of it, hey?" He flashed his fangs, the equivalent of a smile. A drip of saliva hinted at his true thoughts. Trolls *do* eat their enemies, of course, and the worst ones taste the best - namely the maddening little pixies. Atel would fit nicely into that group.

"I'd have sold you some firewood if you asked. You didn't have to steal it".

"We like it this way. Stolen firewood burns better 'cause it's already '*hot*', get it?" The Juggler laughed at his little joke. So did the young troll, who had by now gathered a big armful of dry branches and started back to the knob where they were setting up camp again. The Juggler followed. Atel followed him.

"All the same, I'll expect some payment", she persisted.

"Send us a bill, little boss. That'll burn too".

The trolls quickly got a small fire going and set up their spit. Tonight, a huge kettle would hang there instead of the usual roasting carcass.

"Soup?" inquired Atel. "Are you turning vegetarian? I know some good recipes".

"You might call it that", drawled the Juggler. "We're gonna brew beer. But I'll use my own recipe". He passed his hand through the flames and smiled in satisfaction. "Kindling's going good. Now the big stuff! What do you charge for green firewood?"

"I don't sell it. It doesn't burn well".

"It'll have to do. Put it on our tab. Let's go, Laddie".

The young troll grinned. He was big for his age, big for any age. His Mum had painted him that way - big and ugly - on a cave wall and awakened him, then watched with pride as her brawny toddler broke out from the wall. Now, as a 2-year-old, the lad delighted in breaking things: Rocks were fun. Animals were fun. Trees were the most fun, especially pine trees with lots of branches!

He went to work barehanded on the first live tree and soon encountered difficulty, but that was part of the fun. Green branches don't snap off like dead ones. They have to be twisted and jerked, shaking the whole tree. The Juggler laughed and watched the lad play for a while. Atel backed off nervously. The nursery was close to this upper side of the woods. How many trees stood as a buffer? Only four or five. And now the young troll, a bit frustrated, turned and eyed the next one. But the Juggler tossed him a hatchet.

"We ain't got all night, lad! Use this. You've seen me use it. Watch your fingers now! If you chop them off, you won't get 'em back".

Laddie went after the stubborn branches with renewed enthusiasm. Permission to use the hatchet! Wow! It was the first time, and an accident happened immediately. On the back swing he smacked himself on top of the head, opening a gash. Blood and profanity flowed freely. The Juggler took a look, pronounced it a 'scratch', and rubbed dry dirt into the wound to stop the bleeding. It worked, and Laddie's technique improved from there. Practice makes perfect.

"He can talk, huh?" commented Atel. "I didn't know".

"Sure he can talk", replied the Juggler fondly. The young troll was a pet project of his, like a baby brother almost. "He's a little bashful but he knows all the right words. A fine lad! Don't bug him. Leave him alone, get it?"

"Gladly. I don't know enough cuss words anyway".

"You soon will if you hang around. By the way, I hope you had a nice day? Seen any fairies for us?"

"Nope. If they show up they'd smell you anyway. Do you realize how bad you stink?"

"Everyone has body odor. You're small so the stink is small, but you still stink".

"If you say so, but mine won't spook the fairies. Yours will. You'll have to trap them".

"No problem. We've done it before".

"What did you use for bait?"

"None 'o your business, little boss".

"Oh, come now! The fairies will pick up your scent at the trap. There's only one bait that might tempt them past it".

"Like you're going to give us a tip?" The Juggler chuckled in his throat, a foul, grating sound.

"I'd do a lot of things to get rid of you".

Atel felt his dark look, then it shifted. The young troll was finished up as high as he could reach and swinging wildly at a higher limb. The pine looked like a palm tree now. Only a tuft of small branches remained at the very top. The Juggler shouted to get his attention.

"That'll do! Gather it all up now and let's get a real fire going". That would be Laddie's job. The Juggler grabbed his hatchet back and, with the jug too, had his hands full.

The fire smoldered when they piled green branches on, but when a flame reappeared it flared up wildly through the needles. Sparks scattered everywhere and caught the grass on fire, but the trolls stomped it out. In the old days they might let it go and just watch the fun, but not in the modern world. Home-brewing takes a week at least and mustn't be interrupted by fire trucks.

While the fire burned down the trolls went for water. Atel appraised the damage in the pines and did some figuring. She had observed beer-making before. There were many recipes, but it usually came down to whatever was handy for ingredients and the timetable didn't vary much. The brewmaster would start 'tasting' in a couple days, but good brew takes longer. In the meantime the trolls would be back every night building a new bonfire. At the rate of one tree for each fire they would easily reach the nursery tree, working in a straight line - or they might strip a dozen other trees instead, or miss a night or two. And the babes would hatch any day now. The odds were on her side, but she wasn't gambling with her own life here.

The trolls returned and hung a huge crock of water to boil, then the Juggler got out recipe cards from his pack and leafed through them. He was a chef by trade, having worked in the Royal Kitchen for a whole Age before 'retiring' to the country. Word was that he'd been fired for drinking the King's beer. Another story had it that he tried to poison the King. Whatever it was, the fare at the Royal Table suffered when he left. He was an excellent cook when he had the ingredients. But tonight he would have to improvise.

He needed grits and didn't have any, but corn was ripening in the fields and he sent the young troll to fetch some. In the meantime he wandered over to the pines to gather up a few branches that lay about. As he started back to the camp his nose became animated. He paused, sniffing at a variable breeze, and Atel zipped over to interrupt his thought.

"Do I stink *that* bad?" she asked. "I never knew until tonight".

"You do, but it ain't you I'm smelling".

"Yourself, then?"

"Funny bird. Just shut up now".

She did, but the moment was gone. The nose calmed down and the troll with it. He went back to camp, added a branch to the fire, then got out a tin can and pried off the lid. He sniffed the contents and set it carefully by the fire - not too close, not too far away - to warm a bit while he reviewed his recipe again. He frowned, studying it.

"Missing something?" Atel asked politely.

"A few things. But here he comes with the corn! We're in business!"

The young troll trotted up with his burlap bag and held it open for inspection, eager to please. The ears were ripe, already husked. The Juggler nodded approvingly and looked for a bowl to shell them into, but Laddie dumped the whole ears right into the boiling crock. He got barked at for that, tripped and fell backward, and broke the support post. The spit dropped and the big crock spilled, fortunately splashing the hot water away from the fire and himself. But in the melee the tin can was overturned.

"My *starter!*" bellowed the Juggler, quickly tipping it back up. Too late! The contents were already lost, dribbling into cracks in the ground. He went to his knees and scooped with his hands but all he salvaged was some mud. It was the brewing yeast, saved from the last batch but now lost in the ashes. Both trolls sat down in silence. Now Laddie's nose began to twitch. Atel had a bad feeling about all this. If they couldn't make beer, what would they do with their evening? Trolls are very active at night.

"That's a shame", she offered. "I actually am sorry. I was curious about your recipe".

"Just you wait", growled the Juggler. "I'll figure something out".

"Well, I can't wait all night. I do enjoy watching a good recipe come together even if it's just beer, but you seem to be running out of ingredients. I take it that was the yeast?"

As she spoke he was sizing up the meager remnant in the can, shaking his head. "It was", he admitted. "This won't do".

Atel balanced things out in her mind. On one side she pictured trolls brewing and drinking their beer with all the resulting noise and bluster by the campfire. On the other side she saw crafty, sober trolls with nothing better to do than poke around in the pine woods. It was an easy choice.

"You *are* a Master Chef", she ventured. "Are you not?"

"I am. But this ain't a food recipe".

"But you must have *baker's* yeast in that bag of yours? You could substitute that".

"Ya think? It ain't the same, quite".

"It'll work, but it works better when it's warmer. Set it by the fire".

She got a dirty look. "You makin' fun of me, little boss?"

"Not this time. You know how baker's yeast is".

"I do, but I purely don't trust you! Do you know a recipe that'll work with it - or are you just flappin' in my face?"

"I know an old one, but it might turn out a bit strong. I hope you don't mind".

The Juggler actually giggled. "You don't know much about trolls. No, we don't mind".

"Good. It starts with barley. Do you have barley?"

"Nah. Oats will have to do".

"Well, that's starting off wrong. Barley is better".

"There's none to be had. No one grows it anymore". He waved at the lands all about, shifting the blame to the local farmers. "We can't steal what they ain't got".

"I suppose not".

"Shouldn't make much difference. We'll make one little substitution, but we'll still follow your recipe".

While he was talking he sent the young troll for more water and got busy repairing the barbecue apparatus, straightening the heavy metal spit, and stacking flat rocks to replace the broken post. Then he unbound a gunny sack full of oats and reached in to feel the condition of the grain. He cursed about it.

"Dry as a bone! The lad brung the wrong sack".

"Not sprouted?"

"No! Now we'll have to make 'quick beer'".

"You can't make malt out of that in one night. It has to start growing!"

"We'll skip the malt".

"You *can't!* It all starts with malt and the right enzymes".

"Well, we need to take a shortcut. But it'll still be your recipe".

Atel left in disgust to scout tomorrow's flowers but came back later out of curiosity. The big crock was aboil again and the Juggler was scooping handfuls of dry oats into it while the young troll cracked corn kernels in the bowl. The mood in camp had turned festive and the Juggler hailed her good-naturedly.

"Hey, you! C'mere! It's time to watch your recipe come together".

"It's not mine anymore", answered Atel, keeping her distance. Both trolls were obviously chewing tobacco.

"Oh, bosh! You'll get the credit, but it better turn out good!"

The Juggler laughed. He'd been 'out in the country' for many years now and had wide experience with different folk. He enjoyed matching wits with the hummingbird and was truly grateful for the tip about baker's yeast. Okay then! In with the cracked corn and the rest of the oats! Chaff foamed over the side of the crock and flared in the fire as the heavier grain submerged into the boiling water. Then the trolls made themselves comfortable, the young troll on a stump he'd dragged in from somewhere, the Juggler on an upside-down kettle.

They got out plug tobacco to pass the time while the mash boiled, occasionally spitting into the crock. This they did on purpose and called each other out for a miss. Atel retreated to a tall bee balm flower and looked away.

"Don't worry about your recipe!" the Juggler called after her. "We're puttin' the proper juices into the wort".

"My recipe called for enzymes, not acids".

"Well, we skipped the malt, remember? We gotta substitute something".

There was no answer, nor was any expected. Presently the mash foamed over again, and the Juggler announced, "That'll do!"

They sprang into action, the young troll holding a burlap bag over a kettle while the Juggler poured the hot mash through it to filter out the solids. They scalded their fingers a bit but that's not as serious with trolls and is considered a small price to pay for such an important project.

"There! We've got the *wort!*" the Juggler shouted over to the hummingbird. "*Now* what?"

"Hops, of course. But you may as well skip it. This batch will have bitterness and aroma anyway".

"That's good because we ain't got any hops. But we can still follow your recipe and just use gentian root instead, for the 'bitters'. Old-timers used to do that in a pinch".

"If you say so".

"Yup, and that's not all it's good for..." (he popped some root into his mouth as well) "...it gets rid of gas. Makes grumpy folk cheerful! You should try some". He broke some root into the kettle and added a few whole plants, then set the new kettle up on the spit with a grunt, releasing some of that gas. He hurriedly fanned the fumes away from the fire and winked at the hummingbird.

Atel ignored him but it was getting a lot to ignore. Only a few minutes went by before both trolls started fidgeting. "Now, little boss", wondered the Juggler, "how long should the hops boil, d'ya think?"

"If it *was* hops, several hours".

"Well, that's too long! We'll tweak your recipe and take it off the fire now, but we'll leave the root in there. That amounts to the same thing".

"If you say so".

"Don't put words in my mouth, little boss! This is *your* recipe, not mine! Now then: What next? How cool should the wort be a'fore we dump in the yeast? Timing is critical in brewing".

"It is, and if you do this part right you can still salvage something. The recipe says: 'Not cool, nor still lukewarm, about one hour after the boiling'. That's word-for-word exactly, so have patience for once".

The Juggler frowned, exasperated. "Well—shoot! We've been pretty true to your recipe so far, but the night's gettin' on! Tell you what, we'll skip ahead here. I'll add some cold water...like this..." He sloshed in several gallons, then a little more, til the wort quit steaming, then poured everything into a big vat and got out the yeast from his bag.

"Now, little boss - *how much* yeast?" Before she could answer he shook some out over the vat. "Like *that*, say?"

"I would've guessed half that much".

"You guess? You ain't sure of your own recipe? Then I better add a smidgen..." he dumped it all in... "and that should hurry it up for us".

Atel left for good. The trolls were rowdy the rest of the night. They went off to - wherever they keep it - and came back with a small 'pony' keg, last of the old beer, which they drank up. Why not? A new batch was comin' on! No need to ration anymore. It got so rowdy after midnight that the fairy babes woke up and started crying and the trolls never even heard them. Then they broke into a drinking song:

"Oh!
If we had our wishes
Of all our good dishes,
Like mutton and pork
You can cut with a *fork*
—Or we could pop a cork
And have *beer?*
We'd drink beer!
Hey!

31

Muggers and muggers of beer
Over HERE!

Or,
If we had our wishes
Of all our good dishes
Like gravy and toast
And tender *beef roast*
—Or we could ask the host
For some *beer?*
We'd drink beer!
Juggers and juggers of beer
Over HERE!

Or,
If we had our wishes
Of all our good dishes
Like *manflesh soufflé'*
Or *pixie torte'*
Or we could drink all day?
—Just drink *beer?*
We'd drink beer!
Keggers and luggers of beer
Over HERE!
OVER HERE!!!"

They finished up by bellowing the last lines in the general direction of the pine woods and Atel was worried that the babes would start crying again, but they got angry instead.

"What's *torte'* anyway?" demanded Airy.

"It's a cake. A dessert made of eggs and flour and... usually fruit".

"An' th'want *us*, instead of the fruit?"

"Yes. I wasn't joking. They want to eat you".

"Why?"

"Because they eat their enemies. That means *you*".

"But *why?*"

"Because once upon a time, pixie girls refused to marry them, and insulted their King".

The babes laughed, exactly the reaction Atel expected. Pixies had laughed at King Gorrah back then too, igniting a never-ending feud. It was a grudge taken far more seriously by angry trolls than the mischievous pixies.

"Trolls should marry pine trees", suggested Lolly. "Th'would be more their size".

"Pine trees are too pretty for trolls", said Poo.

"Th'*dirt* is too pretty for them", giggled Airy. "Trolls are too ugly to marry anything!"

They laughed again and Atel swiftly hushed them. The ruckus over on the knob was quieting down.

"Don't laugh. You're too loud. Anyway, it's not a joke. The notion of pixies marrying trolls wasn't out of the question in those days - not to trolls, anyway - despite the difference in size. It happened like this..."

The question of romance had come up when the Lord of Light originally sent pixies to earth - or tried to. He assembled a host of them, explained their origin and purpose on the earth, and dismissed them with their work orders. But they didn't leave immediately. A bold pixie lass pointed out the obvious.

"We're all *girls*. Every one of us".

"Quite true", agreed the Lord.

"Where are the *boys?*"

"On the Green Earth below. Other fairy folk have been there for a while, boys among them".

"*Pixie* boys?" asked another lass.

"No. *Fairies*. They're much bigger than you are".

"What good is *that?* Th'won't even notice us!"

"Maybe not. Just ignore them and do your work".

Thereupon the Lord faced the first work-stoppage, something new in a new world that only compromise could budge. Okay then: If love grew, pixies would be allowed to grow with it to full size. But they had better choose wisely. If the romance diminished, so would they - right down to pixie size again and stay there. Was that fair enough?

Fair enough! One chance is all they needed. Any girl should be able to spot her true love in an instant! On that note the pixies went down to earth where – unfortunately - the fairy boys proved difficult to find, being by now deep underground working their mines. And when the pixies took up their appointed work, *trolls* took a fancy to them, somehow discovering the secret that pixies could grow if they wanted to. Trolls captured a bevy of them with marriage in mind, but the girls were repelled by the idea and refused to grow. Even began to shrink.

Trolls threw them into a dungeon to cure their stubbornness and after some time King Gorrah sent for the prettiest one - a beauty who had by now shrunk to the size of his little finger - to see if prison had taught her some obedience. He held out his hand and she dutifully landed on it. So far, so good. But a troll-wife must be slavish to the boss and bow down to his every demand.

"Now - *curtsy* for me, twerp!" laughed Gorrah.

The lass properly hiked up her skirt a bit, but then spun around, bent over, and rudely greeted him with both cheeks.

In the uproar that followed, the lass escaped - all the lasses escaped, being too small by now for the dungeon bars to hold them. But they never did grow up because the fairy boys were lost in those days. Romance had to be postponed. They didn't know it yet, but their romance would be 'postponed' for Ages.

34

"So we will stay *little* until we meet our handsome prince?" asked Lolly.

"Yes. You'll grow some, but not much. You are pixies, and that's how it is with pixies".

"An' our handsome princes are *lost?*"

"Yes. It's a long story, but all the fairy lasses live in the Night Sky now, in a kingdom behind the Aurora, while the boys remain here below - somewhere".

"But we're here now! We can find them!"

"You are still in your chrysalises. When you hatch out we'll worry about handsome princes".

"At least th'won't be trolls".

"No. Trolls got over that idea. You would be lunch now. Except for your wings, of course".

"Why not the wings?" The babes shivered at an unsettling thought. Their wings were fully developed now, and they were eager to try them out.

"Ishi wants those. You can ask her someday - if she gets her hands on you".

When the babes were asleep again Atel returned to the troll's camp, but they were gone, and the place cleaned up as before. Even the fermenting vat was gone, or appeared to be, but a faint yeast smell lingered. The vat was still there, probably. Stone trolls have no magic but are very skilled at camouflage and other crafts. They're also smart enough to sleep off their hangovers underground. Good! A nanny could get some sleep too.

Near dawn an easterly breeze passed through, the kind that ushers in an early shower and a fine day afterward, the best kind of day to get things done. All day long the hummingbird flew sorties to the flowers until the babes could only sip and burp. That was near sundown when she expected the trolls to return. But this night they didn't come so everyone got decent rest.

They never came the next night either, or the next. For Atel it was like a work holiday. A chance to seriously tend the babes with no distractions. A chance for them to eat, sleep and grow! Their teeth were all in now and she brought berries and fruit. They liked the wild black cherries, which was good. Cherry grows swiftly; the secret is in the fruit and swift growth was needed.

She also brought plum from the thorny wild trees on the hill, but only bits and pieces because the fruits were bigger than she was. They loved it, and that was *very* good. The fondness would draw them to the tree and the protection of the thorns.

Finally she brought grapes because she was worried about the trolls; and because frost, too, was becoming a real danger. The babes must be introduced properly to the Lord of Light, and it had better be done now in case something bad happened. She gave them each a small purple grape and as the last rays of the setting sun bathed their faces she spoke about the grapevine growing upward, seeking the sun and the sky. They ate the grapes, and it meant a lot to her, but babes are only babes. The sweetness of the fruit is all they would remember.

Shortly after sundown the Juggler showed up to taste his brew. As Atel watched from her listening perch he thrust an arm into a stand of tall weeds and dipped a finger into the hidden vat, then licked the finger thoughtfully, sampling several times to be sure. He frowned, which Atel took for good news.

"Slow?" she inquired, paying a visit.

"Sure is! Shouldn't be with all the yeast that went in! What's the matter with your recipe?"

"Too many substitutions. Its unpredictable now".
"It's a poor recipe that can't stand a little tweaking".
"What don't you like?"
"It's *green*. The 'snort' is comin' on fine, but it tastes terrible".
"Give it time. You're less aggravating to the neighbors when you're sober".

She felt his dark look while he sampled the batch once more to be sure of the condition. Then he walked off into the night without another word.

———————◆◆◆———————

At sunrise, the hummingbird awoke to genuine skunk stench drifting into the woods from the direction of the knob and investigated. But the animal had moved on, or possibly been carried off by a Great Owl. It had sprayed several times all around the knob and the west breeze was now ruining a fine morning in the pine woods. But morning was here regardless, and work awaited. She scouted for troll sign, expecting none, but found something. At the edge of the pine woods, beneath a tall elm tree festooned with grape vines, was a new rock - obviously a valuable rock with flakes and speckles of shiny gold. There it sat in the open for anyone to see. It could only mean one of two things: It might be Ishi, except that she didn't like to call attention to herself; or it was *bait*.

She hovered there for several minutes until she figured out the hidden trap and tripwire. It was a net, although she couldn't see it, and the vines were attached to it. High above, a stout branch was bent down under pressure ready to jerk up and pull the net tight around any unwary creature who might pick up the rock. That's what tripped the trigger. It was meant for fairies. The trolls had come back and set it while she slept, and probably brought along a live skunk to cover their own smell. She breathed a small sigh of relief in spite of the bad air. Good! Let them think about traps and larger fairies for a while. Several of them did pass through occasionally. She hadn't lied about that. But she doubted they would touch the big nugget. It was a good imitation, but it was 'fool's gold'.

The holiday from trolls ended abruptly. That very night they came back with a jug of moonshine and got busy making their bonfire, starting with a few dry branches as before and then the young troll stripped another tree. He could have chosen any of several but picked one that led directly toward the nursery.

Atel frowned as she watched from her perch. She wanted to pay a visit, but the trolls had been drinking before they came. Sober trolls could be dealt with a little, but drunken trolls hardly at all - especially when they're drinking hard liquor. But if she thought she could just ignore them, she was wrong. The Juggler chose that moment to turn and bellow in her direction.

"Hey, little boss! I know you're watching. C'mon over and have a sip with us".

"I don't drink alcohol", she said, approaching cautiously. "It makes folks stupid if you didn't know".

"That's only wee little folk who can't hold their liquor. With big folk it sharpens the wits".

"Is that what you call it?"

"Don't spoil the mood now! We're gonna have a turkey roast".

"Well, that's better. The hangover won't be as bad if you eat some solid food tonight".

"Hangovers are for wee folk too. Trolls wake up refreshed".

"Looking for trouble, more like it".

"You're grumpy, little boss. Trouble getting to sleep? Have you tried closing your eyes and counting trolls?"

"I don't have to close them for that".

"Well! There's your problem, then. Try closing your eyes".

The trolls laughed and got busy. The Juggler shook four live turkeys out of a sack, one at a time, as Laddie grabbed them and wrung their necks. It was his job to clean and pluck them too, while 'big brother' set up a heavy grill over the fire. Atel helpfully pointed out pinfeathers that the young troll was missing.

"Stuff it!" he growled, flicking giblets in her direction.

"That's another thing", she replied, dodging the innards. "If you're going to *stuff* these birds you'll need vegetables".

Laddie jerked a thumb at his pal. "He's the chef".

"This is an old family recipe", explained the Juggler. "I *am* stuffing them, but it calls for beer, which ain't ready yet. I'll have to substitute".

He got out four big copper mugs and poured one of them half full of moonshine, then placed it on the grill. Laddie handed him a plucked bird which he set upright atop the mug like a genteel person sitting on a toilet. Then he did likewise with the other three. He even arranged them sociably facing each other. All that was missing was a card table in the middle, and perhaps a deck of cards with four jokers. The Juggler smiled proudly.

"The beauty of the recipe is, the bird stays juicy, and the alcohol gets into the meat, so nothing is wasted. We call it 'slop pail poultry'. We also do chicken like this. But don't fret, little boss! We'd never do it to a hummingbird. There's no mugs that small".

"I'm glad. I'll excuse myself then, so you can eat and do chores and finish everything up before dawn. Don't forget to check your trap".

She flew off to the woods. There was no reply, but she felt the dark looks from both of them. Trolls take pride in their camouflage and rightly so. No one ought to see through it, and no one ever did. But *she* did.

That worried her. If she could see through theirs, they might see through hers too. The chrysalises were protected by a charm and appeared as pinecones, but they did absorb a faint sheen of starlight which was needed for the well-being of the chrysallis. It would not do to cover it up or try to dim it. There were no known spells anyway. That was the province of the Lords of Darkness.

As she approached the nursery Poo cried out in her sleep during a rare quiet moment over on the knob, and it seemed like the whole hill went quiet. Poo was having a recurring nightmare about a woodpecker but had now awakened, fortunately, so that she didn't cry out again. The others had awakened also and all three listened intently for - what? Whatever had awakened them, of course. None of them realized it was just Poo.

Others were listening over on the knob, Atel felt sure. She motioned for the babes to be quiet and waited it out. The trolls had food and drink to occupy them and would soon get back to it. In the meanwhile she whispered to Poo. Was it the woodpecker dream again? Oh yes, that jogged her memory. She nodded and closed her eyes as it came back. It was always the same: The woodpecker knocked, and Poo would ask, "Who's there?" But the bird never answered, just broke right in.

"Woodpeckers don't hear well", Atel explained, "All that rat-a-tatting ruins their ears. But they're not evil, just hungry. They eat bugs that burrow into the bark and cause trees to *itch*. That was appreciated long ago when the forests were awake. Woodpeckers were important and respected. They even took a noble-sounding name to themselves in their rat-a-tat language, meaning 'Flying Physicians'. But they get pretty rough because they can't hear any complaints, so everyone else just calls them 'Drill-Doctors'".

The babes looked silently at each other. "What's a *doctor*?" asked Poo finally, "an' who do *they* drill into?"

"That's a lesson for another day. Just know that the woodpecker won't try it again because you're much bigger than bugs now. That should make you happy".

"I'm happy I didn't sprout up as a little tree".

"You haven't sprouted as anything yet, Poo. That remains to be seen and will require some luck. I think the trolls are listening. Don't let them hear you!"

◆◆◆

The trolls made merry the rest of the night until toward dawn when the food and drink ran out and the racket subsided. That was the hummingbird's alarm clock. She went scouting and found the young troll tidying up the campsite, not one for chit-chat. The Juggler, as she expected, was checking the trap before they left. He didn't care for her company either.

"No luck?" she inquired.

The Juggler growled and turned away, as if he only came looking for a bathroom. "Beat it, bird! This is the boy's outhouse".

"Oh, pardon me! Just don't go on your trap there, or the fairies won't come anywhere near it".

He stood mute for a few moments, then gave up all pretense and waved at the hidden trap. "Okay, what gives it away? It looks perfectly invisible!" He was genuinely puzzled.

"The bait".

"They love gold! That's a thousand carats!"

"Of *fool's* gold".

41

"It's fooled them before!"

"So I've heard. It won't fool them again".

Juggler snarled and stomped back to the camp. Atel followed.

"You'll have to use real gold. What's the problem? All trolls have hidden treasure, so I've heard".

"You hear a lot of things, don't you?" She got the dark look. "Maybe one of these days we'll hear that you came to a bad end". That brought the conversation to an end, too. Night was fading fast anyway. It was time for trolls to be underground.

Morning arrived with a teachable moment, a ghastly one. Just as the hummingbird arrived at the nursery a falcon dived out of the sky and caught a morning dove in mid-air, not twenty feet away. The dove squawked frantically but the struggle was short, ending with the falcon perched on the victim's own nest, eating the owner. Then it proceeded to eat the eggs in the nest as well. The babes witnessed the whole scene.

"Well, now you know how *that* works", said Atel when it was over. "Any questions?" There were none just yet.

"That was a pigeon hawk. They take small pixies too. There are also owls and much larger hawks. They all eat meat. That's the soft stuff you have on your bones. Any questions now?"

Yes. They all boiled down to survival.

"Fairy folk are luckier than some", Atel informed them. "You will find that you have an extra sense, an *awareness*, so that you'll have little to fear in the open air. It's when you sleep that you'll be at risk. Pine trees aren't much protection, as you just saw".

"Where then?" asked Airy. "I don't want to just go into hiding!"

"You'll be able to nap quite safely if you do it right. Wait right here, like good girls!" (she loved to say that) "I'll fetch breakfast and teach you a trick".

There was a honey locust on a nearby hill, an especially ugly specimen of its kind. Thorns like stilettos bristled from the trunk and branches. The fruit of the tree - sweet seed pods - were ripe now but no one dared reach in and pick them. A sapsucker had pecked one open, however, to get at the delicious pulp. Atel stabbed into that and brought a sliver back for the babes to share. It was a hit.

"Oh, my *favorite!*" declared Lolly, but Lolly had many favorites.

Atel was pleased. "It's from the worst thorn tree I know of. That tree - and *all* thorn trees and brambles - will be your best protection and refuge when you need it. The thorns will keep most enemies away. You see? Problem solved".

The babes rolled their eyes, as they always did when they thought 'Nanny' was going nuts.

"What about th'sharp thorns poking right *through* us?" asked Poo finally. "We're soft".

Atel laughed. "I know you're soft, Poo, but don't worry. There's a charm on thorns now, to protect fairy folk. So be glad for the safe haven! There was a time when there were no havens".

"What did fairies do then?"

"Quite a few were caught and eaten. Pixies, especially. Do you want to know more?" There were no requests, but she went on anyway. The babes were already spooked. They might as well learn the gory history.

Phases of the 'Moon'

When fairy folk came to earth it was a more hospitable place in many ways: Less crowded, less noise, much less irritation. The air was pristine. The waters were pure. The forests still remained as

43

the Creator had left them: Orderly and welcoming. One could walk through any woods, for example, and not be snagged by a thorn. There weren't any. But because of this, fairies found themselves in jeopardy. A tragedy loomed.

To be sure, fairies played a leading role in this - especially the little pixies who showed their character flaw right away, stirring up unnecessary trouble with the *Unnaturals*. What did pixies expect? They teased the *Unnaturals* constantly, just for thrills.

They were especially persistent with trolls and soon learned that if nothing else infuriated a troll, 'mooning' him would do the trick! By happy chance, the trick drew the same outrage from natural carnivores of the world also.

Pixies always managed to escape these encounters - but to where? They soon found there were no safe places to nap after a thrilling chase. They could hide, but their foes simply followed their scent and grabbed them. Pixies smell like nectar and honey, understand, and taste like candy, so it was a delight to track them down. Revenge was sweet.

The Fairy Queen saw the carnage and pleaded with her pixies to cool it, but there was no way. The blindness of battle was upon them. It would only have slowed down the slaughter anyway. By now, pixies were known world-wide as a gourmet snack.

The Queen finally sent three emissaries - the fairies Aleta, Hydia and Lorelei - to beg the Lord of Light for help. They couldn't find Him, but they came upon the Artisans of Evermore, the Great Ladies of the Heavens who assist the Lord in His Works. They were busy at the Aurora, talking and stitching extra color into the drapery. Perhaps a dozen of them were quilting away on the big curtain using starlight for thread, but real needles.

One of them, a grandmotherly figure who did a lot of the talking, held up a corner of the curtain for inspection. Several ladies offered opinions. None of them noticed the fairy lasses below.

"It's beautiful!" Aleta called up to her when there was a pause.

The Artisans jumped to discover mice down by their feet, then laughed when they looked closer at the 'mice'.

"You surprised us!" said the grandmotherly one. "We don't get visitors often".

"Folks down below admire your art", said Lorelei. "Some nights everyone stands and watches".

"It shows up well?"

"*Very* well", said Hydia truthfully. "Th'colors are breathtaking".

The ladies actually giggled. "We must be doing the right thing, then", said one. "His original plan was to stay with greens and yellows, but we reviewed it and... well, now we're adding a bit of red. What do you think?"

"I like it", said Aleta. "I would call it 'pink rose'. What do you call it?"

"We were just discussing that. We borrowed the color from your next planet out but *softened* it. Pastels are nice for some of these things. Do you quilt?"

"Nope, no needles", replied Aleta, and a thought struck her. "If you don't mind, do you have any old needles? That you don't use anymore?"

The Artisans looked at each other in surprise. "It's funny you should ask", said another lady. "We have lots: Big, small, tiny, dull & broken, you name it. We keep them in our bags" ...she reached behind and drew forth a canvas bag, medium size (for her), which accidentally swung around and bumped the next lady where she was sitting. The lady stiffened, and her eyes widened but, "Ooo! Careful there, sister", was her only comment. During the apology which followed, the fairies could see lots of needles sticking out through the canvas.

"They're a hazard!" declared the guilty lady. "There's really no safe place to leave sharps, so we tote them along with us".

"I know a place...", replied Aleta.

The fairies told their story while the Artisans stitched and listened, and finally nodded at each other.

"I don't see why not...", ventured the grandmotherly one, "But it would definitely be a change. We really ought to ask. What do you say, girls?"

"I think it's in the 'grey' area", said another lady. "Let's use flower petals and let the fates decide. He knows we do that, in a pinch..."

"Of course".

"And it would be nice to get rid of the bags..."

"Yes. *Very* nice to get rid of the bags!"

The ladies set aside their quilting needles and proceeded to knit a yellow flower with many white petals. It didn't take long. The grandmotherly one held it down for the fairies to pluck out the petals, one at a time.

Aleta plucked one and they took turns as the ladies chanted, "We'll do it! No, we'd better not; We'll do it! No, we'd better not..."

Aleta could tell by their smiles how it would turn out, even while there were quite a few petals left.

"Well!" said the lady then, with every appearance of surprise. "It's meant to be, seemingly! In which case we ought to do it straightaway - don't you think, girls? Then we'll get back to the curtain".

So needles were stitched into the Kingdom of Plants and a charm sewn in with them, making them friendly to fairy folk. Thus pixies found refuges and began to survive.

An understanding about better behavior went along with it: Namely, a ban on the ridiculous 'mooning', or at least a long-lasting truce. That part mystified the pixies, who thought, "Why *now* - when we're *safe?*" They totally ignored it. Pixies simply don't tame that easily. Blame it on the comet dust, what else?

"What means 'mooning'?" asked Lolly. The others perked up at the question.

"I'm not going to tell you. It isn't ladylike".

"We're not ladies yet, are we? We're just pixies".

"No, you definitely *aren't* ladies yet, and you never will be if you don't think nice thoughts. 'Mooning' isn't nice! It makes other folks terribly angry".

"Wow! At least give us a hint".

"Nope. Ask a troll sometime".

The hummingbird left in disgust. Pixies! Lucky for them they had sweet moments to balance out others! All the rest of the day she hauled slivers of the honey locust pulp and during each delivery had to deal with curiosity about 'mooning', especially as it concerned trolls. By evening her patience was exhausted and she gave them the details straight out. They reacted like it was the funniest thing they ever heard.

"Were you even listening to the story?" Atel scolded when there was a pause in the laughter. "It wasn't so funny when pixies were caught! And by the way, thorns will not stop an angry troll or even slow him down! If you ever moon a troll you'll forfeit any safe refuge, do you understand?" The babes nodded but couldn't wipe off the grins. Atel went on.

"One more thing to know about thorn sanctuaries, something to be careful of as long as you're here on earth: Your own 'moons' are at risk among the thorns. The Artisans were unhappy when pixies thumbed their noses at better behavior. They were very unhappy. So they removed the charm from the part of you that you sit on - get it? Watch out behind".

The trolls turned up again as expected and made a bonfire, stripping another pine tree in direct line toward the nursery. That didn't appear random. Maybe the young troll was just extending his beaten path, but it left only two trees for a buffer. Then, even as she watched, he chopped a few lower branches off the next tree in line as well. It was a bad omen. She spent an uneasy night near the nursery, just thinking. But pre-dawn arrived with only one new thought: The wind had swung around to the east. The weather was changing.

She went to check on the trolls before sunrise, but they were packed up and gone. Over at the trap the fool's gold was also gone, replaced by stacks of coins. Real gold coins. That was her smile for the day. The only other sign of activity was the remnant of a deer carcass, no doubt the feast of the past evening, now dragged off and chewed up by coyotes. The hide was missing, to be tanned and sent down to Court, possibly. They wore clothes down there, she had once heard, and King Gorrah fancied fur capes and robes. If true, it had to come from somewhere. All 'country-boy' trolls were required to send in taxes. Gold and silver were expected, but some got by bartering, claiming they had no money.

All day the wind increased. By afternoon intermittent showers pelted the hill. Long food sorties had to be shortened up, but the babes must still be fed. The best berries nearby were grapes, just beginning to ferment: A bad idea for pixies. Instead she brought seeds from the pinecones, very popular with the red squirrels, but the flavor was too strong for the babes. They did like a variety of other seeds, but seeds made them thirsty. It was a difficult day and the evening put a rough stamp on it. The storm arrived in force and buffeted the woods all night. The nursery tree swayed wildly in the wind and several trees blew down on the north end of the hill, but there was some silver lining to the weather: The pixies were able to get a good drink and the trolls stayed underground.

By morning the storm moved on, but a strong wind came out of the north to fill the void, ushering an autumn air mass into the region. It would be colder now, and the babes would need even more food. Good luck with *that*. They were still hungry from yesterday and now the unruly wind limited her foraging range. Cedar berries had to fill out the menu. They were mostly seeds but nothing else was convenient. The babes, very cramped now in their chrysalises, spent most of the day irritably stretching and straining at the walls. Atel took notice and fed them less to irritate them *more* and promote the endeavor. She had a premonition that time was running out.

By evening it was much colder. The wind finally calmed, but it had done its work. Atel went down into the surrounding valley and heard the icy whispers of chillbanes, harbingers of frost and soldiers of the North Wind. Great armies of them would arrive in the months ahead. These were the first. If they overcrowded the valley tonight they would come up the hill, exactly what she didn't need. She went back up to find that the trolls had arrived, not in the best of moods either.

It had rained a lot into the fermenting vat and diluted the beer just as it was nearly ready. Now they stood next to the exposed vat with mugs: Dipping, tasting, and grumbling.

"Well?" remarked Atel. "It should be fine. The recipe was too strong anyway. But - yuck!! - what stinks around here? Is that your supper?"

'That' was the dirty carcass of a fat steer, rustled from some farmer's barnyard, heavily plastered with muddy manure. The Juggler took no offense.

"Patience, little boss. Before the night's over he'll look delicious. You might give up your vegetarian ways".

"I'm not strictly vegetarian. I eat bugs".

"Well, don't bring any to the barbecue! I want things respectable tonight. Special occasion! We're celebrating Laddie's birthday".

The trolls dipped out one more sample each, then the Juggler got out a skinning knife and tossed his hatchet to Birthday Boy.

Here's where it gets interesting, thought Atel, and tagged along with the young troll as he scrounged for dry kindling along the edge of the pine thicket. The rain had soaked most everything.

"Do you still call it 'kindling' if you can wring water out of it?", she asked. "You can't make a fire with that".

"*He* can".

"If you say so".

The kindling was soggy, but the Juggler actually did squeeze water out of it and soon had a flame going. Laddie grinned at the hummingbird and went back for green wood, starting right where he left off last time, while the Juggler finished up skinning. Atel flew up to the nursery and found the babes straining to break open their chrysalises. They could hear the hatchet nearby and knew what it meant. But they weren't making any progress.

Laddie stripped the tree as far up as he could reach. Chips flew everywhere. Then he gathered up the limbs and toted them over to camp. That left one buffer tree. The Juggler had by now finished with the skinning and was building up the fire which was still small. Laddie went for more wood but was called back.

"Enough for now, lad! Help me set things up".

The support posts were first. The Juggler held one, and then the other while Laddie propped braces to keep them upright. It didn't look sturdy enough yet, so they pulled two big branches from the fire and made braces out of them too. Next they impaled the carcass lengthwise with the spit and carried it, one on each end, and set it in place over the fire.

Now it would be time to get more wood, figured Atel.

Wrong. It was time for more beer! The trolls settled themselves comfortably on either side of the big vat and enjoyed a few mugs while occasionally feeding the fire and turning the spit. Tonight there would be plenty of beer. A whole vat. They had even brought an empty cask to fill later. The evening was expertly organized: A lot of time and a lot of wood was needed to roast a whole steer, and a lot of beer to fill up the time, and they had all three! It would be a night to remember.

Presently the wood ran short, and Laddie was sent for more. The last buffer tree didn't yield enough to suit the Juggler, so they both went for still more to make a stockpile. Working together, the trolls stripped the lower parts of the nursery tree and decided to finish up to the top. Atel prepared for a fight, hovering near the nursery in clear view of the full moon. She had considerable skill with light and would reflect a tight beam of it into their eyes with her 'mirror'. It would sting and slow them down, but moonlight isn't sunlight, and there were two trolls. They would surely have their way. Then the unexpected happened. An awful racket suddenly arose from the direction of the fairy trap. Something had been caught and it didn't sound fairy-ish.

◆◆◆

A troll, a big one, dangled in the net upside-down. His nose poked through the netting and scraped against the ground as the suspended net wobbled back and forth. The young troll arrived first and erupted in laughter, setting off a string of profanity from within the net. Then the Juggler arrived, but he didn't laugh. The big fellow in the net called him by name. Ignoring all that, Laddie reached down and tweaked the helpless nose playfully, prompting more oaths.

"Just lemme OUTA here!" the new troll finally bellowed. The Juggler swung his hatchet and cut one of the vines, spilling the newcomer out onto his big nose. There he sat, rubbing it with one hand, still clutching a big handful of 'bait' with the other. He offered the coins to the Juggler with a weird smile.

"Your money, Jag?" he asked.

The Juggler stood mute, finally nodded his head.

The weird smile curled down at the edges. "I'll hold it until I figure the tax. I counted it, but I'm sure there's more where that came from".

This was 'Red', a dreaded 'Biter' from Gorrah's Court. A tax collector. He specialized in tax evasion and stalked the countryside much like an old traveling preacher searching for lost souls, except he searched for lost money. He carried a huge club to encourage sincerity.

Red laughed now and struggled to his feet, every inch as tall as the young troll, and heavier. Now he turned and boxed Laddie right on *his* nose, and the fight was on. The Juggler stepped back, but the violence didn't last long. During a wild exchange of punches they knocked each other out and didn't even remember fighting when they came around again. But they did remember everything else. The Juggler quickly changed the subject to beer, which helped. Trolls love food, drink & fighting about equally, and jump from one to the next in a heartbeat. Red plopped himself onto Laddie's stump and gladly accepted a frothing mug, but it reminded him of taxes. Everything did. Red loved his job.

"Back at Court", he pointed out, "a mug like this would go for 50 cents!" He quaffed it all in one huge gulp and frowned. "Maybe 25 cents. But you're still a rich fellow, Jag. I estimate there's 100 gallons in your possession there, with an assessed value of $100. Property tax is 50%. Add that to the income tax on the gold and there's not enough to cover the whole bill. You'll have to bring in more gold". He held out the mug for a refill.

"Ain't no more gold", replied the Juggler, filling the mug again. "That's my life's savings right there".

"We'll see. Most fellows remember another small stash, the longer I hang around".

"Not here. Between me and the lad we don't have two nickels to rub together".

"No nickels, maybe. But you did have a lot of gold dollars".

"*Did* have".

Red laughed and turned to the young troll. "What about you, Kiddywinks? Mum gives all the new brats a few coins. Where's yours?"

"Up yours!" Laddie drained his mug and went to fetch the cut branches.

"That one will find himself in the slammer someday", said Red irritably. "Rebels against authority".

"He's just young. It's his third birthday today". The Juggler accepted Red's empty mug again and refilled it.

"Ah! So that's the occasion!" Red eyed the spit. "There'll be gift tax on the beef then. Are you giving presents, too?"

"No, but Mum will show up later. She might have something".

Red scowled. That would complicate things! Ishi was the *Real Big Boss*. Even above Gorrah, supposedly. She played favorites and Red wasn't one of them. He wasn't collecting the taxes for her, after all.

Laddie returned with a huge armload of branches and dumped them next to Red.

"Bust 'em up for the fire!"

The Juggler tossed Red the hatchet with a little grin. "Remember, he's Mum's favorite today".

Atel watched for a while and judged the situation to be as stable as it gets with trolls. She went to see about the other danger, the chillbanes, and unexpectedly bumped into them only halfway down the hill. Bad news! They might easily invade the pines before dawn! The departing storm was pulling down waves of them from the north.

She returned to her eavesdropping perch. The Juggler was turning the spit more often now as the steer blackened up on the outside. Trolls like their barbecue rare so it must be nearly done, she figured. But the last of the wood had been put on and Laddie was stoking the coals now, while the others argued.

"You country boys have it easy compared to us", Red was saying. "Ain't no pleasing Gorrah! Don't matter how much I collect for him, it's never enough!"

"Maybe it ain't. You probably keep nine dollars out of every ten".

"Rules are, I get 10 percent and pay my own expenses".

"I'll subtract your expenses off my tax bill then".

"Don't get smart. There would be sales tax on that transaction. And by the way, there's excise tax on beer too. It won't apply to whatever I drink, so you're getting a deal there".

"You already have all my money, so what's the difference?"

"You've got more. Somewhere. And if you plead poverty it'll trigger the 'poor tax'. I'll set up an easy payment schedule but if you fall behind we charge interest. There's penalties for being poor".

"You're making that up! There's no such thing as 'poor tax'".

"Sure there is. If you don't like it, take it up with the big shots back at Court. I do what I'm told. I don't make the rules".

The Juggler turned away and noticed Laddie heading for the woods with the hatchet. It was tempting to join him just to get away, but the steer looked to be done nicely. He stuck it with a knife and blood dripped through the charred outer layer. Perfect!

"Hey! Birthday boy! We don't need any more wood. Give me a hand and we'll lift the critter off".

"Timing is everything!" thought Atel in relief and returned hopefully to the nursery but found things unchanged. The babes were still straining to break out. An optimist might see a little progress, but it would take imagination. She inquired politely about it and came away knowing only that they were in a worse temper.

Lolly even used a troll word. It was better to leave. She went to pay a visit and introduce herself to Red.

"This is 'little boss'", chuckled the Juggler, doing the introduction for her. "She owns the hill, so if you want anything, ask her first". Red snickered and held out his mug for another refill. Then he launched a sudden gob of spit at the cheeky hummingbird hovering right in front of him. It nearly hit her, and she returned the favor, reflecting bright light from the grease fire with her 'mirror'. The beam hit the mark. Red yelped and rubbed an injured eye.

"I could've warned you", laughed the Juggler. "She does tricks. But it's best to learn the hard way. Then you'll remember".

"So *this* is what you caught in your trap?" inquired Atel mildly. "Not pretty like a fairy, but he must like gold".

"If you only knew."

"I do know a little. I couldn't help overhearing your talk. He wants more money, I gather? Well - shake loose! *Give* it to him so he leaves! Seems simple to me".

She left them with that, feeling helpful. They needed something to talk about while supper cooled and now they had it. Back at her listening post she almost had to plug her ears from the angry voices. But the barbecue soon cooled enough to rip into and rip they did - tearing off a 'drumstick' each to start with and tossing the bones to a coyote when they were done.

The night was getting old when they finished the carcass, gnawing on the bigger bones and swallowing the small ones. The trolls stretched out their meal, drinking extra beer to wash it down. The mood mellowed. Red and the Juggler traded hair-raising stories about King Gorrah and shared a laugh. They had come to some agreement about the overdue taxes. The young troll just drank steadily and listened, which is how young trolls get most of their education.

Clouds that had moved in earlier now moved east, exposing the moon again and putting the trolls in a serious drinking mood. They don't like the moon. It reminds them of the sun for one thing, but also of the hated fairies. They see a face in it and believe it to be the Fairy Queen Yoyanneh, up there in the Night Sky watching them. It really bugs them that she watches, but they have a way to get even, a trick learned from the fairies themselves.

The Juggler suggested it and they all got up and faced the moon. Hoisting their mugs in a toast, they bellowed:

"To Yo! High Ho!

Hey, Yo!

Look down below!

We drains our cup,

And bottoms up

To Yo!

High Ho!

Our shiny, heinie ho!"

Then the big bruisers gulped down their beer and stuck their rumps high in the air, right at the moon. They laughed so hard the hummingbird retreated in disgust with just one backward glance. Red and the young troll were rolling on the ground and even the Juggler sat down so he wouldn't fall.

Circling around the hill to the east she flew unexpectedly into the chillbanes. A shift in the air currents had pushed them into the pines and they were coming much faster now. It wasn't a matter of hours but only minutes before the frost reached the nursery. She hurried there and found the babes at last making good progress. They had each forced open a crack and were elbowing it wider, still in no mood to talk but obviously sensing urgency. They should easily win the race against the chillbanes. She breathed a sigh of relief.

That left only one serious threat. The Juggler. He was distracted right now, but she feared him because he could hold his liquor better than the others. He was probably napping. All she could hear was a lot of terribly loud snoring over there now, the worst danger being that they might wake each other up. With a last glance at the babes (halfway out of their chrysalises now) she zipped off to double-check on the trolls.

That was a mistake. Red and the young troll were sprawled where they had been, unmoving except for the rise and fall of their bellies with each breath and the flubbering of their lips with each snore. But the Juggler was gone! Where was he?

At that moment she heard little shrieks of delight from the pines. That's what happens when fairy babes hatch and unfold their wings to dry. They hop up on the branch and dance to celebrate. Oh Joy! But clever old trolls know this. It's exactly what the Juggler was listening for all summer. He too had smelled frost in the air and guessed that this would be the night, acting sleepy and drunk minutes earlier only to fool the hummingbird.

Even as she reversed direction and dashed for the nursery the happy shrieks turned to cries of distress. She had failed at the last moment! The Juggler had got there ahead of her, pulled the treetop down, and grabbed the pixies in the vulnerable minute before they could fly. Even as she flew at his eyes scratching and clawing he stuffed the pixies into his jug and jammed in the cork with a pop, muffling their cries.

"I've got 'em!" he bellowed.

CHAPTER

2

PIXIE TORTE

Atel stared helplessly at her little charges inside the jug, noses pressed against the glass, wings aglow from the dust of the chrysallis. The sparkle would soon be doused by the beer. They stood on tiptoe in home brew up to their necks.

"Let them go!" she demanded.

"Fat chance, little boss", chortled the Juggler. "That means no chance". He slung the jug carelessly over his shoulder and made off in triumph to the camp where he kicked the young troll in the rear to awaken him. His snoring skipped a beat, but he never stirred. That disappointed Big Brother immensely. He was in a mood to boast, and rightfully so! The whole summer was now a success and himself the mastermind.

What's more, with pixies in hand it would be easier to deal with Red! He booted the tax collector in the butt and got a better reaction, but not much.

Red sat up bleary-eyed and slapped himself on both cheeks. Ah, that helped! Then he focused on his sore rump and noticed the Juggler who stood there grinning and figured out what had awakened him. That *didn't* help. Then he noticed what was inside the jug in front of his nose and smiled. He had horribly chipped and blackened teeth and he fogged up the glass when he leaned close. When he wiped off the glass the babes had swum to the far side, and his head was beginning to swim too. He hoisted his big rear just high enough to plop it down on the stump and held his head in his hands, not fit to be an audience. Soon he was snoring again.

"What are you going to do with the pixies?" demanded Atel.

"I'm inviting them to dinner!" said the Juggler, pleased that he could brag to someone. "It'll be for dessert, actually. They won't say 'no' to that".

"I'm sure. Fetch them out then, or they'll drown in there!"

"No. They're marinating. It's part of the recipe". He jostled the jug to be sure they were all wet and felt pretty cocky. As a gourmet chef he knew words like 'marinade', 'tablespoon', and 'cream-of-tarter' as well as anyone. He wasn't born yesterday. But then, neither was the hummingbird.

"What are you making, if I may ask?"

"An ice-cream torte. The weather is perfect for it".

"Ah! And where do the pixies fit into the recipe?"

"At the very end. It's Laddie's birthday. (He kicked Laddie again and got the same non-response.) The torte will serve as a birthday cake, but of course there must be candles. That's where the pixies come in".

"You don't mean to light them on fire!"

"Maybe, maybe not. Depends on what Birthday Boy wants, but he sure likes his fireworks!"

"Well, they won't burn in their present condition".

The Juggler frowned a moment. "No. But when the time comes we'll warm 'em up over the fire, like browning marshmallows".

"They'll be pickled by then".

"Nah. That's just beer in there. They'll be fine".

"They'll be drowned! Do you want limp candles?"

The big troll uncorked the jug irritably and took a long swig, nearly sucking the pixies out with the beer. He plopped the jug down again and the beer only came up to their bellies. "There!" he grunted. "Happier now?"

"Much. I want them to enjoy the party".

"It'll be fun, you'll see. We'll eat the wings first. They're the best, but it's tricky. They brown up pretty quick".

"They'll burn! How long has it been since you ate pixies?"

The Juggler frowned. "Yeah, good point. Maybe we'll pluck the wings and eat 'em raw, then. The wings are *very* sweet".

"You're forgetting your Mum. She wants the wings".

"What she don't know won't hurt her".

"My goodness. You seem to have it all figured out. Do you have the cake ready?"

"No, but I have the ice cream. I'll whip up a quick pound cake for the torte. Just back off!"

Very efficiently he sprang into action. Everything was in his sack: Measuring spoons, a mixing bowl, flour, butter, eggs & sugar. In short order everything was in the bowl. Atel was startled by his speed.

"Odd recipe", she commented. "Aren't you forgetting a few things?"

Ignoring her, the Juggler produced vanilla and measured out precisely one teaspoonful. He even had nutmeg, which isn't always included, and added a bit of that, then whipped it all together. Finally he set up a makeshift grill supported by stones. As he worked at this the young troll rolled closer to the fire and flopped out an arm that whacked Big Brother in the hindquarters, nearly pitching him onto the grill. The Juggler showed remarkable patience and simply moved Birthday Boy's arm back down by his side. Atel took interest and bided her time.

"You're pretty good", she said. "I never knew trolls were much at baking".

"I've flipped a few hot cakes".

"I suppose you have a pan..."

"Naturally". He dug one out and went to pour in the mix.

"It'll stick without grease!" warned Atel, hoping to slow him down. It did. The frown reappeared. But only for a moment.

"Can't have everything. I'll have to substitute". He spat liberally into the pan. "There! Nuthin' sticks to that".

"Not knowingly", agreed Atel, looking away. "But the taste will be...*off*".

"A little. But Birthday Boy is a little off too, just now".

The Juggler quickly spread the mix out in the pan, set it on the grill, and blew on the coals to stoke them. Then he jostled the jug once more, mostly to irritate the hummingbird, and went to refill his mug. Atel adjusted her position slightly, arranging her breast feathers to reflect the firelight and focus it tightly on the end of Laddie's nose. The Juggler came back with his beer and squatted on his haunches, leaning forward to sniff the cake.

"Perfect!" thought Atel. Birthday Boy's nose was just beginning to steam. Then the Juggler leaned back again. Rats! But the aroma was so tempting! He leaned ahead for another sniff just as Laddie's hand decided to rub his overheated nose. The arm swung up smacking Big Brother in the rump a second time, but this time he went head-first into the cake pan and collapsed everything into the fire. He roared from the sting of the coals, or maybe from the loss of the cake. He didn't say exactly, but he said a lot of things. Red awoke from his stupor, but Laddie snored on even when Big Brother kicked and rolled him completely over.

"Brat!" the Juggler finally shouted and sat down rubbing a stubbed toe. He eyed the pixies hungrily.

"You can bake another cake", suggested Atel quickly. "Why not angel food?"

The Juggler brightened a little. He was genuinely fond of the young troll in spite of everything and wanted to do something nice. He glanced at the eastern sky. Still dark. He relaxed and reviewed the recipe from memory: "Eggs - yup; sugar - yup; bit of flour - yup, yup..." He drummed his fingers as he went down the list of ingredients, then rummaged in the big bag. When he had everything together he kicked the cake pan out of the coals and let it sizzle in the frosty grass. In a few moments he spat in it again to test the temperature and went ahead and licked it off.

"Angel food doesn't call for grease", said Atel.

"I know. That's why I licked it clean. Don't interrupt!"

Into the bowl went eggs, sugar, a little vanilla, and cream-of-tartar. He took special care to squash each yolk with his finger, then whipped everything up with the same finger. It worked surprisingly well. Next he poured sugar and flour into one hand and ground both hands together over the pan, spreading it out evenly.

"Powdered sugar", he explained.

"Very nice, but you're supposed to use a tube pan for angel food".

"Doesn't matter", he growled. "I've made this hundreds of times! It was Gorrah's favorite". He proceeded to demonstrate a delicate skill, sifting a bit of flour into the bowl, folding it in, sifting a bit more and folding that in, over and over. Not for nothing had he been Top Chef of the Royal Kitchens for almost an entire Age! Finally he dumped the mix into the pan.

"Oh my! It's the wrong color", said Atel. "You didn't leave in the egg yolks, did you?"

The Juggler frowned. Blast! He had forgotten.

"That's bad", said Atel. "You've got a *Devil's Food* mix. That's for Halloween, not birthdays!"

"Doesn't matter!"

"But it does! Pixies are like little angels. If you stick them in *that*, your cake will fall! You'll have flatbread".

Juggler scowled fiercely and dug into the bag once more. To his relief there was another mostly full, mostly unbroken carton of eggs! He licked out the bowl and cake pan and started afresh.

"The sign of a good cook!" observed the hummingbird. "You eat your own mistakes".

"It happens. Even to the best of us".

"Do you still have enough ingredients?"

"Yeah. But if this one flops we'll have pixie-pretzels and just leave it at that!"

He whipped up a new angel mix, slurping out the egg yolks with his tongue, and re-set the grill, carefully placing the cake pan on it. Then he blew on the coals hard. Sparks flew everywhere, as he intended, stinging the sleeping trolls and awakening them. Birthday Boy just rolled over and went back to sleep but Red perked up, cold sober again. He spotted the jug.

"There's a reward for pixies", he said. "A big one".

"I know. I thought about it".

"That's all? You just *thought* about it?"

"Yup. How much is it now?"

"Not sure. He raises it every now and then. Gorrah never forgets".

"Well, I ain't interested. If I tried to collect, he'd have me in the slammer. Thinks I tried to poison him, he does".

"Did you?"

"Nah! He loves beans, and then he blames the poor cooks for the gas".

"Yeah. Well, listen. They say it's a *huge* reward! We could all retire! Even the brat". He kicked ashes over at the young troll.

"No way, pal".

"*I* can take 'em in! I'll bring back your shares, next time out. Minus my ten percent, of course".

"And some tax too, I'm sure".

"Some, sure! That's why he makes the reward is so big. He'll get most of it back anyway, in taxes".

"No thanks. We're gonna eat 'em and that's reward enough".

"Not me. I get one for my share! I'll take the little redhead and collect the reward on her. She's cute". He stuck his pinky into the jug and tickled Poo's cheek. She bit his finger. "Oo! Little twerp! I'll stuff you in a bag!"

"Nope. She's for the birthday cake. We need three candles".

"Idiot! He won't pay if the wings are burned up. That's what he wants most!"

"Tough. I want the cake to look nice".

"No wings, no deal! Now we're talkin' taxes again".

"Okay! Take the wings! But leave the girl. I'll light up her hair for a candle".

"Deal! But dry the wings off first. They're soggy".

"Yeah. Well, it's time anyway". He uncorked the jug and gulped down the contents - pixies and all. Atel had barely time to gasp before he belched them up again into his hand and dangled them by the hair over the fire. The wings took on a healthy glow almost immediately.

'NO YOU DON'T!' shouted an angry voice. Ishi had walked up unnoticed and stood at the edge of the firelight holding three wax candles in one fist and shaking the other furiously.

'I'll have the wings!" she hissed. "Were you going to burn them?"

"Oh Mum! Don't be silly", protested the Juggler. "We're just warming 'em up for you".

"Good boy! Nip 'em off for me then, so the little darlings can't fly away".

"The wings are no good if you rip them off!" warned Atel. "They die, and the pixie too. It has to be *voluntary* - didn't you know?"

Ishi hadn't noticed 'the bird'. She narrowed her eyes. "What do *you* know about it?"

"More than you, obviously".

Ishi must be excused here, having never played with live pixies before. Atel was right. All fairies can take off their wings, and they frequently do to clean and groom them. But removal by force is the same as murder. You might as well rip their heads off.

Ishi thought it over. She needed crushed pixie wings for a very special paint mix, *not* whole pixies that would gum it up. The wings had to come off!

"Clever", she replied. "But I think you're bluffing. I'll take the chance".

"Why not make a deal? Let them go if they give up the wings".

Ishi stepped forward and leaned nose to nose with Airy, still dangling by the hair from the Juggler's fist. "What about it, little brat? Give up the wings and you can run along".

"What do you want them for?" asked Airy defiantly.

Ishi just smiled. The pixies flapped their wings frantically, straining at the leash of their own beautiful locks to no avail. Finally they just scowled and crossed their arms.

"Rip 'em!" ordered Ishi.

"Give them *up!*" Atel shouted to the babes. "We'll get 'em *back!*"

That drew mocking laughter, but it was their only chance. The Troll-Mother took possession of the wings and the Juggler held up the wingless babes in triumph, still by the hair. Obviously, they wouldn't be allowed to just 'run along'. That was just talk.

The grand moment called for a toast, and they enjoyed several. Mum wasn't about to leave anyway without sampling the home brew. But there's a party pooper in every crowd, especially a drunken crowd.

"Don't forget your tax obligation", Red informed Mum when the hoopla had quieted a bit. "I'm authorized to withhold one third of your profits. Payment-in-kind is satisfactory, so one pair of wings will go to the Treasury".

"I don't pay taxes."

"So I hear. But one day you'll be audited. Do you know what that means?" He smiled.

Ishi glared. As his mother, she knew Red better than anyone and never liked him from the beginning, never trusted him. She'd had a notion once to put him to sleep permanently. It would've been easy. Most trolls spend the daylight hours napping in the walls of their caves, in the very hollows they originally stepped out of. Light from fireflies, who also spend their days down there, gets in their eyes and re-awakens them in the evening. All she had to do was hang a dirty towel over his eyes while he slept! Well, she hadn't and here he still was, thirsty and sassy.

"Sorry, Mum", he was saying now, "but in the eyes of the Court you come under the tax laws like anyone else, and it seems we can't find your records. I've been instructed to ask a few questions, should I happen to see you".

"Tell your Court if they look my way again I'll scratch their eyes out!"

"I *did* warn them, Mum! I stuck my neck out for you! But rules are rules. You're gonna get a whopper of a tax bill".

"Listen, boy! I painted every troll in your phony 'Court'! If not for me, you never would have stepped out of the wall!"

"I know it, Mum! But when they run short of cash they send out the poor revenue agents. I can't help it. I have to assess the pixie wings for taxes. The valuation will be high".

"You got that right. They're priceless".

"I'll put down a number. I don't make the rules, but I'm authorized to make up numbers".

"So what? I'm not paying!"

Red was nervy enough to pick up his club. Years of bullying gets to be a habit. "Don't make it hard on yourself!" he growled.

Ishi finished her mug and approached him quietly. Red smiled inwardly. "Works every time!" he thought to himself. Then she touched his nose with a finger. The light in his eyes went out and he turned back to stone. Ishi did tricks too. But unlike the hummingbird, she worked with rocks. The Juggler whistled softly.

"Didn't know you could do that, Mum," he said with new respect. Ishi handed him the empty mug to refill and fumbled for the candles.

"Now that you know, shut up about it!" she snapped. "And wake up my baby. I want to sing 'Happy Birthday' to him before I go".

That wasn't easy. A mug of beer in the face finally got him up into a sitting position and the Juggler went ahead and decorated the cake. To please Mum, he popped the pixies back into the jug and used her candles. They sang then and toasted Birthday Boy in the best tradition, draining their mugs afterward. For Ishi it was her fourth mug, which she could normally handle, but the batch *had* turned out extra-strong as Atel had predicted. Ishi was tipsy when she tottered off toward the sinkhole clutching the wings.

The Juggler watched her go, then turned and studied Red. He walked over and touched him on the nose out of curiosity. Nothing happened.

"What'll you do with him?" asked Atel. "He'll be found. Men will start poking around".

"Ahh, let him sit there for a while. Mum will wake him up anyway when she gets over it. She's pretty soft-hearted".

"If you say so. That's the first I knew of it. But what about the candles? Isn't Birthday Boy going to blow them out?"

"Why? They look pretty".

"You don't know much. Hey - Laddie! Make a wish! If you blow out all the candles in one 'POOF' you get your wish".

The young troll perked up. "Really?"

"There's only one way to find out".

Laddie closed his eyes, concentrating, then opened them and blew at the candles. They went out and half the cake went with them. He grinned in triumph. The Juggler smiled too.

"Well? What did you wish for, Kiddo?"

"I get all the pixies".

"In a pig's eye!"

"That was my wish!"

"-----!"

Atel backed way off and let them argue. Dawn was awakening in the east behind low clouds, and they didn't notice. The clouds would hide the sunrise until the last moment, but that moment would be delayed until the sun rose above the clouds. All she could do was wait.

Now the argument took a curious turn. The Juggler fished out the pixies one by one and tied them to the spit by their long hair. There they dangled, and the coals beneath them still far from cool. School was declared in session and the subject would be arithmetic.

"We'll settle this fair and square", the Juggler explained. "How many pixies are there? If you guess the right number, you win. You get three guesses".

What could be fairer? Laddie wasn't good at math but the number had to be pretty small...

He counted on his fingers: "One?"

"Nope".

"Two?"

"Nope".

"Three!"

"Close, lad! But wrong. Redheads count double because they're rare, so the correct answer is four. But how will two of us share up three of them?"

"Cut the redhead in half?"

"That's good arithmetic, Lad. But they're more fun to swallow alive. You want 'em to squirm a little! Tell you what, Red was nice enough to leave the money. We'll flip a coin for the extra pixie". He shook some coins out of Red's fat purse and tossed the purse over by his own bag. It was his own money after all, some of it.

Atel rose to a higher altitude. The argument was resolving quicker than she had hoped. Where was the sunshine? Still too high up! She dropped back down to interrupt the argument.

"You're too late if you want them *squirming*", she noted urgently. "They're almost gone! Get them into cold water - fast!"

Alas, it was true. The pixies were overcome by heat and smoke and dangled limp, possibly lifeless. Laddie threw a kettle on the spit and splashed in some cold water while the Juggler untied the pixies and tossed them into it. It helped. They began to show signs of life. Red flipped the coin and caught it on the back of one hand, glimpsing 'heads' before he covered it with the other.

"You call it, Laddie", he said. "Heads or tails?"

"Heads", replied Laddie, scratching his own head in doubt. He was right to have doubts.

The Juggler lifted his hand and grinned. Somehow it had become 'tails'. He grabbed a saltshaker and reached for Poo. Atel landed on the kettle right in front of him.

"That wasn't nice, cheating Birthday Boy. I'm going to let him eat *me* to make it even".

The Juggler stepped back in surprise. "No! We'll flip for you too! Heads or tails, Lad?"

"*I get her!*" hollered Laddie, struggling to his feet.

"Make up your minds", said Atel. "But you'd better hurry".

The Juggler reached for her, grinning. "What's the rush, little boss?"

"Because you have only moments to live".

In that instant the sun peeked above the clouds and found Laddie, even as he threw up an arm to shield himself. The Juggler, safe for one moment in the long shadow of a tree, was struck in the next moment by reflected light from the hummingbird. Both suffered the same fate as Red, touched by the unexpected.

CHAPTER

3

ISHI & COMPANY

Atel turned to the pixies. "Come, little foot soldiers! No time for baths! There's a war on".

There was a mad scramble out of the kettle up onto the hot spit, a quick hop, skip and jump along that to the support post, and from there the babes jumped straight to the ground landing with a bounce, unhurt. Pixies are fearless and acrobatic with wings or without. But they cannot go to war on empty stomachs. Nobody can.

But what to eat? The frost had killed most of the flowers. Already they were wilting instead of opening under the morning sun. That would be a problem for the hummingbird, but the babes needed solid food anyway. Atel searched her memory, but there was nothing nearby that they liked, and time was fleeting. An anecdote from somewhere popped into her mind: Was there nothing for them to eat? Then let them eat *cake!*

"You can't mean *that!*" said Lolly pointing at the birthday cake, still bravely sitting there with its top blown off.

"I certainly do! Hop up there like happy little candles and try it".

They finally did, and liked it. Atel was not surprised. With any luck the Juggler would never bake another cake, but his final one was a masterpiece. A lot of sugar went into it, more than the recipe called for probably, but perfect for pixies. And speaking of sugar there was the sugar bowl, not yet put away, and a bit of water in the bottom of Laddie's bucket. Atel mixed imitation nectar for herself and the pixies soon caught on to that trick too.

While they gorged themselves, Atel outlined an initial plan. Ishi would have gone underground for sure, with a special purpose. The hummingbird knew where she would go, having spied out that part of the Underground in earlier years. There was a room with a large stalactite a mile or two down below as the tunnels twisted and turned (and dived). The stalactite overhung a deep pit and orange liquid oozed slowly down the sides of the formation, making it look like a giant carrot. Ishi hung a cast iron pot at the bottom to catch the drip, and this was the dye she used to paint new trolls on the rock walls, mixed with crushed fairy wings – boy fairy wings, up to now. It was the fount of Ishi's power.

The orange ooze stank and was partly the cause of the trolls' body odor. Where it came from was unknown, but it seeped down from above, from some kind of mess up at the earth's surface. Ishi came here often. It's where she would be going right now and might already be.

"But I doubt it", Atel finished. "This has been her dream for the past Age: Actual *Pixie wings!* But she's slow and we might catch up.

Let's go! There's a sinkhole entrance but it's a ways off and you'll have tough going through the brush".

That's where she was wrong. The pixies were quicker than rabbits and didn't stop like rabbits do. They soon found that it was true about thorns, how they let fairy folk pass, and they took shortcuts through brambles wherever they could. But sticker weeds were not as friendly. One might think prickly stickers should fall into the friendly category, but most didn't. And nettles are friendly to no one.

Still, they reached the sinkhole a whole lot sooner than big folk could do it. It was a widely sloping pit strewn with old junk and overgrown with vegetation. Lots of sinkholes have that much in common. But there was no hole at the bottom, which usually means there's a troll-cave entrance. If there is an open hole, trolls don't use it.

The answer to the missing hole is concealment, of course. The entrance is there, but not at the very bottom where everyone would look. In this case it was under a big plum tree partway up the slope. The tree had long, exposed roots under the brush. Big trolls simply lifted up the entire tree and stepped down into the entrance below. Once inside they reached out through the roots and arranged the brush nicely again. This morning there was an obvious gap left open. That would be Ishi, too drunk to cover her tracks when she entered earlier. It looked pitch black through the gap. Atel rose up into full sunlight to rearrange her breast feathers, to absorb as much light as she could hold, while the pixies fidgeted below.

"We'll start in!" Airy called after a few moments.

"You'll do it in the dark then. A minute, please! In the meantime find *sticks* - stout ones! - to bring along."

They grabbed up what was handy and by then their patience was all used up. They plunged into the cave. Atel let them go and listened as the quick little feet slowed and stopped in the darkness. Trolls can see very well in the Underground. That goes without saying. But fairy folk need light and the pixies had lost their glow. Atel brought some light with her, a shimmer. With luck it would last throughout the trip and that would be short. She entered behind them.

As the pixies paused inside, something took a whiff of them. A loud whiff. The hummingbird uttered a few words of acknowledgment to someone - pair of 'someones', one on each wall:

"Greetings, *Snufflers*. Are you satisfied?"

It was the door wardens, Ishi's foxes. They appeared to be satisfied of their duty, but unhappy about letting three little snacks go by. Ishi had painted the foxes too, but unlike her trolls they were anchored in the walls and never slept. They didn't challenge the big trolls but made sure to identify anyone else who came and went - or tried to.

"What was that about?" asked Airy when they went on.

"Getting to know you. Making sure you're not rats. They don't like rats".

"Can't they see?"

"As well as you can, but their noses are better in the dark. Be happy you don't smell like rats! These passages are sometimes crawling with them and Ishi doesn't allow them out. That's mostly what the foxes are for, so the rats can't leave. The rats are bad news. I hope we can avoid them".

But around the very first corner their luck deserted them. Rats were waiting and saw them. They chittered and skedaddled toward the interior. These were the Arsi, the peculiar rats of the deep troll halls with their oversize ears and bulging eyes: Eyes and ears for the trolls, their masters, while the trolls slept.

"So much for surprise", said Atel. "They will hurry now to report trespassers in the tunnels. Maybe it won't matter. We don't know what lies ahead".

"Don't you know?" asked Airy.

"Put it this way: "I know *what* is ahead as far as I plan to go. But I don't know *who* is up ahead. We'll be expected now. The rats answer to Gorrah, King of the Trolls".

"That's what th'sticks are for, then? The rats?"

"Yes. Next time we see them they might not run".

"Th'might so!"

"Don't overestimate yourselves. For now, running is your only job. Forward, foot soldiers!"

The pixies moved off grudgingly, expecting a chuckle from the hummingbird, but there was none. A guide knows when not to, and that is what the hummingbird had become: A serious guide on a deadly serious quest. Ishi's grand scheme to multiply the race of trolls overshadowed their own problems. She must not to be allowed to bring it to fruition. Trolls had long been a scourge upon a decent world, but *rumored* more than actually *known*, and limited in numbers. If her plan worked it would soon lead to trouble with mankind. Sooner than Ishi wanted, most likely. Then trolls and other *Unnaturals* would be discovered and destroyed - or driven out. But so would fairy folk. Men barely put up with each other on this earth. They would never tolerate another race.

The cave passage was large and mostly natural but hewn wider in tight places by the big trolls. It was an important route, leading to Gorrah's Court far below. Atel led the way, and the pixies followed her shimmer as they passed over deep fissures. They could only guess at the murky depths by the faint echo of their footsteps far below. Trolls stepped right over these chasms but laid poles for rats to scamper across, with a special handrail for 'Mum'. The pixies had no trouble, being as agile as rats themselves, but larger animals would find it chancy. Even

'Mum' was at risk, handrail or no, when she was drinking. Judging by the disarrangement of the poles Ishi had nearly suffered a fall earlier on unsteady feet.

The thought gave Atel a moment's pause, no more. Her focus was needed for the way ahead. It had been a long time since she was here, and then only once. The memory wasn't perfect. Things may have changed. And then they did change.

A section of the original passage had collapsed in recent years, exposing a new steeply climbing tunnel. Trolls had begun clearing the blockage but given that up in favor of the new way. Atel followed and the pixies scrambled to keep up.

Presently they came to a series of rooms, very un-trollish, all partially caved in, that might once have been living quarters. Remnants of the largest room were open to the sky, or appeared to be at a glance, but it was only a domed, crystalline ceiling where a shaft of sunlight came in from outside. Trolls had ransacked and trashed the place, but a few flowers and weeds still grew in a central garden, bathed in that life-giving light. The flowers were huge, giving a hint of what once had been. All around were crushed wooden chests and broken pottery, mostly covered over by the rubble. Rats gnawed the wood now, in shadow, eyeing the newcomers with interest. The pixies remained in the doorway, such as it was, while Atel spoke to the rats.

"This place is new to me. Did your masters break in to steal treasure?"

"They took back their own!" chittered a large, flop-eared rodent. He pointed to the door. "The pixies are welcome, but not *you*. Beat it!"

"I'm traveling with them. Don't get your tail in knots over it".

There was no rush to enforce the bluster, just gnawing noises and sullen silence. Atel tried again.

"This place looks *fairy-ish*. Is it?"

There was still no answer.

"Okay, just asking. But I see how this works now: The fairies were kicked out and your masters took the food and treasure. Your kind get to chew on empty boxes".

The rat grinned suddenly. "Yes! It *was* fairies. We gnawed their bones!"

They all grinned then, half a dozen of them, peeking out from their ambushes. Like their masters they loved to gloat. Atel was waiting for it. Now she knew where they were and put her mirror to work reflecting the sunbeam at them, exposing a weakness she was aware of: They turned back to stone in the sunshine just like the big trolls.

The Arsi specialized in waylaying trespassers. That was their job. They crawled the walls and ceiling as easily as the floor and could ambush fliers as well as walkers. But not this gang anymore.

The pixies were speechless for a moment. Then they laughed.

"You're *awesome*", said Airy. "This should be easy!"

"Wrong. The light here was unexpected, no doubt the last daylight we'll see. I'm going to borrow a bit more of it and have a word with our friends". She looked to the crystal ceiling where a cloud of fireflies circled aimlessly.

"You talk to *bugs?*" asked Poo in surprise.

"Don't call them 'bugs', please. They are friendly to fairy folk. And yes, I do talk to them".

She did this while her foot soldiers loitered below, and the fireflies began to drift off toward the far doorway. In a few more minutes Atel settled back down, her shimmer recharged.

"They're confused", she explained. "Fireflies go underground in daytime like trolls. *Following* the trolls, some say, but that's not really true. These simply have not got used to the detour here and are dazed by the light in this room. I showed them the exit. Don't laugh about it. We may need to follow them".

"Did fairies live here, then?" asked Airy. "The garden must have been pretty, but it should be outside. I get the willies down here".

"You're a girl, so that's understandable. But fairies did live here. *Boy* fairies. They like the underground".

"And they were eaten up?"

"I greatly doubt it. The rats are liars. Let's go!"

Beyond the crystal room a dark emptiness yawned that Atel's shimmer could not measure. A steep rubble path led down to a wide fissure, now bridged to overflowing with rock from the cave-in. Beyond that the original tunnel picked up again, joined by side passages from - where? There were no signposts or maps. The Underworld has an extensive road network, but no courtesy desks.

A *trollway* commenced, a main passage with sculptures hollowed out within the walls. Here is where Ishi painted her 'boys' and awakened them with the light of fireflies in their eyes. The fireflies didn't mind, being fooled by the paint which contained the dust of fairy wings: *Boy* fairy wings, and thus *boy* trolls. Once awakened, the brutes stepped out to take up a life of mischief, leaving a niche - a void in the wall. There were many niches, and other trollways too, in the Underworld.

A lot of fireflies loitered in the passage, attracted to the paint probably. Ishi was crude with her brush and outlines of luminous paint still clung to the edge of the niches where she had painted sloppily. Arsi were everywhere too, some posted as lookouts but most watching from within the empty troll niches - one in each, obviously holding the space for their master - or curled up in their own niches at the feet of *occupied* ones, sleeping like their master above them. Sleeping trolls and rats appeared as luminous outlines on the walls, eyes darkened. But when faint light touched the eyes - rat or troll alike, which have no lids - they stared angrily at passersby.

Poo suddenly stopped and pointed at an empty niche. "Look! The Juggler!"

There could be no doubt about the familiar figure, even without his jug. The caretaker rat, faintly outlined with paint residue like most of them (and most live trolls) raised up and hissed at her. Poo laughed.

"Th'Juggler will be out for a long time", she said. "I hope you brought a lunch?"

"You'll be my lunch if you come any closer!"

The rat took a threatening step or two and Poo moved on, but not far. The next empty niche belonged to Laddie, the young troll. He had been painted in a sitting position and the rat - young like his master - skittered around on the 'lap' making false rushes at the unwelcome party.

"Your masters are delayed", Atel informed him. "You should make plans in case they never come back".

"Iggli doesn't talk much", sputtered the Juggler's rat, answering for the young one. "Do you have *news?*"

"Your masters got drunk and careless. They're *stoned*", answered Atel. She turned to the young rat. "You must be Iggli?"

The rat bared his teeth, eyes bulging as if they would pop out. The pixies backed away, worried about being hit if it happened. The Juggler's rat answered for him again.

"You're marked now, trespassers! We'll get you".

"I'll put you on the list", said Atel wearily, "but others are ahead of you".

She moved on. Laddie's niche was the last in the line, Ishi's newest creation for the local gang. They counted over thirty troll-niches in all, but Red's wasn't here. The size and shape of the niches varied depending on the height of the wall and ceiling. Ishi was very efficient. On high walls she made them tall. On lower walls, short and fat. Most spaces were occupied by sleeping trolls at this hour - an ordinary, run-of-the-mill bunch in Atel's opinion. Gorrah and his gang of cutthroats would have their own special trollway, she guessed, and crossed her toes that she would never find out.

"Will they come out after dark to search for us?" asked Poo.

"The rats? No. Remember? Ishi doesn't let them out".

"An' what if she *sends* them out? Th'would not be safe to sleep at night!"

"Just hush, please! Don't worry about it now".

"Okay, but we need to plug up the sinkhole!"

"Save it for later, Poo! We'll be lucky to get out of here ourselves".

"But----"

"But HUSH! There is something ahead, maybe a place I remember. Ishi might be there".

A dull orange glow came into view not far ahead, although distance is hard to judge in total darkness. The eye can be fooled in such a vacuum. They went on and the glow hung there seemingly in front of them for quite a while, the only sounds being the hum of the bird and a light pitter of pixie feet, until without warning other sounds barged into the tunnel: A scream up ahead of them and a shrill chatter behind. Atel recognized both instantly.

"Run for it the best you can", she urged. "That would be Ishi throwing a tantrum ahead of us. We can deal with her somehow, but not the other! You can guess what's chasing us".

Indeed they could. The rats had gathered in a pack and pursued. A shimmer wouldn't even slow them down, nor would sticks. Not a pack of them. Maybe the orange glow could provide enough light for Atel's mirror. It had better; they would need to defend themselves very soon. The rats were catching up swiftly in the dark passage.

Ahead, Ishi's screams became even louder and congealed into oaths sprinkled with her worst profanity. Atel had last minute doubts. *That* is what they were racing to face? If Ishi was the lesser of any two evils, they were in bad trouble. But it would get worse. They burst into a room filled with the glow.

The phosphorescent stalactite drooped wetly from the high ceiling. Orange-colored wetness oozed slowly down the sides. And there was Ishi's black kettle, hanging at the bottom to catch the drip. Fireflies swarmed around the stirring sticks, attracted to the mess in the kettle. Below the kettle was a pit in the floor where the stalactite dripped when the kettle wasn't hung.

A second glance suggested that the drip had *made* the dark pit, instead of a corresponding stalagmite. How? Ishi would know that but wasn't saying. She was hopping around a stone barrier that encircled the pit, kicking at it in a fury. If she could speak coherently she might have explained that the ooze was acidic and melted away the floor. But she had more important things on her mind.

She hadn't trusted her own balance to lean out and grab the troll-pot when she arrived earlier. Too drunk. She might slip! So instead of crushing the pixie wings into the paint kettle right away, she took a nap. But someone stole the wings while she snoozed! Right out of her lap and made off with them. And she knew who did it: The *rats!* Threads of her dilemma punctuated the tirade and Atel guessed most of it, but that would be for later. Right now a life-or-death battle was upon them!

The rats burst into the room, snapping at the pixies' heels even as they leaped up onto the stone barrier. From there they tried to defend themselves with the sticks. That didn't work at all, and the hummingbird could do little to help. In desperation they threw the sticks at their attackers and leaped up to the stalactite. It stunk, and it stung too. It was also greasy, so they immediately began to slip. They hollered so loudly it caught Ishi's attention, but in her surprise she did nothing.

"Grab them!" Atel shouted into her ear. "You know why!"

Indeed she did, but before she could act the babes slipped off the stalactite. They managed to grab the rim of the kettle, but all three on the same side, causing it to swing. Bad idea with greasy fingers. Worse yet, the back swing would bring them within reach of the grasping rats.

"Last chance!" shouted Atel.

The Troll-Mother reached out and touched the first rat that might get them, then another. They turned to stone, for she was also the Rat-Mother. The pack spooked and skedaddled - not back to where they came from but into the passage ahead. Ishi tipped the stoned ones into the abyss with pleasure. She was their mother, but her motherly instincts were badly frayed. The Arsi had turned out to be loyal to the big trolls instead of her, and this business was the last straw!

On the next back swing she plucked the pixies neatly off the kettle rim and glared at them. Yes, the dratted bird had a point: The pixies would make trade bait. But they were filthy! She tossed them into a pool of water near the wall.

"Wash up! Don't run off or I'll call the rats".

There was no argument. The stinging ooze washed off and the cold water helped their burns. They almost felt grateful but as girls they understood Ishi's real motive. She didn't want her dress messed up when she handled them. Atel saw a chance to offer sympathy.

"Bad luck, huh? I suppose the wings will have arrived at the King's Court by now".

"Yes. Rats, you know! Can't trust 'em".

"No. But we're going your way. It's lucky we met".

"Maybe". Ishi jerked a thumb at the pixies. "Will they be a lot of trouble?"

"No trouble at all. They want the same thing you do".

"Ah, yes. We'll sort that out later. I'm surprised they're still alive. What about my boys, upstairs, then? Did morning sneak up on them?"

"It did. They're basking under the sun right now. The beer turned out to be bad luck, but I guess you already know that".

Ishi didn't reply right away. She wasn't at her best with the hangover and a pack of troubles. Losing the wings so soon after winning them was maddening. Losing them to the rats and trolls - her own creations! – was infuriating. Gorrah, *King of Trolls*, had them by now of course. She refused to utter the words but that's what he had become. A *rival*. Well, she would see about that! It seemed only yesterday she had painted him on a cave wall - her very first troll! - but a disobedient brat from the moment she woke him up. Even the name was *his own* idea, not hers! If she hadn't needed him so badly she would've left him in the wall! But she did need him. Fairy folk had blockaded her in the Underworld, and she had no way out.

The Torrillogge

Who would guess that the *Outer Smuttysphere* - the cloud of polluted dust left over from earth's formation - would ever cause trouble for the pretty Earth far below? Not the Artisans of Evermore who sorted out the unwanted grime and expelled it, or even the Lord of Light, maybe, who approved of their decision. The smutty stuff ought to have remained in orbit, being too light to ever fall down again or to be cast off by the spinning planet into a clean Universe.

But way out there in limbo it fell under the influence of the Darkness. Resentment festered and spread through the dust. Sullen particles clumped together and began to grow, layer by layer like hailstones, until *Night Hags* appeared - first of the *Unnaturals* - who were heavy enough to fall down to the earth's surface.

Some Hags perished on arrival, splashing into the ocean. Others fell apart on the way down or broke up on landing, being little more than a collection of dust after all; but many survived in serviceable shape. They were despised and avoided by the *Naturals*, not taken seriously until they were everywhere, and by then it was too late.

They hated the Green Earth with its privileged inhabitants and overwhelmed it with dust and filth. It got so thick the sunlight dimmed and decent life struggled to survive - a dark period in earth's history often referred to as the *Smuttsee Minimum*.

Luckily for the young human race and other respectable life, the Lord of Light intervened and sent the Tempest, a mighty wind to clean things up. Hags couldn't withstand it. Many disintegrated in the first gusts. Some rolled with the punch but were battered into bits when they hit trees or rocks. Others tumbled into sheltered nooks and emerged later missing limbs or other faculties, but still capable of mischief. A few - a dozen hardened malcontents - were solid enough to endure the wind and went on to become the Great Witches of lore. And one Hag was blown into a hole in the ground and survived unharmed: The hag *Ishi*.

The Tempest blew most of the dirt back up to the Smuttysphere where hags are still being recycled to this day, but at a more reasonable pace. The Age of Hags was over. The young human race could begin to grow. But fairy folk would dominate the next Age, an Age of Enmity between themselves and the Hag-creatures.

The New Age began with a purge of surviving Hags. The 12 Great Witches, already in league with the Darkness, couldn't be gotten rid of, but ordinary hags could. Some had picked up a bit of crude magic and proved difficult, and a few were smart enough to blend into the human population, but most were hunted down. Hags never again seriously threatened the face of the earth. But all the while a different threat was building in secret. Ishi spent the entire Age brewing trouble underground.

She had fallen into a common sinkhole where the opening at the bottom led directly into large caverns. Happily for Ishi, her sinkhole drained a polluted area near a dump and the cave system was as dirty as the Smuttysphere. She felt right at home. The passage walls were grimy, and she spent years luxuriating in the touch, licking nourishment from the stone. Please understand, hags do not have normal bodies with blood vessels and digestive systems. They are packed together entirely of dust and dirt requiring mostly liquid to bind it together, although they do partake of certain foods. Just don't expect their food to look like your food.

She learned tricks that could be done with the stone. She discovered the stalactite room and caught the orange drip in her fingers to draw pictures on the walls but suffered burns from it and had to quit. That made her mad, as it would make any artist mad. But art will find a way. One day she stumbled onto a cave-in where the dump had fallen through the cave ceiling into a pool of water. A junk pile of treasures! She fished out a small kettle and a paint brush - Oh joy! - and even a plus-size black dress. She wrung it out and put it on. It was fairly clean, which should have revolted her, but didn't. Her feminine instincts approved of that much cleanliness, but no more.

She also grabbed an old gas streetlamp, the kind with a flip-up lid, and ventured above ground on a fine summer evening to collect fireflies. She could see decent enough in the caves, owing to her origins, but the artist in her yearned to see better so she could paint better.

A century passed, and her skills greatly improved. There were limits to her own cave system, but she learned to trace doors with her paint and open them into new passages - and shut them behind again so no one would know. Shutting them was perhaps unnecessary but she was cautious, suspicious that fairies - the *boy kind* - visited the new passages. In this she was proven correct and stayed out of their way until she had perfected her best trick: The art of folding herself inside a rock for concealment. For this she selected rocks that resembled noses - *big* noses - because they looked like her own nose.

With practice came perfection. The rocks actually took the place of her own nose, each new one replacing the last. She was thrilled with her do-it-yourself beauty secret! But more importantly, revenge against the hated fairies now seemed possible.

Oh - she had dreamed of revenge! Every hag knows about the awful wind and the atrocities that followed. Even new-formed hags floating down tonight know the horrible details because the news spread through the air. The Smuttysphere chafes with it yet, and a full load of resentment gets packed into each new hag. If Ishi lived a thousand years her goal would never change: Pay the fairies back! Now she could snoop on them and figure a way.

It was a while before her snooping paid off. Fairies had once mined these tunnels following veins of gold and silver-bearing ore, but the deposits were played out, gone. And so were the fairies, except a few local lads who used the tunnels simply for travel. She learned nothing from them that she didn't already know. They were just typical boys fascinated with treasure, and their tunnels led only to dead ends. That part irritated Ishi because she suspected that she was being fooled, that the dead ends weren't really dead ends. Fairies are clever that way.

She never learned that secret, but her dumb luck won out. One day she painted a door and it opened into a dark anteroom just off the old mine entrance. Stacked against the back wall, unused for years, were fairy wings covered in dust: A half-dozen pair. She would have ignored them, but the original stardust still glowed faintly through the dust, enough to cast an eerie glow against the wall. A thought struck her. It seemed to make the wall come *alive!*

Ishi paused. Her inner artist was intrigued. She thought about her vile orange 'paint', the only paint available. It had one outstanding quality: It ate into the stone and never faded. But it had become boring. She stared now at the pretty glow and imagined mixing prettier paint: Something worthier of her talents!

Gathering her hem to make a bowl she shook the wings off into it, collecting most of the sparkly stuff along with ordinary dust. Then she left boldly through the front entrance and discovered she was not too far from her own sinkhole. What a great day! She whistled all the way home, catching fireflies in her lamp and dreaming what to paint first, while unwittingly leaving a faint trail of sparkles behind her.

Local fairies found the trail that very evening and followed it to her sinkhole. What she possibly wanted with the stardust they couldn't guess. That part was very un-haglike except for the thievery, but they had known from her lingering smell that a hag frequented the area. Now her smell and the *esporellia* trail both went into the sinkhole together. She was trapped! There was no other way out: No air went in or out of the entrance, signaling a closed system. They went right to work plugging it up, much to the dismay of Ishi who could hear the commotion from down below. She abandoned her paint-mixing plans and hurried to see if her fears were founded. They were! Her front door was plugged. Worse yet, when she opened other 'doors' after that, the fairies were waiting on the other side. All her ways had been figured out.

She was doomed, because hags - even hardened ones like herself - have no muscles to speak of. She could never dig her way out. She was left with only curses and thoughts of revenge to keep her company, until finally she grew bored and remembered her paint pot. Aha! She would mix the sparkles into her paint as she had intended and paint her revenge on the wall! It would be only a picture of course, but it would be better than boredom. Hags live in fear of being trapped in boredom. A hag could live in a cave like this for hundreds of years with absolutely nothing to do. That frightened her. She went down to the stalactite room and mixed up her sparkly paint, then wandered the deep passages until she found a perfect wall: Sheer and tall, and smooth enough for the brush!

By the light of the firefly lamp she painted a powerful figure, huge and ugly with a nose to match, and stepped back to admire it. There! *There* was a creature strong enough to break out! She imagined the brute kicking boulders aside and grabbing the dratted fairies as they laughed at their little prank. *He* would throttle them! Bash their heads together! Of course it was a 'he'; nothing so ugly could ever be a 'she'.

It was uncanny the way the new paint glowed, made the wall 'come alive' just as she had hoped. She thought about what to name him and climbed up her stool once more, holding the lamp to his face, lingering about the eyes. The fireflies grew restless, thinking they were in the presence of fairies, and flashed ever more brightly. The eyes absorbed the light and suddenly lit up. Ishi climbed down in surprise and stepped back to see the effect. She smiled, wondering how far she could push the fantasy. There was only one way to find out.

"You are a '*Torrillogge*'", she said, using a word favored in the Smuttysphere to incite violence and mayhem. The creature heard, but the word contained too many letters for a disgruntled brute-in-the-wall just waking up.

"*Troll?*" retorted the brute instead. Ishi was delighted! It wasn't the answer she wanted, but that seemed trivial next to the accomplishment: A giant stone ruffian! She wondered what else it could do.

"*Troll*, then. Whatever", she replied. "But I'm your *Mum* and you do what I say. Don't forget it! Can you climb out of there?"

"No, Mum. Unless you tell me to".

"Good! First, promise you'll do whatever I say – *always!* Then I have a job for you".

"Sure, whatever". The troll grinned out the side of his mouth.

Ishi paused a moment. That sounded insincere coming from a slave. She prompted him several more times until it became clear he might say anything she wanted, but probably meant none of it. She scowled. A relationship like this must begin properly!

"I name you '*Guttifoul*'", she instructed him, which meant 'Ugly Boy' in her native tongue. "Say your name!"

"*Gorrah*", replied the troll with a smirk. That did it.

"Have it your way!" snapped Ishi. "It'll be '*Gorrah*', and you can stay in your wall until you crack!" She turned on her heel and walked away.

Smart alecks usually know when they've gone too far, but then it's too late. Ishi took up her brush and painted a second troll on the opposite wall where Gorrah could watch every stroke. She spent several days in the labor (as time is counted in the outside world) purely to irritate him. She gave the new one smoother features, thinking he might turn out more agreeable that way, and made him every bit as big as the first. She finished up with a short ladder, giving him a longer neck so he would be taller than the 'Gorrah' creature. By this time, her fireflies were getting old and gave off much less light, barely enough to awaken the new troll.

"You are a '*Torrillogge*'", she informed him.

"*Torrillogge*", he answered obediently.

"I name you '*Guttifoul*'. Say your name".

"*Guttifoul!*"

"Good! I'm your *Mum* and you'll do as I say, understand?"

"Yes, Mum!"

"Very good! Climb out of the wall. I have a job for you".

"Yes, Mum!"

Guttifoul led an obedient life, but it was a short one. As he leaned out from the wall a hairline crack in his neck opened up - a flaw in the wall unnoticed by Ishi in the fading light - and his head fell off, smashing into pieces. The rest of him reverted to solid stone and became part of the wall again. Across the way Gorrah laughed.

"It's just you and me now, Mum, so we're pals again! What's the job?"

'Mum' saw no further reason to quibble and loosed a scourge upon the world. Gorrah made short work of the plugged entrance and stepped right out into bright sunshine. He didn't even have time to shade his eyes before he turned back to stone. That would prove to be a handicap for all stone trolls, but an unavoidable one: They spring from deep stone that was never meant to see the light of day, and daylight will have its revenge.

It slowed Ishi's plans a little, but not a lot. After sunset she simply woke Gorrah up again and turned the bad experience into motivation.

She explained that light was bad, and creatures of the light - *fairy folk* - had done him wrong!

She went on to make many trolls. Recruiting her own army now became simple. But the army turned out to be mutinous.

Gorrah had gone his own way even before the end of the lecture figuring he knew everything he needed. Out of frustration, Ishi painted a rat on the wall below Gorrah's niche and awakened it also, sending it out to shadow him and report back to her. It worked well, and she adopted the practice with all her trolls, but eventually Gorrah caught on and made a pet out of the snitch, even getting him to spy on their Mum until she caught on to *that*. She put an end to it by dunking "Snitch' in her paint pot to light him up permanently. Presto! No more sneaking. Very amusing for Mum. But it highlighted a bigger problem: Ishi had founded a troll empire only to find it uncontrollable.

Gorrah set himself up as leader of the trolls down deep where rock is warmer and fireflies gather to overwinter, calling it his 'Court' and himself King. That had a noble ring, but Ishi imagined it to be nothing more than a gang headquarters where the toughest trolls lived it up. She had never been invited, which always struck her as rude. She would pay a visit now!

Ishi blinked away the irritations. Someone was talking to her, one of the pixies. *Demanding* something. Well, what next!

"You never answered me!" repeated Airy. "What do you want our wings for?"

As before, Ishi only smiled.

"She would crush them and mix the dust into her paint", said Atel. "She wishes to paint *lady* trolls, but she needs something prettier, more *feminine*, to mix in. Her plans have suffered a setback, however. The Troll King has your wings right now".

"An' what does *he* want them for?"

Atel left that one alone, but the Troll-Mother had no qualms about answering. She didn't smile this time.

"Frosting".

The cavern went quiet for moment. Then Poo asked, "For cake?" She was rewarded with an angry nod.

The pixies laughed. Ishi became upset and moved off toward the 'exit', the down-sloping passage into the Greater Underworld.

"What's so funny?" asked Atel when she left. "Your wings would be crushed for that purpose too".

"'T'would be a sweeter ending", giggled Poo. "Wouldn't you rather be frosting than *trolls?*"

"Enough! You might have to make that choice yet. Just don't upset her *needlessly!* She plans to trade you to Gorrah for the wings, but she has a bad temper and might throw you to the rats just as quickly".

They caught up to her at a fork in the passage where Ishi stood undecided, thrusting her lamp back and forth. She rarely ventured beyond the stalactite room, hadn't for a good many years, and was paying the price of forgetfulness. Now a lone firefly hurried past into the right-hand passage, and she hurried after it. The fireflies went where the trolls went, and so must they! She remembered that much. But at this hour fireflies were few, just stragglers in a hurry, and Ishi was slow. They lost sight of it until they turned a corner and saw light again far ahead, but not quite the same light. It didn't move, didn't switch off and on, just glowed. The cave passage tilted steeply downhill now, necessitating caution, and the light proved farther away than it had seemed. Farther away and somewhat larger. As they finally approached, it moved. It *wiggled.* Ishi halted and leaned forward suspiciously. Her nose twitched.

"Snitch!" she barked. "Is that you?"

The only answer was laughter - a chittering, giggling sound that plainly irritated the Troll-Mother. Drawing closer, the light turned out to be a large rat, glowing like moonlight, standing alone at the dead-end of the tunnel. It was Gorrah's personal rat come to check them out for his master.

'Snitch' looked them over disapprovingly. No one was ever permitted to enter the King's Court uninvited, although it happened sometimes. There were occasional rogue trolls and once in a while some creature from deeper in the Underworld, but this group was very suspicious. A visit from 'Mum' would be awkward, not at all welcome, and the bird was out of favor with the Boss. Even now as Snitch glanced at her she reflected his own glow back into his eyes, the foul thing!

But the pixies, now! That was different. Pixies were always welcome (on the menu), but none had ever been stupid enough to volunteer like these.

"Eeek-k-k! Hullo, Mum!" he chittered. "What brings you down here? Lost?"

Ishi laughed at him. "My dear Snitch, who could get lost with you around? You're a walking lighthouse! Given up your sneaky ways, I suppose?"

The rat scowled. "Insults won't get you an audience before the Court".

"I'll get that much without your help."

"Yeek-k-k! No-no! You need an *appointment*, Mum. That's the rule! But Court is adjourned now, anyway".

"Don't give me trouble, rat! Tell your boss to put on some underwear, he's getting company! I've got business with him".

Snitch leered. "A swap, huh? Pixies for pixie wings? Ha! Too bad! The Boss ain't available..." (here Snitch smiled broadly) "...but I might deal. He's got the wings on his lap. What'll you give me? I'll steal 'em for the right price".

Ishi studied him. "How do you figure to get away with that?"

"The Boss takes naps".

"And when he wakes up and the wings are missing?"

"We'll leave your pixies for him to play with, but I'll be out of here. *Way* out of here! All the Arsi go free! That's the deal".

"Forget it. The foxes will eat you".

"Eeek-k-k-k! No, Mum! You'll put them to sleep for us. That's *your* end of the deal."

"No deal! I'll talk to Gorrah first".

Snitch shrugged. "Too bad, Mum. Like I said, he's sleeping. All the trolls are sleeping. And when they're asleep rats rule! This is *our* time!"

On this signal, a vicious pack of Arsi issued from hidden cracks and went for the pixies who barely avoided the snapping teeth by scrambling up onto Ishi's shoulders. Rats scrambled up after them, almost more than Ishi could swat off. These were a larger, more belligerent type: The personal rats of Gorrah's worst bully boys, accustomed to scraps of fresh meat. The pixies kicked at them with little effect.

Atel went after the ringleader, reflecting his own bright glow in a narrow beam that found his toes. Snitch yelped and danced, and suddenly turned and whispered something to the wall, which swung open in the middle. He shouted an order and beat a retreat through the opening, followed by the whole pack. The doors immediately slammed shut and they were alone again, almost like it hadn't happened.

"Now what?" blurted Airy. "They know the way! We should follow them!"

Ishi chuckled. "Stick with me, little one! I'll make sure you find all the trouble you want. Are you comfy there?"

Airy shifted position a bit on her shoulder. "Yes, ma'am. Very comfy. Except for your whiskers".

Ishi stiffened. "Nice girls don't talk about that".

"Well - sorry! But th'*poke* me when you take a step".

"Suffer through it! Not many steps now. Soon you'll be out of your misery".

"I don't think so! One more step and we'll bump our noses. Can you open it like they did?"

Ishi didn't answer. The huge doors, when shut, looked exactly like the cave walls. A spell would open them, but she hadn't caught Snitch's exact words in the confusion. None of them had. No matter! Ishi tapped here and there with her lamp pole, listening, then dug out a small bottle from her pocket, a fingernail polish vial with an artist's brush inside, and painted her own little door at the foot of the big ones. It was her troll paint of course, and she used it sparingly. A narrow line worked as well as a wide one for this. The real trick was to trace it properly over a thin part of the wall, adding hinges so the door could swing freely. A doorknob wasn't necessary. When she was satisfied with her artwork she leaned close and whispered. It flipped open like a doggy door. Ishi stepped through with the pixies into a brighter passage, but when Atel tried to follow the door flipped shut in her face.

Ishi knew that would happen. The big doors were loyal to Gorrah. They could be broken, or tricked like she had just done, but would in no way admit someone without legitimate business, like Atel. Ishi glanced back to be sure. Good! She was rid of the bird! That had been a worry. Now she had the brats to herself, and they were unhappy. Ha-ha! Ishi enjoyed this. They were at her mercy! But she was in a tricky spot too, locked in just now with the very worst of her own creatures.

The brighter light on this side revealed a scene from Ishi's past. A whole Age had gone by since she toiled here painting the first trolls. The first niche was Gorrah's, with Snitch's just beneath. After her initial success she had painted a long row of very big trolls along the same wall, the tallest, smoothest wall in all the caverns. The opposite wall she left vacant after *Guttifoul's* accident. Later she had painted rats for all of them, and here they were now - hissing and spitting at her! Ungrateful vermin! They were guarding their masters who slept in the niches at this hour.

The stone was different at this depth, speckled with quartz which reflected and diffused the trollish glow into every corner. The room held no shadows except an imaginary one behind her. She thought about that now because of the creepsy noises back there. Like most mothers she could usually spot misbehavior as if she did have eyes in the back of her head, but of course she didn't.

"They're sneaking up behind", reported Lolly, "in case you didn't know".

"Thank you", replied Ishi, and she meant it. "Keep me posted. It's *you* they want, and I need you for something else".

Ahead, at the far end, the passage broadened into a wide room that glittered with calcite speleothems. Stalactite and drapery formations caught the eye immediately among other beautiful crystal deposits. But the main attraction was a raised, coned stalagmite that dominated the center, perched atop ripples of flowstone that spread across the floor. A huge troll sat there as if on a throne and glared through a partition of column formations that served to keep beggars and petitioners at a respectful distance. Now he reached down and grabbed a fresh bone to crunch and vent his irritation on, one of many strewn on the pretty floor. On his shoulder, whispering in his ear, was Snitch. He had awakened the Boss in the middle of his nap, and someone would have to pay for the disturbance! Snitch was promising that 'Mum' would pay, that the rat pack would grab her pixies and Gorrah wouldn't have to deal with her at all.

"Here they come!" yelled Lolly.

They swarmed Ishi again, scrambling up her dress as before but in greater urgency. The lead rat lunged at Lolly but missed and bit Mum instead. Enraged, she jabbed him with a finger, and he dropped stone cold. She jabbed several others and they also turned to stone. The assault backed off, but Gorrah had now witnessed the little trick she planned to use on *him*. He grabbed up a club with one hand and hoisted the pixie wings with the other, shaking them defiantly. Water shook off them. He laughed, and water flew from stalactites on his chin. The 'throne room' was damp and dripped endlessly from the ceiling feeding calcium to the beautiful formations. The most persistent drip fell onto the big, coned stalagmite, or had before Gorrah sat there. After that it dripped on him. Well, calcium must stick somewhere and for the past Age it mostly accumulated on the King of Trolls. He liked it, being related to the mineral anyway. It gave him mystique. Eventually it would seize up his joints like arthritis but until then it was no worse than humans with a lot of body jewelry.

"Ho-ho-ho!" he bellowed, still shaking the wings. "Look who's come to visit! You want *these*, Mum?"

"Yes. Snitch stole them from me. I want 'em back".

"Too bad. Your claim expired when he gave them to me".

"Don't quote me the law, Sonny! They're mine! But I'll trade the pixies for them, even up".

Snitch whispered into the King's ear again and a smile contorted Gorrah's lips. Calcite icicles broke off from the seldom-used muscle contractions and he grinned wider.

"Why should I deal when I can have both?"

Ishi looked sharply at him. The grin turned into a sneer.

"You were trapped underground once before, Mum - in the Old Days. I dug you out then, but I'll plug you in now!"

"Oaf! I want to paint *girlfriends* for you and your pals, don't you get it?"

96

"Sure, I get it. But would they be cute? I don't think so! Your little redhead there is cute! I might even give her wings back if she promises to grow up and marry me".

Ishi changed tactics. So Gorrah still fancied the pixie girls? The Troll Mother knew all the old stories. That hadn't played out very well for him, once upon a time.

"What about the other two? Don't you like blondes or brunettes?"

"Sure, I like 'em all! But pixies are rebellious. It'll be tough enough to keep even just one in line".

"Maybe you should see them dance before you choose".

"Hoo! *Now* you're talkin', Mum!"

Gorrah leered at the pixies. Mum was right. The more he thought about it, the others were really cute too. It might be a tough decision after all. He bit off a huge plug of tobacco and settled back grinning to watch the show.

Pixies love to dance even in times of danger, as we have seen. It's just in their blood. But this was disgusting. At Ishi's suggestion they hopped up onto her hat brim and grudgingly formed a queue to audition. But Gorrah had other ideas.

"No! Not by turns. Make a *chorus line!* But hold up with that. Hey, Snitch! Get some music going! Fetch beer!"

Partying and drinking had gone out of style at Court long ago and been replaced by arguing, drinking, and brawling. Good humor had been lost. What was to laugh at anyway except the losers? And they were usually the same bums.

But now: *Dancing girls!* The King of Trolls would be entertained like a King ought to be! Snitch scurried and squeaked orders. Several rats headed for the cellars, the rest slipped past Ishi and chose instruments from among the scattered bones. A few went to rouse their own masters for the show, but Gorrah nixed that. *He* would be entertained first! His bully boys could get in on the fun later.

Beer was brought in the Royal Mug, a dented 10-gallon milk can from the same dump where Ishi found her treasures. Gorrah chugged it, sent for a refill, and drummed his fingers on the throne waiting for the music to begin. Where was the conductor? Ah, there he was!

Snitch appeared from behind a drapery. It had to be him because of the glow, but that was the only clue except for the tail. He wore a polished skull, or animated it if you prefer, setting the teeth a-snapping and a-chattering in the usual ghoulish rhythm used for teasing prisoners. The other rats joined in, whacking loose ribs against shin bones or whatever. The pixies covered their ears and Gorrah threw his bone at the conductor. It glanced off the skull with enough force to pause the performance.

"Stop! They don't like it. *Sing* for them".

Pity poor Snitch. He had no idea what to sing. Drinking songs had been popular in the Old Days when Gorrah entertained visitors, but they were vulgar. The Boss obviously wanted the pixies to enjoy this. That was a new twist. Okay! He shrugged off the skull and tried to carry a tune while the musicians gnawed their bones for gentle background music. He crooned in a dialect of the Underground which the pixies didn't understand. That helped - since the only lyrics he knew were meant to frighten and shock. In this the Arsi were ahead of their time and likely their music escaped the Underworld at some point. How else to explain our modern rockers and rappers? Snitch even did a little tap dance on top of the skull that looked comical and made Gorrah laugh.

Only pixies could choreograph such gibberish into a line dance. It didn't bring out their best, but the King of Trolls was pleased as punch. The poor guy had waited nearly an entire Age for another gander at cute pixie girls, and now he whooped and whistled and made up for lost time.

"YEE-HA! Shake them tushies!" he boomed, and they certainly did. Insulted and angry, they all mooned him at once, re-enacting the most humiliating moment of his life. He roared, shattering one of the restraining columns with the sound waves, and grabbed for the pixies through the gap. There would be no more dancing! No more stupid romance! He would eat them right *now* and put an end to the foolishness!

The pixies ducked behind Ishi's hat, and he missed them, but he didn't grab nothing. Ishi was waiting to touch him with her finger, and he got *that*, anyway. His roar cut off suddenly as he returned to stone. In the moment of hush the Arsi stood amazed, but not the visitors.

Ishi lunged desperately for the wings, now fallen to the floor, but the columns were in the way and her fingers scrabbled inches from the prizes. In fairness to her, no one could have gotten between the pixies and their wings in that free-for-all. There is a magnetism at work. Pixie wings, unspoiled, are as alive as their owners and drawn to them. In a moment, the pixies were flying again like they had never lost them. But where to fly? From the talk of 'cellars' and 'kitchens' there must be other routes through this part of the Underworld, but who would know? Not Ishi. But she did know where they came in. The pixies were foot-soldiers no longer, but they were stuck in Ishi's company, and she knew it.

"Follow me, little ones!" she cackled. "It's your only hope".

She moved off into the trollway waving her finger of doom, pixies close behind, and the rats yielded right of way. There were more of them now, hundreds of them. Clearly, Mum couldn't stop them all if they mounted a determined rush - so why didn't they? It seemed odd.

Not that it mattered so long as they gave way ahead, but there would be no escape to the rear. The Arsi swarmed the hall behind them and climbed the walls. Rats with the longest, sharpest claws crawled the ceiling. Everything depended on Mum and the chances of reaching her private door, but she seemed in no hurry at all, declining even to look behind when Poo warned her about the rats.

With little mincing steps Ishi passed through the gallery of sleeping trolls, as confident as you please. But surely Snitch could awaken these, as he had awakened Gorrah! Ishi was giving him all the time in the world to do it. Why didn't he? The brutes might easily block the doors ahead.

But now they passed the last sleeping troll and approached the doors, which appeared as ordinary doors from this side. The Arsi closed in behind, blocking out most of the light. Well, that shouldn't matter. All that mattered was Ishi's little door. When that opened, the pixies would bolt past. They could find their own way out from there. It seemed simple, even odd that Ishi would risk it.

Of course she didn't, although she carried the charade right up to the door and kicked it gently in mock dismay. "Oh dear!" she chuckled. "It doesn't open! Maybe Snitch can help".

"That's what we're here for", said he. "You know what we expect for this".

"Yes. But pixies will decide your fate, Snitch, along with their own. They will choose! What do you say, little ones? Mum has stumbled into a dead end and can't save you unless you choose wisely. Which will you give up this time: *Life* or *limb?* One or the other has to go".

"We wouldn't live long without wings", replied Airy. "We'll keep them this time".

Ishi was annoyed. "Still don't trust Mum? What's missing? I've arranged this so everyone gets something: I get the wings, the rats go free into the Upperworld, and three little pixies live happily ever after!"

"Pixies aren't happy without wings".

"You'll get used to it, in time".

"We don't have much of that". It was obvious. The rats were creeping forward, drooling. Ishi's vise was closing.

"Sad, but true. So give up the wings and you can perch on my shoulder again".

"I don't think so! Th'would have no reason to keep us alive".

"But I do! I've become almost fond of you scamps. Isn't that a reason?"

"*Almost* a reason isn't one."

"Well - I'm *almost* sorry! But giving up the wings again is your only chance. Otherwise, the rats can have you. I'm not bluffing".

"Get us out of here, then we'll deal".

"No. I want them *now*".

"We want some assurance".

"Don't argue so much! *Mum knows best!*"

As soon as she said it she regretted it. Of course it was the password she used for everything. The little door swung open and Atel appeared in the opening.

"*Shut up!*" barked Ishi - speaking to the door, not the bird. The door slammed shut on the countermand, but the pixies had already zipped through. The rats squealed in disappointment. Ishi stood amazed at her own blunder. Snitch quickly gave the big doors a little shove and from that they opened by themselves, going out, being designed for convenience in a busy passage. Ishi gave the order to charge through in pursuit.

CHAPTER

4

THE DOORWARDS

"Well, look at you now - wings and all!" said the hummingbird, some ways ahead. "It must've been pretty easy. Don't lag now. Keep up!"

The pixies fled up the passage trying to stay abreast and argue, but they were ignored. Atel didn't allow a stop until they reached the stalactite room, and then only for a short breather. They perched on Ishi's stirring sticks, up away from the occasional drip and splash.

"Everything else can wait", said Atel, "but I'm dying to know why Ishi opened the door for you. I can't believe she did that".

"We couldn't either", laughed Lolly. "I'm sure she didn't mean to".

"By rights we should be rat chow by now", said Airy more seriously.

"Whatever happened to *you?*" asked Poo.

"I'm sorry", confessed Atel. "Ishi outsmarted me. Her door wouldn't admit me, and I couldn't guess her password. What was it?"

"*Mum knows best.* Th'was the last thing she said".

"Aha! I *did* guess it, then. But the door heeds only Ishi's voice. Doesn't matter now, it's behind us. But the next door will be more difficult".

The pixies looked at each other. "Th'*aren't* any more doors", said Airy. "What's to stop us?"

"You're forgetting the stone foxes".

"All they do is *sniff*".

"Yes, to learn who you are. But they do Ishi's bidding. What do you think that would be if they sniffed out three little pixies going in? You can be sure they're waiting for you. Is everyone rested? Let's go!"

"No rest here anyway", grumbled Lolly. "Why do these sticks tingle so?"

"They're *wands*, such as only the Great Witches have. I can't guess how Ishi came by them. If we were big enough to use them our escape would be easy". Atel laughed. "What about it, pixies? Can you just grow up for a few minutes and bring the wands along?"

It isn't that easy, of course. Growing up was for romance only, and only *once*. The pixies did their best to ignore her.

"No? Then we'd better hurry along. Maybe we can deal with the foxes before everyone else shows up".

Unfortunately, the idea of speed soon had to be abandoned. The hummingbird's 'shimmer' was fading out. There would be no light at all through a long stretch coming up. They had a lead on the big rat pack, but there were plenty of other rats who might ambush them in the dark. Atel led the way almost like a bat, listening for echoes. The pixies followed single file, guided only by the hum of her wings in front of them.

After the pitch dark, the light seemed dazzling in the Juggler's trollway when they reached it, though it was only the outlines of sleeping trolls and empty niches. The rats were all gone, even Iggli and the Juggler's rat. Good riddance to them.

Beyond, the trollway darkness closed in again, less frightening maybe, but more boring. A change of air alerted them to each cross tunnel, but these too were deserted. There were no ambushes nor any sound at all - not a pebble falling or drip of water - and they gained confidence as they passed them by.

They came to the steep rubble slide that had been so difficult to clamber down and it was easy now, going up with wings. A friendly light beckoned them, the true light of the fairy ruins with its domed ceiling. Here they expected to find no active Arsi but heard one gnawing in the shadows.

"Hello!" called Atel cheerfully. "I missed you earlier. Where are you hiding?"

There was no answer. The pixies laughed, and that drew a response.

"Laugh, little sun dogs! You'll never get out. No one *ever* gets out. Mum has a surprise for you".

"The foxes?" replied Atel. "We know about them. They eat rats, don't they?"

There was a faint rustle behind the debris and the rat clammed up. The foxes were a taboo subject among the Arsi, far more frightening than being 'stoned'. Rats had learned years ago about being stoned by the sun. Some sat for months or years before fireflies discovered and re-awakened them, while other rats used their statues like dogs use fire hydrants. That was humiliating. But the foxes were death. The rats feared them.

Atel went up and re-charged her shimmer while the pixies poked around the crystalline dome looking for a way out. There was no way. The window was thick and seamless. Perfect for light to pass through, but nothing else.

They went on, retracing their steps through the natural cave passages, across the rickety 'bridges' still disarranged where Ishi had disturbed them. There was no sign of recent activity, no sign of life. It was eerie. Surely the rats were pursuing them, but where were they?

<hr>

Ishi wondered the same thing. The rats had ignored her order to pursue and suddenly charged *rearward* instead of forward. Left by herself, she had trudged all the way back to her troll pot and rested there to catch her breath. So be it! The rats were undependable, but her foxes would stop the pixies. *They* would follow orders. They had no choice! The thought cheered her, and a new plan began to take shape.

She knew several routes from the stalactite room to the foxes, mostly shortcuts she had opened herself. *Private* shortcuts, not for rats. She grabbed her stirring sticks - mustn't forget those! – and chose the shortest route, mumbling to herself, "Where are the stupid rats??"

The answer was simple. It was their lunchtime. By coincidence, at the very moment the pixies escaped through the door a bell had rung way back at the kitchens - their dinner bell - and on that note the rat horde charged to the rear.

It stumped Ishi, but she wasn't familiar with everyday life in the Underworld. The rats must eat too! Though not as well as their masters, naturally. Gorrah and his bullies ate late at night, near dawn outside time, and it left quite a mess for the stewards. The King demanded freshly roasted meat, so there were always leftover bones and gristle as well as remains from the butchering. Most days the cleanup finished around noon and the garbage was dumped into the tunnel behind the kitchen. The cook then rang the bell and quickly shut the door to keep the mayhem outside. Instantly, rats came from everywhere and everything looked like food to them. Even the cook's hairy legs would be chewed up if he were slow to shut the door. But it got even worse. When all the scraps were gone, the cook tossed out a pail of blood and the mayhem redoubled.

The Arsi thirsted for blood. Maybe the native stone was dry in most of the Underworld and that would explain the thirst, but the blood-craving was unnatural. A small pail never satisfied them, so the horde dispersed searching for more. Pity the occasional *warm bloods* then, who wandered into the troll caves and were discovered. The rats made short work of them, which is exactly what their masters wanted. Or sometimes the *warm bloods* might get back to the exit only to be devoured by the foxes. Either way was a happy outcome for the trolls. They were never threatened while they slept.

So trespassers were allowed - even welcomed! - but none ever got out alive. Nor did any rats - since the falling-out with their Mum - and the foxes enforced the rule as Ishi's only loyal servants: *Very* loyal servants, though not of their own free will. They once were Great Witches, now just Ishi's doorwards locked up in stone.

The Stone Foxes

The familiarity between a witch and her fox (or any animal) that has spawned so many fanciful interpretations, was never between two separate creatures but simply the witch herself at different times of the day. The witch, who is nocturnal, becomes the fox at sunrise, and then reverts to herself again after sunset. The practice was begun by the First Coven, a group of scattered, bitter hags who came together a hundred years after the Tempest when hags were thought to have been wiped out but weren't. Not quite.

Twelve loners had survived so long by staying out of sight and practicing their rituals quietly. Each believed they were the last hag on earth, soon to be the final innocent victim of unfair persecution. There was no tolerance! No *sufferance* in this world! They were hunted simply for practicing *live human sacrifice*. And also *live fairy sacrifice*, which was even more fun.

Alone they were doomed, but over time that changed. Voices from the Darkness whispered to them, and they became aware of each other.

A thirst for companionship and revenge drew them from their lairs to a common hilltop under a new moon where they came together and swore oaths, with no other witness but a locust tree. Voices from the dark sky bid them to touch the tree and behold: Silver thorns sprouted grotesquely from the trunk, but the longest ones felt useful in their grip and they took these to use in their demon worship. Thus, both wands and witches came into being all in one unfortunate evening.

The wands inspired black magic, a vast improvement over the crude spells that hags pick up on their own. Better yet, the wands became aware of the likes and dislikes of their masters - especially the dislikes - and served the witches well in their vendettas against everyone else. Life became fun again and their gruesome ceremonies more common, but the newfound success did attract a lot of attention. All too soon, anonymity became desirable again and the wands provided them with a trick.

Witches by nature are most active at night anyway, and it was only during daytime that they feared trouble, should a mob discover them. But an animal would arouse no suspicion, so they conjured up a simple spell to change their appearance. They favored the fox as an alter-ego during daytime and the ruse has worked well ever since. Witchdom went on to reach its greatest heights although the Coven suffered some turnover. Membership is limited to 12, but fortunately for new hags with ambition, a vacancy doesn't have to be natural.

The fun lasted until Ishi invaded their comfort zone with her trolls and troll rats, determined to make life miserable for everyone in the Upperworld. Black magic had no effect on creatures from the stone, so Arsi tracked down the witches at night and trolls hassled them for sport. It upset the Coven so much that two witches went to see Ishi one evening to broker a peace, but she brushed them off at the cave entrance. They left with threats and a dire warning that she'd better think it over.

Ishi did think it over. The Arsi had recently turned against her, and she wished to punish them, to lock them up! But how? The visit by the witches gave her an idea: Far-fetched maybe, but extremely useful if it could be accomplished.

She had learned enough from her daily prowling to suspect the witches of employing an alter ego, much like she used a rock. It must be an animal, she figured. But which one? Hmmm! Well, she herself dressed like the witches and even had similar features. Which animal did *she* look like? She studied her mirror.

Crows seemed a possibility. They mimicked her all-black outfit. But they were very clannish, unlikely to put up with an impostor in their territory.

Cows had big, bulging noses, almost as pretty as her own. But they *licked* them. *Very* un-ladylike! And they were clannish too. It had to be a more solitary animal.

Ishi finally decided it must be foxes. They were quite attractive with their protruding snoot. They had all-black feet just like her boots and tall, pointy black ears like little witch hats. Close enough! Ishi went home and stirred up her troll pot.

A little way inside her cave entrance she began to paint a fox on the wall - the head and front quarters of one - taking several evenings to get it right. In truth, her skill was much improved by this stage of her career. It turned out quite lifelike except the eyes which looked empty, obviously lacking finishing touches. The next evening as she began a second fox on the opposite wall, the witches - *Bella* and *Louella*, she called them - returned, asking her to come outside (where they could hex her in the moonlight.) Ishi, no fool, replied that she was busy, and they should come in if they wished to talk.

The two stepped just inside. This was Ishi's ground where her big trolls might physically grab them. But there were no trolls, and they were impressed with the painting. They had a low opinion of her artistry, being familiar with her crude trolls: Amateurish! But they liked *this!* (As Ishi noted out the corner of her eye.). She continued to paint, more confident now.

"So! What are you crones bellyaching about tonight?" she inquired politely.

They rehashed the main points: Spying, harassing, betraying their activities to enemies, etc. etc. But they lacked the usual hard edge in their voices, watching her. Ishi teased them.

"That's all? Have my boys quit stomping your hats?"

That sore spot had been brought up at their first visit. Once in a while trolls did get hold of a hat and squished it underfoot like naughty boys. It was trivial among serious complaints, but it angered the witches more than anything else. Bella mummmmphed! Louella harrumphed! They stalked out, but Ishi called after them, inviting them to return again.

"Just a little joke, you'll get over it." she cajoled. "Come back tomorrow! We'll bargain".

Great Witches are not easily fooled but the paintings piqued their curiosity. Next evening they found Ishi working with her brush again and the second fox taking shape nicely. The haggling resumed and Ishi feigned stubbornness to drag it out. The witches showed remarkable patience, hoping to see the finished portraits, but dawn arrived with artwork and bargaining both unfinished.

Artwork shouldn't be rushed, maybe. Even witches know that. But they were angry at the slow pace of negotiations.

"Do you want to *deal* - or *not?*" demanded Bella. "You'll have to give up something if you want a truce!"

It was empty bluster. The witches had precious little leverage to bargain with and Ishi knew it. But she needed them to come back one more time.

"I'll have a word with the rats if they're bothering you", she offered innocently. "I'm an artist now. I want to be a good neighbor".

"Trolls too, or no deal!"

"Can't help you there. My boys don't listen to their dear old Mum. I could ask them to lay off the *hats*, but boys will be boys".

"Harrummph! We'll think about it".

The witches left and quickly changed into their own foxes as the sun was coming up. They were in good spirits. Ishi was finally showing her stupidity and they laughed about that, but mostly they speculated about Ishi's plans for the foxes. Would she turn them loose like her rats and trolls? Or (hopefully) keep them where they were? Stone creatures were nothing but trouble. In any case they would soon find out. Only the eyes were left to be painted and the witches were eager to see them. The next evening should find both foxes finished!

But they weren't, not quite. Ishi was being very fussy with her final touches.

"Please come in!" she bubbled, as if by now they were old friends. She had expected them and even set out a small table with beer for herself and extra glasses in case her guests might accept a bit of 'juice' to pass the time. Sure enough, as she fiddled and dabbed they grew bored and helped themselves. Of course, witches know nothing about beer. They hate humans (who invented it) and purposely avoid all human habits.

111

The night dragged on and Ishi worked feverishly, or pretended to, while the witches got drunk. So far, so good! But the timing would be tricky. As dawn approached the witches got ornery. Beer does that to some humans too and it's not any prettier. They smashed the glasses and demanded that Ishi should finish the eyes! Ishi re-traced the outlines once more, keeping her own eye on the growing light in the entrance. When she couldn't stall any longer she suddenly shouted: *"Dawn!* Look! It's *dawn!* Get into the foxes!"

They did, but in drunken confusion they jumped into Ishi's stone foxes. Boots and wands clattered to the floor, for the stone does not accept hard objects. Ishi grabbed up the wands and ordered the witches to *'STAY!'*, and they did stay. They were locked inside. That was obvious from a sudden change in the foxy eyes. They no longer appeared empty. They had Bella and Louella's eyes now. Ishi winked at them, but they didn't wink back. That gave the Troll-Mother another idea. She grabbed her paint brush and adjusted their eyebrows, raising them higher so the eyes could never shut. Perfect! She smiled happily. If they were going to work for her they'd better stay awake!

◆◆◆

Now, years later, Ishi still smiled when she thought about her obedient door wardens. The wands were the key. They had done her bidding as soon as she touched them. Maybe they would work for anyone, but they were forever out of reach for Bella and Louella. That posed a problem for the Coven, with just ten witches to cover twelve moons each year, leaving two moons wide-open. Well, that was their problem. Just now as she entered her shortcut Ishi mulled a problem of her own: How to corner the pixies without her rats? Bird and pixies would reach the foxes before she did, that was for sure. Ishi knew how slow she was, even with shortcuts. But the foxes wouldn't let them out. It would be a dead end. They never let anyone out without her permission. But they knew now that she valued pixies. Things could get tricky. They might use the pixies to bargain against her. Ishi scowled and tried to speed up - but couldn't.

Atel approached the foxes alone and was immediately challenged. They stepped silently out of the wall with their front quarters and blocked passage.

"Excuse me", said the hummingbird. "We're just leaving".

The foxes laughed, an annoying *yip-yipping*, and lolled out panting tongues.

"I've come and gone before. I'm sure you remember".

More *yip-yipping*, then whispers between them.

"Well?"

"Go ahead. Leave."

Atel moved closer. The foxes allowed a small gap for her. She moved into it, almost to their tongues, and held there. Exactly as she expected they did nothing, probably preferred that she did leave. It was the pixies they had their eyes on.

"You have bad breath!" commented Atel. "Do you follow a healthy diet?"

"We eat what we please", growled Bella, licking at the hummingbird's cheek. Atel moved back a bit.

"You eat whatever Ishi says, more like it".

The foxes leaned together again, closing the gap. Louella snapped her teeth.

"You had your chance!" she barked. "Now we'll eat you too and round out the diet. Hummingbirds are sweet, they say".

"Sweet, but small".

"Together with the pixies you'll make a nice snack".

"We may, but it won't be your snack. The Arsi will be arriving soon. We'll be *their* snack".

Louella whined and strained forward as far as she could, a matter of only a few inches, which is exactly what Atel wanted to know. Bella shot her sister an angry look.

"Rats would rip you into a hundred pieces", Bella warned, speaking to the pixies. "We'll be much nicer if it comes to that".

"How?" asked Airy. "Less pieces?"

"Don't get smart", snapped Louella. "You're supposed to be kept safe. That's our orders. We'll swallow you in *one* piece".

"We'll be gentle", said Bella sweetly. "You won't be any trouble, will you?"

"I don't know! I've never been swallowed by a dog before".

That upset the foxes. They strained forward but their rear ends were anchored inside the wall. Atel hardly noticed. Bella's last comment reminded her of Ishi who had uttered the same words not long ago.

She studied the foxes in a new light: They had black 'boots' like Ishi, a long nose, and a sly look. One could almost picture the Troll-Mother in these creatures. And what was Ishi if not a witch? It was the answer to a riddle.

"I know where your wands are", she said suddenly.

The foxes settled back in surprise, into their blocking mode. A different look came into their eyes.

"If you know, why didn't you bring them?" inquired Bella. "We could all go free!"

"You wouldn't help us. Witches don't like pixies".

"Don't like you either, but we could overlook that".

"Too late. Your Boss will have the wands in hand by now. She's coming to the party too".

"Oh, swell. Special occasion?"

"Yes. You know what *she* wants. The rats just want blood".

"We'll keep the brats alive. The rats can have *you*".

"Tsk! Be nice! I'm not here to help you, but it might happen accidentally. Can anyone use your wands?"

No answer. Then Louella whined. Bella scowled at her again.

"Excellent!" laughed Atel. "I'll take that as a 'yes'. Goodbye then and do be gentle! Ishi will expect the pixies in perfect condition when she arrives".

As she turned back to the pixies a dreadful chatter arose from the deeper passages. The Arsi were indeed coming.

"Do exactly what the foxes tell you", she instructed them. "Remember, anything is better than a rat's belly!"

"Where are you going?" asked Poo.

"To make sure Ishi arrives safely. You saw what shape the bridges are in".

"Which side are you *on*??" demanded Lolly.

"Everyone's, at the moment. Let's get the party started!"

Atel disappeared in the direction of the approaching chatter. The babes edged closer to the foxes who lolled their tongues out, licking and slobbering.

The hummingbird didn't have far to go. A melee had broken out at the first bridge below and Ishi was caught up in it as she edged her way across. Crazed rats barged past her and scrambled over the top of her. She lost her lamp for a moment, grabbed it again and tossed it onto solid footing, past the end of the bridge.

There! Now a couple more steps and she would be across too! But it was not to be. The last rat clambered over and knocked her hat askew, blinding her. She lunged forward, somehow managing to land with her elbows on the stone edge of the abutment. Now she clung there, cursing, legs and feet dangling helplessly into the void. It was a dangerous position for anyone, but hopeless for a hag with little strength of muscle - and for others too, if she fell.

Atel arrived and checked out her dangling feet, then hovered in front of the hat (which still covered her face) and interrupted her tirade.

"Hullo Mum! Are you hurt - or just hung up?"

There was a pause, then: "Is this the bird?"

"Yes. How long can you hang on?"

"Not much!"

"Do you have the wands?"

Another pause. "Why?"

"We'll need them. Tell me now. Or I'll let you fall".

"I got 'em. But you can't pull me up, little twit!"

"True. But you can *climb* up. Poke around with your left foot. There's a narrow step down there. Do you feel it?" She did and grunted with relief.

"Very good, Mum! Now reach up a little higher with the other foot. You'll find a good step there, too. Feel it?"

Ishi struggled up onto the ledge and lay there panting from possibly the hardest work she ever did. It didn't earn her much respect.

"That's a start. Now - up on your feet! Or can't you?"

Without comment Ishi heaved herself up, retrieved her lamp, and set off with little steps. Atel took a seat on her shoulder. That bugged the Troll-Mother, but she refrained from comment.

"Didn't think you'd mind", smiled Atel. "So! You'd better put your boys to work on that bridge, eh?" ... (Ishi mumbled something best left at low volume.) ... "And do something about your rats, too! Not my business, maybe, but they don't show proper respect".

As she hoped, Ishi got mad and squeezed out a little more speed. She also put a hand in her pocket, fingering the wands. Atel changed the subject.

"I'm impressed with your foxes, madam. I didn't know until today who they really are. Neat trick there! I hope they mind better than your other creatures".

"They mind perfectly".

"Good! Then by now *they* - and not the rats - will have the pixies".

"Ah! We want the same thing again, don't we?"

"Yes. We could make a good team, Ishi. What shall we do next? Teach your trolls to eat salad?"

"Ha-ha. All good things must come to an end, bird. Don't think too far ahead".

"Well?" said Bella to the pixies after Atel left. "You heard the bird. Come here!"

"We'll see", replied Airy. "There's no rush".

"There soon will be".

"What are you going to do with us?"

"We'll put you in safekeeping". The foxes laughed and opened their jaws wide. Even at some distance the pixies whiffed a strong alkaline breath.

"How do we know you won't swallow us?"

"Don't tempt us! We have orders, but we don't like them!"

"That's not very comforting".

"Don't worry, you'll be comfortable. We're *limestone*. That's organic, just like you".

This subject also needed to change and the Arsi did it in a frightening way. Dozens of yellow buckteeth suddenly appeared rushing up the passage toward them. Behind the galloping teeth a churning mass of rats charged forward, leaping for the pixies who hovered up near the ceiling. It wasn't high enough. Rats piled on top of each other to launch themselves, quickly closing the distance. The only escape was back toward the waiting jaws of the door wardens.

Louella whined and licked at them. Bella laughed, enjoying the spectacle. They were bound to save the pixies, that was true. Ishi had ordered them, using their own wands. But if they *couldn't* - if the rats got them first – they wouldn't cry about it. Pixies were fairy folk and deserved it.

Obviously, one side or the other would eat them in the next few moments, and then it became painfully obvious: Poo lost a toe to the rats and the foxes dutifully licked the babes right out of the air when they came close enough. Louella got Airy & Lolly; then Bella got Poo, bleeding from the foot, and savored the taste of blood before slurping the pixie into her mouth.

That still didn't stop the rats from attacking, which greatly amused the foxes. They grinned, exposing spike teeth like bars in a prison window and pixies peeking out through the bars. That inflamed the mob. Ishi had a full riot to deal with when she arrived minutes later. She grabbed Snitch by the ears and shook him until he squealed loud enough to get everyone's attention. The mob scattered then and regrouped a respectful distance behind Mum, except for Snitch who collapsed at her feet in a daze. The foxes clammed up, scowling. Atel left Ishi's shoulder and approached them urgently.

"Give the pixies some air!" she warned. "They're worthless if they choke in there".

The foxes stalled, hating Ishi almost enough to defy her. But Mum produced a bag with one hand and whipped out their wands with the other.

"Spit!" she ordered, stepping up to them, and they did. She caught the limp pixies neatly in her bag and stepped back again. Sensing opportunity she pointed the wands at Atel next.

"Stay!" she ordered. It had exactly the effect she wanted, but on the wrong victim. Atel expected it and reflected the energy back at her. Ishi froze with a sneer of triumph on her lip. The pixie bag fell from her grip and the wands as well, right in front of Snitch's nose just as his mind was clearing up. He grabbed the wands but hesitated, not quite believing his good fortune.

"You'll need to move the foxes out of the way", prompted Atel. "They're still blocking".

Snitch got it and pointed the wands in their direction. "Move!" he ordered.

The foxes growled and snapped their teeth at him.

"Try *BACK*"', said Atel.

That worked. They shrunk back into the walls.

"Now: *STAY! BE QUIET*"'.

That worked too. The way was open! But Snitch sensed opportunity just like his Mum and turned on Atel, thinking to settle old scores. She preempted him, flashing him in the eyes again with his own light.

He dropped the wands at Ishi's feet and retreated back down the passage with his mob. That saved them all from disaster since the sun was shining outside. In the evening cooler rat-brains would prevail. Their escape would mean trouble for the Upperworld. Ordinary rats had been a problem for Ages, but the murderous Arsi would certainly make things worse.

The pixie bag showed small signs of life. Atel went down and bounced on it, calling to them until they wrestled their way out.

"Come along!" she announced. "The fun's over here. You'll have to make your own mischief outside now".

They flew warily past the foxes who followed them with wild eyes, perpetual motion machines now but with only one moving part. The eyes shouldn't move either, technically, but it's difficult to totally shut down a Great Witch.

The rats ate Ishi's leather bag later but gave the mysterious wands a wide berth when they departed after sundown. The wands would lay there out of reach, just a few feet from their previous owners, for - who knows? - eternity, maybe. But at least it gave the foxes something interesting to look at.

As for Ishi, she found herself wide-awake and able to speak, yet otherwise stiff as stone, eyes fixated toward the entrance. She knew that one day someone would come, someone she could trick into helping her out. That was a happy thought, and there was one other: In the meantime, she could lecture the foxes with no interruptions.

PART TWO

THE PIXIE EFFECT

CHAPTER

5

THE STORM CROW

I t was a cocky flight of pixies that emerged from the sinkhole,
battle tested and ready to assume their rightful place in the world.
But the first place they had in mind was the noses of the stone
trolls, to moon them and gloat over them. Atel was not impressed.

"That kind of behavior brought a lot of trouble down your race",
she reminded them. "Now you're asking for it again?"

"Oh, Nanny! These fellows are harmless", declared Lolly. "We'll
be fine".

"You worry too much!" laughed Poo.

"Maybe you're right", decided the hummingbird. "The worst dangers should be behind you now, the ones that couldn't be avoided. Now you can stay back from trouble when you see it. That will be your own job from now on, by the way. As for me, I'm going to find something to eat. Maybe some flowers escaped the frost – or gnats, at least. It's turned into a beautiful day. The gnats should be out everywhere".

"You eat *gnats?*" asked Airy incredulously. Lolly and Poo just gaped.

"Certainly", replied Atel, irritated at having to explain herself. "You could too. It wouldn't hurt you one bit".

"Do they tickle?" asked Poo." Do they...*struggle?*"

"Never noticed. But then, I only pay attention to the flavor. Some are tastier than others. Shall I teach you which are best?"

They didn't answer. Atel laughed.

"You'll learn to eat lots of things now that it's your own responsibility. It's called 'survival of the fittest' by those who survive, and you'd better get started. It'll give you something productive to do!" She turned to leave.

"Wait!" called Airy. "What should we look for...that isn't alive?"

"Fruit. You've tasted a lot of that. Today - just to be safe - find some bramble berries or thorn apples. Something with thorns to protect you. That kind of fruit tastes good to fairy folk anyway. See you later, maybe!"

The pixies waved and fell to frolicking again, but after talking about food their stomachs wouldn't let them forget. Now they had to face up to it on their own. It was their nanny's way of informing them she was no longer a 'nanny'. Pretty soon they couldn't ignore the hunger pangs. They took off and circled the hill.

There was no sign of Atel but many signs of the frost, especially on the lower hillsides. The day had turned out warm, as

Atel had noted, and many green leaves had wilted under the hot sun giving off a sweet, pungent odor.

The first fruit they investigated - orange berries on a mountain ash tree - tasted sour, notwithstanding that birds seemed to love them. But the tree had no thorns and perhaps that explained it. Next was an apple tree with delicious-looking red fruit, but a hook-billed shrike eyed them from a high branch, obviously interested in *them*, not apples. So much for that tree. They departed through the underbrush.

A third tree was the charm: A hawthorn rich with both fruit and thorns. They made themselves comfortable and found the fruit delicious but were unable to actually pick the stubborn 'apples' and had to eat them clumsily on the stem.

"Like wild animals", complained Lolly. A small red squirrel overheard and took offense.

"If you mean me, I'm better than that", he chattered, and plucked one off the tough stem to demonstrate. "So that means you are weaklings! What are you, anyway? Can't be dragonflies. Dragonflies are smarter".

"And rats are smarter than *you!* So watch out, mister".

The squirrel laughed. "You've got a lot to learn, nitwit! Rats don't climb trees".

"Ours do! They'll climb up and get you some night".

"Cha-cha-cha! There you go again, nitwit! What are you, really? You must be just out of the egg".

"We're fairy folk. *Pixies!*"

"Cha-cha-cha! Never heard of it".

The squirrel took off with a mouthful of the little apples and didn't look back. Why should he? There were only apples and pixies in the tree, and not a brain among them.

Lolly opened her mouth but didn't quite know what to say. Airy finally spoke up. "Forget it. You can't win any argument now. The squirrel's gone".

"I want to be ready when he comes back!"

"What if he doesn't? Then you wasted your time. C'mon! Th'fruits are delicious, an' we have th'whole tree to ourselves".

But only minutes went by until they got more company. The shrike had caught a sparrow and was trying to impale it on a spine up on a high branch of their hawthorn. The sparrow - about the same size as the young pixies - fought back furiously before finally succumbing to the ordeal. When things quieted down the shrike looked directly at the pixies as if sizing them up for spines of their own.

"Don't touch the meat!" the shrike rasped.

But then - instead of eating it herself - she took off, leaving the lifeless sparrow to bake in the sun. The spectacle took away the pixies' appetites.

The sparrow was clearly dead by now so there was no thought of freeing the poor creature, but their own position suddenly felt exposed. They moved toward the interior of the tree where fruits were fewer, but it felt more secure. Poo, whose appetite was totally gone, volunteered to keep watch. It wasn't long before she sounded the alarm.

"Here she comes again!"

The shrike was having a good day and landed now with a small mouse in her talons. She stuck the wiggling thing on a spike just like the sparrow and not far from it, holding it casually in place with a claw until the wiggling slowed and finally stopped. Poo shivered with revulsion.

"Why don't you eat apples?" she shouted. In her anger she managed to pick one and threw it at the shrike, narrowly missing. "Stick *that* on your spike!"

The shrike threw a hissy fit, shrieking and snapping her beak. She was *Ny-ku-kuu!* Ny-ku-kuu eat *meat!* Then she suddenly calmed down and became sociable. What were they? What kind of meat? Did they live in the neighborhood? She was full of questions. Her talons flexed and clenched on her perch.

"Just passing through!" sang Airy. "Stopped for an apple, that's all".

"Yes, yes – *apples!* Puts meat on your bones! But where from? Are more of you?"

"No more. Just three 'Sour-Susies'. We're bad meat from sour apples".

"Not to worry! Ny-ku-kuu eat good meat, bad meat, *any* meat!"

That reminded the shrike of something, probably on another spike somewhere, and she was about to leave when a much larger bird swooped in knocking her right off her perch. The crow pecked once at the off-balance shrike and the battle was over. The mighty Ny-ku-kuu fled the scene. The pixies cheered.

The new master of the tree peered down in surprise, spotting the pixies below. "You like?" he asked.

"Yes", replied Airy. "She wanted to eat us".

That upset the crow - not for humanitarian reasons but simply because the shrike hadn't asked permission.

"All food goes to the *Caw!*" he blared, meaning his own Family. "The *Caw* get first choice!" This is an ancient litany. Crows have claimed the food since the very Beginning, and rightly so according to the legends of their race.

"We're not *anybody's* food!" sputtered Poo.

"Not for you to decide", shrugged the crow. "Bigger folk decide that. Hey! Are you eating those apples?"

"Sure. Is something wrong?"

"Well! I guess so! Weren't you listening? The shrike didn't ask, now *you* didn't ask. You have to *ask*. It's not hard. I'm right here!"

"Okay, okay," said Lolly. "Can we please have some apples?"

"I don't care. They're sour anyway".

"Then why all the bother?"

"They *belong* to me, to my *family!* We get first choice! But you can have them. I'm going to eat these sun-ripened treats".

He tore into the sparrow and soon feathers were floating down, some with skin and pieces of meat attached. The crow wasn't efficient like the hook-beak, but so what? It was easy food, the best kind. He loved to harass the shrike.

The crow belonged to a large Roost nearby, home to several hundred of his family. They dominated the entire area during daytime and policed the food. Most inhabitants deferred to them anyway, especially in the morning, but some tried to cheat - like the shrike - and must be made examples of! It was a responsibility and really a noble undertaking: Crows don't just *own* the food they also inspect it for safety. All food needed to be inspected. Like the sparrow, for example. It tasted great. And the mouse was proving to be fine as well. He finished, wiped his beak on a twig, and regarded the small, winged creatures below.

"What kind of birds are you, anyway?" he inquired. "I didn't catch that part".

"Not birds at all", said Airy. "We're *pixies*".

"Never heard of it. Are you safe to eat?"

"No. The Ny-ku-kuu wanted to eat us and you saw what happened to her".

"Haw, haw, haw! At least you have a bird brain in your head. But it doesn't answer the question".

"Okay. The trolls tried to eat us too. Have you seen what happened to them?"

He certainly had. The whole Roost had seen the trolls this morning and been amazed. The two species had known of each other but never met before, being diurnal and nocturnal. Some of the *Caw* had already perched and pooped on the statues and the trolls didn't move a muscle. It was the big news of the day. He looked at the pixies suspiciously.

"Did you do that?"

"Who else?" said Airy. "Do *you* want to eat us too?"

The crow decided he'd learned enough and took off.

The pixies left immediately afterward in case the shrike should return, and made their way back to the troll's camp, which was the safest place they knew of at the moment. As they drew near crows were raising a ruckus, caw-cawing and flapping above the campsite, scolding a pair of furry shapes that were disappearing into tall grass near the pines. Atel hovered near the trolls in the midst of the racket.

"You're too late to meet the bandits", she shouted, "but that's just as well. Ferrets might be a bad influence on three innocent pixie babes".

"An' what are *ferrets*", inquired Airy, "if we may ask?"

"You may ask, but I can't give you a definite answer. Only a ferret could describe another ferret. I will just say they are friendly, entertaining animals when in the right mood".

"An' what means 'bandits'?"

"Crooks. Robbers. They steal things! But sometimes that's okay. Just now I asked them to steal Red's purse and loose coins and hide it all before the crows take it. We're poor country folk with no present need for gold, but one never knows..."

"Never knows...*what?*"

"Exactly! That's what we don't know".

'Ferrets are like hummingbirds' thought Poo and changed the subject. "Is it safe here? Th'crows sound angry!"

"They *are* angry. They had just discovered Red's purse when I arrived and would've made off with every shiny coin if I hadn't stopped them".

"An' what do *they* want it for? Honestly, money seems so silly".

Atel laughed. "Spoken like a true fairy lass, but most folks love the stuff and trade it for things they need. Crows love it too - if it's shiny - but not for trading. To them, every shiny object is an heirloom piece of the Great Egg and belongs to them".

"They think a lot of stuff belongs to them", grumbled Lolly.

Atel laughed again. "Have you talked to crows?"

"One of them. He said they *own* the food! Like it's all theirs, an' we have to ask!"

"It is theirs, if one goes by the old tales".

"Well, phooey to that. I think th'make stuff up".

"The tales are very old, Lolly. These crows didn't make it up. They believe the stories of their race and we have to deal with it. Who's to say, anyway? You've met Ishi and the trolls. They go back a couple Ages, and your own people go back even farther. Some of the old stories really *are* true, and they all have *some* truth to them. Just don't argue with crows about their ancestry or you'll have big trouble".

"You better tell us about the *Great Egg* then, so we can laugh now instead of when *they* tell it".

She laughed even before Atel began. So did Airy and Poo, which angered several crows still within earshot. They became aggressive and the pixies were obliged to take the only shelter available, underneath Red's rump, on a narrow edge of the stump he sat on. It was left to Atel to arrange a truce and she was in no mood for small talk when she rejoined them, launching directly into a lecture.

"The story goes back to Crow Mother, who bravely sampled all the food on earth so others could safely live here. Unfortunately, she didn't stop until she had consumed the earth, the sun and even the moon. She fell mortally ill from the deed but left a bright, shiny egg behind. When it hatched the world was renewed and pieces of shell were scattered everywhere. They are still being found today. They're not hard to find. They glitter in the sun".

The pixies knew enough to keep straight faces when she was in her lecturing mood. Atel watched closely to be sure they were listening. Good! She hoped they had learned a lesson.

"There's much to learn about crows", she finished up, "but the most important thing is to stay out of their way!"

She left to see about the ferrets, a wise decision anytime. The crows didn't hassle her but kept a close eye on the pixies - or at least the troll they were hiding under - until boredom set in around mid-afternoon. Crows are not grudge-holders, as a rule. They are far too busy.

Later, the pixies emerged hungry. They'd had a nice view of the Juggler's cake the whole while and built up an appetite, but now found it covered with insects. Ditto the sugar bowl. Same with all the baking supplies. They would have to forage for supper like other wild creatures, and maybe even fight for it.

They found the blackberry brambles picked over. Jays were chowing down on a few good berries that remained and defended their territory. One of them helpfully pointed out small trees in the area rich with blue berries: Lots of bluish berries and no one else eating them.

They looked delicious, but a brown thrasher loitering nearby offered a bit of prudent advice: The trees were *buckthorn*, and no one ate the berries unless they were desperately hungry. They were known locally as 'starvation' berries because they raced through the stomach and out the back door so fast they left no benefit.

"Did the jays send you here?" she asked. "I thought so. Never trust a jay! But if you're hungry, the grapes are good now. Really good. There will be crows to put up with, but crows are everywhere anyway, and there's lots of grapes".

There were a lot of crows, but they weren't belligerent. Or maybe these hadn't yet heard about the trouble over by the trolls. The pixies asked politely for permission to eat but were ignored.

"I don't think they even heard us", said Poo.

"What's that? I can't hear you!" replied Airy.

"That's what I mean!" hollered Poo. "I don't think they *heard* us. Ask again!"

The crows didn't hear the second time either or didn't care. Pandemonium reigned, almost like their Roost in the morning with all of them talking at once. Well, about half were yackety-yacking; the other half were munching fermented grapes. The fruit was overripe, and the hot sun was speeding up the fermenting process, contributing to the festive atmosphere. Later, a less sociable reaction would occur, but for now they were happy bunch.

Young pixies have little experience with alcohol, but there was a regrettable period in history when fairy folk imbibed with the worst of them. Trolls tricked them into it, and fairies that couldn't fly straight were easy prey. But that was all about the evils of *drink,* which these lasses had been warned about. It wasn't about eating delicious grapes off the vine.

"Mmmm, good!" said Lolly at first bite, and went after it with gusto, eating the grape as fast as she could peel it.

Poo peeled hers quickly too, and they each finished one before Airy even got started. It was necessary to peel back the tough skin, but the fruit inside was juicy and delicious with an uplifting aroma.

132

They'd been given grapes in the chrysallis of course, but not like these! Airy finally got a taste just as they were interrupted.

"Haw! Looky, fellas!" said a large crow above them. "The fledglings are here! They think they can hang with the big boys". The pixies recognized him from back at the trolls. Not friendly.

"Maybe they can, Gronk", said another. "Maybe they can hang with you. That don't take much". Everyone laughed except Gronk who took it as a challenge.

"Only one way to find out!" he blustered.

This drew a few catcalls and a lot of interest. Whoo-eee! A *berrydare!* There had been several entertaining challenges already today, but all of them between crows. This would be more exotic: Gronk versus *unknown species!* A crowd began to gather. Gronk hopped down closer to the pixies, called out Airy, and strutted. The crowd loved it.

"What's this about?" asked Airy. When told it was an eating contest she objected. "Not fair! You're ten times as big as me".

"Okay, sissy. I challenge all three of you!"

"That's better but still in your favor. What are the rules?"

"I eat a grape, you eat a grape, and like that. Whoever falls down first, loses. Choose your bunch!"

That needed more explanation: "Your bunch of *grapes*, dummy. See? They hang in little bunches". Gronk chortled. "As for 'falls down', that's when you get dizzy and fall off the branch. That's when *you lose*, and *I eat the losers*. Get it?" The crowd cackled. It was unusual to challenge for such high stakes. Much more fun!

"Oh!" Airy looked over the clusters with no idea what to look for. Poo pushed some dark, wrinkled ones aside and chose the next bunch underneath because they were 'prettier'. Gronk chose a wrinkled bunch out of bravado. The crowd appreciated it. Everyone knew the older grapes were 'spiked' stronger. Let the game begin!

Gronk flipped up a grape, caught it neatly, and swallowed it whole. The pixies were impressed, but the crowd wasn't.

"Cheat!" they crowed. "Chew it up!"

This was a veteran crowd. Everyone knew the rules. A whole grape would retain its alcohol way too long! That was no fun. A *berrydare* was about getting *drunk*. Hey! No cheating! Gronk was obliged to eat another one correctly.

Now it was the pixies' turn. Poo chose a small grape and the three peeled and shared it, chewing correctly and spitting out the seeds.

"Your turn", said Airy. Gronk couldn't believe it.

"I challenged the three of you! You gotta eat *three!*"

Airy refused. "You challenged us as a team. We count as *one* and we *ate* one. Your turn!"

"You spit out the seeds too! No spitting out seeds!"

The crowd booed. This was nit-picky. Several crows even turned and lifted their tailfeathers at Gronk. He was expected to win easily. Just get on with it! The fledglings could count as one and who cared about seeds? Seeds didn't make anyone drunk.

Gronk angrily chewed up three grapes at once and swallowed them seeds & all, hoping for a better reaction from the butt-feather birds. They turned around properly again. Good! Gronk strutted some more but slipped a bit on the branch. Oops.

"Your turn, little ones", he crowed.

Lolly picked another small grape and they shared it as before. This bunch had less of the 'lift' aroma, probably due to less sunlight, but even a small amount of 'lift' was a lot for a pixie. Poo sat down afterwards. Lolly plopped down too. Gronk side-stepped on his branch for a closer look, slipped again, but caught himself.

"Your turn!" called Airy. "Don't fall off th'branch!"

The crowd tittered. This was better than expected. Hey Gronk! You got 'em now, buddy! Put 'em away Gronk!

Gronk tilted his beak proudly. Yeah, this was more like it! The crowd was with him again! The last cheer reverberated in his ears: *Put 'em away, Gronk!* Huh? What did that mean? Grapes? Okay, he chewed up three more big ones and 'put 'em away'. Haw! How about that!

"Your turn again!" he belched and put a wing on the branch to brace himself. Wind seemed to have come up.

Airy peeled a grape and began to eat. The others, being already a full grape ahead of her, finally joined in. When the grape was finished and the seeds spit, Poo went right to sleep and rolled off the grape vine. She tumbled to the forest floor six feet below, waggling her wings uselessly. Gronk claimed victory!

"No, no, no!" protested Airy. "One fell down but two of us are still standing!"

That was a stretch with Lolly hanging on to a grape for support. The crowd was split. Some waved their tailfeathers at Airy, but she simply looked away. Others buttfeathered Gronk again, infuriating him. He raised his steadying wing to make a point and nearly fell off without the support. Oops. That persuaded him to just get on with the challenge. He popped in a grape, pretended to chew it, and swallowed it whole again. This time he got away with it.

"Yer turn, kiddo!" he crowed.

Airy saw him cheat but there was no use complaining. She peeled another grape, leaving as much flesh on the skin as she dared, and jogged Lolly in the ribs.

"Just eat this one more", she said brightly. Lolly groaned, took a few big bites, and got sick. Gronk called a foul and the crowd agreed, but then Lolly rolled off and landed with a 'thump' in moldy leaves and crow poop just like Poo, so the foul was vacated.

"*I'm* still here!" shouted Airy and before anyone could argue she finished the grape very sloppily, being sure to let most of the juice dribble down her chin. Everyone saw that except Gronk who wasn't seeing well anymore, but since he didn't object the crowd let it go.

"Back to you!" said Airy with an effort. It was all she had. If Gronk made it through his turn he would win. He probably would. The crowd was getting behind him again, encouraging him.

"C'mon Gronk, show us what you got! Hey, Big Boy, show off a little! Eat three again!"

Gronk basked in the glory for a moment, mostly to regain his balance. 'Eat three' again? Better not. He stabbed for a single grape and missed. Egads, the crowd started to laugh. Okay, he would show them! It took a few tries, but he got three into his beak finally and pretended to chew. That's when his wing slipped, and he chomped down hard on the grapes in panic. Gulp! All the 'lift' juice washed down his gullet.

He froze for a long moment wondering if he might pass out - but no! He cocked his head toward Airy, not daring to speak. The crowd considered this a fair signal. Her turn!

She clutched the vine with one hand and tried to pick a grape with the other. It refused to come loose. She tugged harder. It popped loose and she did too, falling over backwards right off the grape vine. The last thing she remembered before blacking out was a big reaction from the crowd. Then she hit the mucky leaf-mold and bounced and that woke her up again, but only to see crows bending over her, beaks horrifyingly agape.

"Hey! Nice going, fledgling", said one, a lady.

"You beat Gronk. Way cool!" said another, her sister. "You okay now?"

Gronk had lost his grip and fallen moments before she did, clearly hitting the ground first. He was still out, which didn't evoke any crow-tears from the concerned sisters.

The 'dare proved to be a turning point in crow-pixie relations. That was the good news. It would show up in the next day or two.

The bad news kicked in right now: None of the pixies could fly and only one could move at all.

Airy stumbled back and forth ministering to Poo and Lolly's needs, but their needs were too much. Only sleep and better habits would make a difference and she needed those too. She gave up and collapsed next to the pooped-out pair, and for the rest of the afternoon their snoring was the only sign of life; but the crow sisters watched over them by turns and kept Gronk at bay when he awoke with an ornery hangover.

About sundown the pixies awoke with their own hangovers and the crows winged off to their Roost. A Great Owl hooted deep in the woods warning other predators that this was his territory. The pixies shook away bleariness and trudged off to find better cover than just an open forest floor. But where? Not back to the trolls. That was a long way off, and they were stumbling badly. Mustn't stumble into any open clearings. But looky here, now! Rock faces sprang up in front of them, low, broken cliffs with cracks and fissures. The big owl hooted again, closer, and they scrambled into a shallow cave. The floor was bare rock, but dry leaves and grass were tucked into the back end, blown in by the wind probably: A perfect bed and they made use of it.

Early next morning the rightful inhabitants of the den - a mother skunk and her litter - found them there. The skunk babies took fright at the bedraggled pixies and Momma was about to spray some 'protection' when Atel happened by on her search.

"A moment, please", she suggested to Momma. "Let me line them up for you outside. No need to mess up your home".

Skunks don't mind their own smell. They like it. Momma would've ignored the hummingbird, but the notion of 'lining them up' struck a chord. She sometimes did this with her own babies, to scold them. With this thought in mind she moved her rump aside and allowed the pixies out.

"Stop!" ordered Atel when they were directly in front of Momma's nose. "You must apologize for messing up their bedding. Let her smell you!"

They did, reluctantly. "Armpits too!" Atel ordered. Everything smelled like crow manure. Momma made a face and backed up into the den.

"*That's* what your bedding smells like now", stated Atel. "Hadn't you ought to freshen it up?"

The pixies made a break for it when she commenced housekeeping, but they still couldn't fly. It was all they could do to run, and not far at that. Meanwhile, the baby skunks tattled to Momma. *They* never escaped a chewing-out! Why should the stink-birds? But Momma was busy with her air-freshener.

"Forward, foot soldiers!" urged Atel. "Momma may come looking. You need to put some distance between you".

'Foot soldiers' was getting pretty old, but it's hard to argue with the truth. The pixies slogged onward.

"My plan for the day was in two parts", continued Atel. "First, I was going to take you on a tour of all the edible nuts and berries in the area. You could've sampled lots of delicious food. We still could. Would you like to?"

She had to settle for a silent answer, the kind that won't improve.

"I'll take that as a 'no'", decided the hummingbird. "Now, the second part involved introducing you to the crows since you got off to such a bad start with them yesterday, but there I think you are way ahead of me. You smell of crows and fermented grapes, among other things. Crows and grapes go well together this time of year. Would you like to tell me about it?"

No one volunteered. The hummingbird had led them a quarter mile through the woods by now and they were exhausted.

"Tomorrow, then", Atel went on cheerfully as they approached a spring bubbling from the hillside. "For now I'm going to leave you here. You'll have everything you need: Water to wash in, and also to drink. Hangovers can be very thirsty I've heard. The water can suffice for breakfast also. I don't think you'll be wanting any solid food. Any questions?"

"Just so you know, it wasn't our idea", mumbled Airy. "They made us do it".

"I believe you, but that doesn't help anything right now. Stay under the bushes! See you later!"

The pixies washed a little, but mostly drank water. A lot. It got rid of the bad aftertaste and allowed them to fall sleep. They curled up in dry leaves under a hazelnut bush and slept until mid-afternoon when a bad smell - and a bad word - brought them wide awake.

The local fairy boys had come by for a drink and were puzzled by a strange odor in the area. There were three of them: *Noggin* (a sturdy lad who had uttered the bad word), *Nary* (quieter, a bit smaller), and *Boo* - a skinny, active fellow. They were a tad shorter than the Troll-Mother for comparison, but obviously much stronger. Now Noggin wrinkled his nose and used another bad word.

"Well?" responded Boo. "Are you cussing the smell - or your own self for not knowing what it is?"

"Both. And you, too! How's that? You don't know what it is either".

"That's where you're wrong. It's wood nymphs. They stink just like that".

"There ain't none around here. I believe it's goblins".

"If it is, they've been eating wood nymphs. So it's not. You just said there ain't no nymphs".

"It's goblins. You're just wrong about the nymphs".

"I ain't wrong! Goblins *do* eat nymphs".

"That's not what we're arguing about!"

"Then don't argue! It's true. They *do* eat nymphs!"

Noggin turned away and loosened a canteen from his belt. Nary grinned at him and that was a lot of words for Nary. He could speak and had been known to but found life easier this way.

When Noggin had filled the canteen he sipped a little, very suspiciously. So did Nary. Boo put his hands on his hips.

"Now what?" he demanded. "Water tasted fine to me!"

"Well, I'm fussier", said Noggin. "Someone has to be. I was hoping that whatever stinks didn't get into the water".

"And what did you decide?"

Noggin deferred to Nary, who stuck a finger by his nose.

"Water's dirty", translated Noggin.

It finally dawned on the pixies that these louts were talking about *them*, and yet the louts themselves were the source of the bad odor *they* had awakened to. But who were the louts? The pixies remained hidden and debated in whispers.

"Can't be trolls", said Lolly. "Trolls wouldn't be outside in the daylight".

"Too runty anyway", said Airy.

"Can't be witches either", said Poo. "Th'don't have wands".

"I think all witches are girls", said Lolly. "These are too ugly to be girls. They're boys".

It wasn't hard to narrow it down that far. The 'boys' certainly weren't easy to look at with their ragged clothes, big ears and scruffy hair. They did have cute, curly beards but didn't bother to brush out cobwebs they picked up in the woods. They went barefoot too, and the hairy feet were even dirtier than their beards.

"*Hop-goblins?*" suggested Poo, a little too loud.

The boys seemed not to notice, but ears that size pick up everything. The pixies hushed and didn't move, but the boys did hear them. Heard a noise, anyway, and knew exactly where it came from. Noggin began to work his way up the creek "looking for crayfish", While Boo casually circled around their bush inspecting the hazelnuts and Nary got out a gunny sack from his pack. Suddenly Noggin and Boo dived under the bush grabbing leaves and whatnot and Nary came quick as a rabbit with the open sack. But they weren't quick enough. The pixies exploded out of the leaves like a covey of quail and up out of reach.

"Leave us alone, bozos!" shouted Lolly. The boys were flabbergasted.

"Sharp-tailed grouse - or what?" wondered Noggin.

"Sharp-*mouth!*" said Boo.

"*Pixies!*" exclaimed Nary and clammed up again. So did the others. So did the Pixies. Boo stood up, hands on hips again to make a point.

"Darned if it ain't true!" he marveled. "Funny, I always expected pixies would smell better".

"Aww, they're just wee babes", said Noggin. "Been living with crows at the bottom of the Roost. *That's* what the stink is".

"Don't be *bottom birds* all your life", advised Boo, wagging a finger at the pixies. "There ain't no future in that. Crows know the weather, but that's all they know that's worth knowin'"

"Find some new friends!" said Noggin pointedly. "*Better-smelling* ones".

"That leaves you out!" shot back Airy, but it was only a parting shot. There was no way to win this argument while smelling like *bottom birds*. The pixies followed the spring down the hill and washed up in a narrow pool overhung by grass where no one could see them. Cleaning up was a big job, especially their hair, and they were thankful for moving water that carried the smell downstream. When they had brushed out the last burrs and dried their wings in the breeze it should have been enough, but a new-found modesty nagged at them until they found something to wear.

They braided dresses - Lolly's and Poo's from leaves and grasses, Airy's out of thistledown - short enough to avoid catching on everything, yet long enough to enforce the modesty. Then they flew back to the stone trolls and mooned them (which they had not yet done today) and wound up feeling good about themselves once more. That's how Atel found them later, dressed like polite schoolgirls and acting nice.

"Well! Very pretty! Who gets credit for the new look?"

"Oh, just us", said Poo. "It's nothing special".

"Well, I'm proud of you! We must groom ourselves out here if we want to look pretty. Everyone has to".

"The hop-goblins don't".

"The - *what? Hop-goblins?*"

"Yes, three hop-goblins, dirty and ugly. Th'tried to catch us in a bag!"

"What did they look like – besides just dirty and ugly?"

The pixies gave an exaggerated description and Atel tried to sort it out. There were no goblins around that she knew of, and only one hop-goblin who didn't fit the description at all.

"Hop-goblins don't usually wear clothes", she replied doubtfully. "Did they call themselves that?"

"No, but it wasn't hard to guess".

"I see. Well, all's well that ends well, and it leaves a beautiful evening! Come along. I'll show you some edible acorns and you can tell me what happened with the crows".

Atel was irritated when she heard the full story. Gronk in particular was known to be dangerous and there were other villains too, but there was just no avoiding them because of the permanent local Roost.

"But they *do* know the weather", Atel admitted. "I'm going to ask them tomorrow. There's been a big change with this warm-up and I'm not sure what it means. Crows will know".

"I doubt it", said Poo. "All they know right now is grapes".

The acorns, white oak and burr oak, but *not* the red oak, were very tasty, but it was a race with the squirrels this year. The mast was poor and the sound of each nut hitting the ground drew scavengers. Atel showed the pixies how to pick ripe ones off the branch by wiggling them out of the husk, but cracking them required rocks, so they carried them back and used the trolls for anvils. They dropped some from altitude onto Red's big skull too, and that worked even better.

They slept overnight at the trolls, inside their open mouths for safety. It was Atel's idea because of the usual early morning crows. There was room for one pixie per mouth, she calculated - and no place at all for a hummingbird who wanted none. But the pixies wouldn't get close to Red's teeth for any reason, so Airy took the Juggler and the others doubled up in the young troll's open mouth. His tongue was sticking out and they used that for a pillow.

"Comfy, I hope?" inquired Atel. "Just don't sleep like them, with your mouths open. Crows will be out and about early, looking for mischief".

Morning came and the hummingbird was proven correct. The first crows to arrive were Gronk and some pals who'd been up all night and had grape juice on their breath. They still remembered the pixies laughing about the Great Egg and wanted to make a wager. Atel didn't trust them, but they wouldn't leave until the pixies took up a bet.

"You laugh at the Great Egg, but Gronk challenges!" said he, strutting atop Red's bald head. The tipsy pals peeked slyly from behind him. "We'll show proof of eggshell", he boasted. "And then you go tell everyone how dumb you are!"

"And if you don't show proof?" asked Atel. "Then what?"

"We go away, sweet as sugar. You be the judge!" He stomped his foot in glee and fell on his rump but never lost focus. Gronk was a tough bird even with a gizzard full of grapes.

It all seemed ridiculous to Atel, but if she could be the judge... "Well?" she said, turning to the pixies, "It's your call. He's not challenging me".

The pixies didn't hesitate. "Sure! Go get your shiny things. We'll show how dumb *you* are!"

Too late, Atel guessed their trick. The morning sun found the spot where the Juggler had mixed cake batter and cracked all those eggs. Of course he never had time to clean up the mess. Eggshells galore glinted in the sun and the crows presented their 'proof' right away.

They hawed and guffawed until they went to sleep, perched ridiculously on Red's nose and ears. The pixies protested but Atel in good conscience could only rule that they had seen proof of eggshells, so technically the pixies must follow through on their end of the wager.

It was a long day for unlucky gamblers. Most of the crows laughed at them and wagged their tailfeathers, but some did show sympathy. Gronk was an important crow, but his wisecracking ways were starting to wear thin. Out of curiosity the pixies asked the friendly ones about the weather and received identical forecasts every time, but the forecast was boring.

Crows take pride in this skill and particularly enjoy forecasting bad weather just like modern meteorologists, but the forecast to the pixies was simply 'warm' and 'windy', although they hinted ominously about a 'Storm Crow' in the longer range. When the pixies asked who that was they clammed up, refusing to give any details yet - a technique employed by all forecasters to build suspense and keep folks tuning in.

"Pretty safe forecast", commented Atel. "The warm breeze is here already and that will lead to other changes in the weather. I could predict that much. I don't like the Storm Crow, though. He can go somewhere else". But she wouldn't offer any details either.

◆◆◆

The forecast verified during the day. The warm sunshine got even warmer. The South Wind gusted, blowing down leaves and even small branches. It was a dangerous time for the *imps* who do the leaf-coloring, for they have no wings. If their branch goes, they go with it. On a day like today it was hard to get any work done.

"Why don't you quit until it lets up?" suggested Airy. She was breaking unwritten rules by speaking to them at all. Atel had advised against it and everyone else agreed. Imps are just anti-social. Not *grumpy*, maybe, but terribly busy. They do not take kindly to interruptions. But today they were tempted to interrupt themselves, these two at least: 'Ink' and 'Puk'.

"Thinking about that!" snapped Puk but kept working. He had a brush but no paint, which didn't seem to matter. Wherever he touched a leaf it bloomed into autumn display. But the leaves were flapping around like crazy: Now he got one! Now he missed. Now he got the other imp on her cheek and *that* bloomed into display. It was time for a break whether they could spare it or not. And then their branch broke - not quite off, but it hung by just a strip of bark. The imps scrambled up onto the remaining stub where their long coats didn't blend in so perfectly among the leaves. Now they were easier to see.

"That does it!" vowed 'Ink', referring to the autumn blush on her cheek, not the close call they had just survived. It was a red oak tree they were coloring, on top of the hill where frost had been light, and leaves were still in good shape. Down the hillside many leaves were already turning to a dirty brown and that would be their color for the Fall Fest. Too bad. Imps try anyway, sometimes, but frozen leaves don't take color well.

The imps plopped down like construction workers everywhere and got out their lunch, which looked like bars of some kind but smelled like honey. The grumpiness evaporated and they even offered extra bars to the pixies, who politely accepted just one. The imps were only half their size, but the bars were big. Imps need the food. They work overtime in the fall, and round the clock after a disaster like the frost.

Atel stopped by and made a mirror for Ink to touch up her complexion. That was appreciated. Atel knew them a little.

"Rough day?" she asked.

"Seen rougher", replied Puk between bites.

"I'm sure. I love your work! Everyone does".

"Won't last. Just ask the crows".

"Yes, I will. They never miss a chance to put out a warning, do they? What have you heard?"

Puk scowled. "Big *blow!*"

"They must mean this, right now".

"Nope. Worse tomorrow".

"Oh? Well, in that case I have things to do. Thanks for the tip".

146

The hummingbird left and the pixies jumped back into the conversation in alarm. Worse than *this* - tomorrow? What would the imps do for shelter? They shouldn't be in the trees!

"Have to!" said Ink. "It's a rush now, and we're not all here yet. Some are still Down Under".

"Under what?" asked Airy. An absurd vision of imps struggling under felled branches leaped into her mind.

"Under the world, I suppose. It's called Down Under. We come up here, Up Top, when we finish down there, but winter is lingering down there. Imps are still needed to do frost designs. That's our winter work".

Airy did the math: One year divided into 2 equal parts leaves no remainder. "So you don't get any vacations?"

"Who cares? We like to be busy!"

"We could help. Do you have extra brushes?"

The imps laughed. Sorry! No extra brushes. Imps are issued only one and better not lose it. The Boss was stingy that way. Anyhow, they expected to finish by evening and move on to a more sheltered location.

"We're about done here anyway", said Puk "There's a few late trees we'll come back for, and we'll have to skip the frost damage. But the Boss gave us a waiver on the Crow's Roost".

"You don't paint those trees?"

"*Won't!* They paint it themselves, know what I mean?"

The pixies laughed. They had made an apology tour through those trees just yesterday and never found a clean place to perch.

The pixies brought acorns back to the trolls and found Gronk there with his ill-favored pals, cracking their own. They'd had a few grapes again and were dropping the nuts from up high like the pixies had, to smash on Red's skull. At least they were in a better mood. The pixies stashed their own acorns in the young troll's mouth and perched on his ears.

"This is how *we* do it", boasted Gronk. "You should try it sometime". They had seen the pixies do it and learned a trick. But hey! If no one challenges, crows *own* the idea! Lots of big reputations have been made that way. All it takes is muscle. The pixies wisely let it pass.

"We'll wait our turn", said Airy. "You can give us your weather forecast while we're waiting. We'll compare it to the other ones".

"*What* others?" demanded Gronk. The pals glared.

"Just gossip we've heard around the hill. But everyone hears it from the crows first, don't they?"

The pals relaxed. Gronk even smiled. It was fun to forecast for the stupid *Yaccaw* (not crows). They listened up. Other crows didn't. "Windy today, worse tomorrow!" he rattled off, watching for a reaction. That was the fun part, the looks of worry and astonishment.

"That's it? Just wind?"

Gronk cocked a stern eye. "Isn't that enough? Don't you think it's windy *now?*"

"Yeah, but...that's all? No rain or anything?"

The crows huddled a moment, then Gronk flew over to the young troll's arm and spoke quite seriously. "What more do you want? Lightning? Thunder? The Whirlwind? I could put them all into the forecast".

"So? We could make wild guesses too".

Gronk became angry and stalked along the arm, studying his audience murderously. The pals hopped up and down, hissing. The pixies prepared for anything.

"Crows know! Crows know!" blustered Gronk. "We are the *Caw! You* are the silly *Yaccaw!*"

"Okay, we get that! So what's the forecast?"

Gronk looked to the west, smelling he air. He paused a few moments for theatrical effect.

"The *Storm Crow*", he said reverently.

"We've heard of him before", said Lolly. "Who is he? King of the Crows?"

"No, no, no! There are no kings. We have *Heroes!*"

The pixies giggled. Fortunately, Atel showed up at that moment and jumped into the conversation.

"*Storm crow* would be one, I'm sure! And *Crow Mother* before him. Are there others?"

"'*Are there others*'?" Gronk mocked. "*All* Great Heroes are of the *Caw!* But we don't expect wee little folk to know much about it".

"Then it's lucky you're here", replied Atel. "I was about to tell the pixies what little I do know. Now you can tell it correctly".

That turned Gronk on. He strutted back and forth, recalling the historical facts to mind. Atel left immediately, having heard the story numerous times.

"Listen up, fledglings!" blared Gronk. "You got a lot to learn!"

Storm Crow

In the Beginning, according to the *Caw*, the world was in three parts: The Light of the Great Spirit, the Darkness all around, and a narrow twilight between, inhabited by the Great Heroes.

Then Great Spirit created the earth, the sun, and the moon, and brought forth the *Yaccaw* to dwell upon the earth. But the *Yaccaw* proved weak and timid, not daring to explore or even taste the food. The new world desperately needed a Hero.

Great Spirit summoned Crow Mother from the twilight to sample the food - a risky assignment even for a Hero, but she fulfilled it. To make sure, she consumed everything: The moon, then the sun and the earth. She perished in the deed but left behind a Great Egg from which the world would eventually be renewed - made safe for the *Yaccaw*. She made sure her own family, the *Caw*, also hatched out of the egg.

For her martyrdom crows claimed rightful ownership of the food. Great Spirit agreed and stirred up the Four Winds to produce good weather. Satisfied with this, He moved on to other works throughout the heavens.

Thus the First Age commenced in perfect order and bounty spilled upon the lands. But the Winds grew bored and went to sleep. The atmosphere calmed and weather stopped happening. Plant life withered, and the food failed.

Great Spirit saw and chose another Hero to put things right, summoning Storm Crow from the twilight to flap his huge wings and reawaken the weather.

"Stir up the winds!" commanded Great Spirit.

"Sure. But I'll do it *my* way", replied Storm Crow.

"Just do it", said Great Spirit. "I'll watch".

Storm Crow decided to stir up just the North Wind first.

"Don't do that!" advised Great Spirit. "It's too cold!"

Storm Crow did it anyway, and winter descended upon the earth. Blizzards raged without end and glaciers advanced. Storm Crow noticed his mistake and calmed the North Wind, but what to do about the frozen planet? He decided to awaken the South Wind and turn it utterly loose.

"Don't do that!" advised Great Spirit. "It's too hot!"

Storm Crow did it anyway and the ice melted way too fast. Floods devastated the lands. Great Spirit was dismayed but knew the floods would eventually end. The lands should still recover.

Then Storm Crow decided to stir up all the winds at once.

"Don't do that!" warned Great Spirit. "It's too much!"

Storm Crow did it anyway and flew out front, leading the new weather around the world. But the winds became uncontrollable. Monstrous whirlwinds formed. Storm Crow himself was drawn into one and drowned in the ocean.

When the storms finally blew themselves out Great Spirit was pleasantly surprised to see a return of normal weather. The atmosphere and oceans had formed sustainable currents. Storm Crow had done all the right things! Bounty returned to the lands. Once again a Great Hero had guaranteed the world's food supply!

Great Spirit worried that it wouldn't last. Mortal matters seldom do. But Storm Crow's descendants have kept up his work throughout the Ages. Even today it is they who bring the rain, expecting only first choice of all the food that grows. It's not too much to ask.

Remember that next time they steal yours.

The treacherous pals flapped over to join Gronk on the stone arm, cawing and squawking in applause, so it seemed. But while the pixies

critiqued the story quietly among themselves, the crows suddenly raided their lunch stash, snatching the acorns out of the young troll's gullet and making off with them. It was a well-planned robbery, swift and soon over, and the thieves made their getaway. The surprised pixies could only watch them go.

"I didn't see that one coming", admitted Airy.

"We should have!" said Lolly. "Th'whole story led up to it".

"Oh, let's just go get some more", said Poo. "An' maybe we should find a safe place for us too, in case the Storm Crow does come".

Atel returned and listened to the bellyaching, but her advice was the same as Poo's. She too had been thinking about shelter. Her choice was the troll caves – just inside the sinkhole entrance. That would be safe from both directions, she figured. But the pixies had no intention of ever again venturing near the stone foxes.

"Very well. Find your own shelter", said Atel. "Just be sure you do! Don't ignore the forecast. And while you're out and about this evening, collect some esporellia for your wings - some of the stardust that sifts down. It will keep you warm when winter comes. Your wings have lost all of what you had from the chrysallis. It's a blessing to your race, but it rubs off. Don't neglect it!"

The pixies had been acutely aware of the loss. The wings had lost much of their beauty along with the dust. Well, another lesson to learn! Hardly surprising. Their education had been interrupted by adventure. Sooner or later they must get back to basics. But right now basics meant lunch.

They headed for the hawthorn apples but happened upon a real apple tree with golden yellow fruit. A buck with ragged velvet antlers was eating the fallen ones, rolling them first to check for bugs. When he liked one he seized it whole in his mouth and crunched it, throwing his head back to swallow everything. Shreds of the velvet shook and dangled when he did so, presenting an untidy appearance, but that was the least of his worries. The fighting season approached now! He'd been jousting with small trees, practicing his moves.

152

The pixies avoided him and went to the hanging apples which were sure to be more sanitary but found the skins too tough to chew through. They went to the fallen ones reluctantly, some of which were split open, but the buck was belligerent and swiped at them with his antlers. The pixies quickly fluttered up out of reach.

"Find your own tree", snorted the buck. "This is mine!"
"You can't eat all those apples!" said Airy. "We only want one".
"Tough! These are all mine, and then I'll pick some more!"

The pixies laughed and clapped their hands. "You can't pick anything!" pointed out Airy. "You don't have *hands*". She waved hers at him. That was trouble.

The buck reared up on hind legs and hooked viciously close to them with the antlers, knocking down several apples and impaling one on a sharp point. That wasn't intentional and irritated the animal. He tried to shake the fruit off, but the first try didn't dislodge it, whereupon he stamped his hoof and threw his head violently. That did it. The apple flew into the brush, which worked out well for the pixies too. They found the freshly broken pieces and were able to dine in a more peaceful setting.

Later, when the buck had his fill, he noticed them over in the brush and challenged them again.
"I thought I chased you away!"
"Just leaving", said Airy quickly.
"We're looking for a nice hole-in-the-ground", said Poo innocently. "Do you know of any?"
The buck snorted in surprise, catching them with droplets. "That's stupid! Birds should nest in the trees".

"It's just for tonight".

"Slumming it, eh? There's an old fox den if you're not fussy". He gave directions and stalked off muttering, "Dirty birds!"

The den was roomy and deep with a back door, and that was enough. It was only for one night anyway. But there was nothing nice about it. The hole still stunk of fox waste though it obviously hadn't been used in a while. There were chewed bones and hides underfoot and a layer of matted hair under everything. Well? What did they expect? A vixen had raised her litter of kits here with no vacuum cleaner or garbage disposal.

"Let's go up in the trees", suggested Lolly. "If a storm does come we'll duck back in here"

"But first, a bath!" suggested Poo.

No one argued, and when they were washed and dressed again with new material it was sunset. They perched atop the tallest tree they could find, a huge elm in a grove of tall elms, and enjoyed a bit of breeze at the end of the day, maybe the last of several hot days. It had been 'stuffy', to quote Poo, and a change would be welcome.

A fox appeared far below them with her three kits, trotting along a game trail in single file. The trail would take them nowhere near the pixies' foxhole, which they carefully noted, but the vixen stopped directly under their elm for a bit and tested the air, waggling her ears in all directions. The young ones soon began to play and that reclaimed her attention. She spoke sharply to get them back in line and trotted on, but the pixies were no longer paying attention. The view of the heavens was far more interesting to fairy girls.

Stars had appeared in the darkening sky - more and more of them, even as they watched. The Milky Way traced its arc across the heavens. It was time for their chore. The pixies entered the Night Sky, searching upward for the esporellia belt, that region where stardust is common and sparkles easy to see and catch. It was cold up there, but the stardust warmed them. 'Nyo', this part of the Night Sky is called by those who live there, and that means nearly all the fairy girls who formerly lived down below. All this was known to the three pixies once, in an earlier life, but that was before the forgetfulness. Tonight their thought was simply for the warm dust and finding their way back down again. Gravity played a part in that, and a sense of direction known only to their race.

They decided the great elm was a better place to pass the night, being fairly close to their foxhole anyway. It was also the best lookout perch available to watch the weather. But as yet there was no weather to watch, not even on the horizon, and they fell asleep.

The witching hour came and went with no sign of weather or witches, and the moon fell below the western horizon unchallenged, but in the final hour of darkness things changed quickly. The wind calmed entirely as though the woods held its breath. Storm clouds suddenly loomed high in the west, devoured Mercury, the morning star, and advanced upon them. But the pixies snoozed.

Dawn grew in the east, angering the oncoming storm. The first high clouds hurried ahead to do battle with the light, snuffing it out like a matchstick and restoring the darkness, but still the pixies snoozed.

Dawn appeared in the west, as it shouldn't: A false dawn of lightning and fire in the sky; yet still they snoozed.

A churning shelf cloud dipped past and loud rumbles of thunder arrived. That awoke them, but for nothing it seemed in the dark. The hill was perfectly quiet and still in that moment. Then the Storm Crow cawed ominously, passing overhead in advance of the gust front. The pixies winged it for the safety of their hole-in-the-ground, but wind suddenly forced them down and sheets of rain caught them in the open. A bolt of lightning blasted the top out of the tall elm behind them, but in the bright flash they found their hole and crawled inside, tumbling headfirst down into the mess.

"Who are you?" said a voice in the dark.

"Lolly", said she, being closest to the voice. "Who are *you?*"

There was no answer, or if there was the storm noise drowned it out, but the voice had come from the passage leading to the back door. A faint glow from the pixie's wings revealed a dark shape there, blocking the darker tunnel. No one moved or spoke again. The storm was rapidly becoming violent outside and seized everyone's attention, including the toad.

Yes, it was a large toad whose home this now was, in his opinion. The storm thrilled him, promising a rich buffet. Worms and bugs would be coming up everywhere out of the soggy ground! He was just on his way out when *this* prey came in. He could hardly believe his good luck: *Dragonflies,* he guessed, though they weren't admitting it. *Huge* dragonflies judging by their wings. That was all he could see. Three of them this size would make a fabulous meal, with leftovers! He braced himself and loosened his tongue.

The violence increased outside. A whirlwind indeed tore through the woods knocking down trees, sucking up anything that lay loose. As it passed over the foxhole the suction reached inside and snatched at the pixies, pulling them out. But at that moment the toad let fly with his sticky tongue. It latched onto Lolly's cheek as she was beginning to float away. She screamed, and the others grabbed her, arresting their own departures.

Whoa! This was way more than the toad had bargained for! But the sticky tongue would not let go. They never do. He dug in with his feet and the tongue stretched almost to the breaking point.

In the fury of the moment other breaking points demanded attention: Lolly's cheek was being sucked away by the tongue - ouch! And Airy held onto Lolly's hair for dear life - ouch! And Poo gripped Lolly's ears fiercely as the whirlwind surged past.

But all storms finally come to an end or move on. The suction lessened and the floating pixies flopped onto the floor, into a trickle of water from the entrance. Poo and Airy let go to Lolly's partial relief; but the tongue didn't let go. Lolly felt herself being dragged through the mud toward the creature.

With the passage of the storm and new light from the entrance the toad now saw his mistake. The prey was too large to swallow! He wished he could drop it but only the saliva in his mouth could melt the bond. He couldn't even talk or explain his predicament, he could only act. He must draw the giant dragonfly to his mouth - *lips to cheek* - and *drool!*

"Oh, Lolly!" giggled Poo suddenly. "He wants to kiss you!"

That didn't help. Lolly, a romantic soul any other day, was aghast. She resisted desperately but the toad was dug in, and the tongue was strong, pulling her forward. Arrgh! Made it look like she was attracted to the creature!

The toad was no happier about appearances. He already had a girlfriend. What if she hopped in right now and saw this? Arrgh! Must get it over with! He pulled harder.

The toad would've had his way, but Lolly's face found a puddle of muddy water. The sticky tongue didn't like that and let loose. The reluctant sweethearts broke apart. The toad reversed and headed out the back door. Lolly washed away as much of the stickiness as she could, but a big red spot remained. Airy called it a 'beauty' mark.

"Icky!" said Lolly and put an end to the subject.

It rained for a while longer and lots of water trickled in. When the rain stopped the pixies were quite ready to leave.

"It's over with!" said Airy. "Let's go!"

But someone outside overheard. A fox poked her face into the entrance and looked them over.

"Well, well!" she said, and showed her teeth. "Here's a bit of luck for me".

CHAPTER

6

FOX AND KITS

The vixen, the same one they had seen, was not about to eat them. She was beside herself with worry.

"Please, can you help? My baby is up in a tree!"

In the tall elm where lightning had blasted away the top part of the tree the whirlwind had deposited the kit in its place, seventy feet above the ground. There she clung to splinters of the broken trunk. Could the pixies fly up there and rescue the kit? The vixen stood helpless with her other two girls.

"We can try", ventured Airy, "but we've never done such a thing. I just don't know!"

The kit was frozen with fear and a wild look in her eye persuaded the pixies not to lift her by the ears or tail, or to go anywhere near the teeth. Rope was needed. They found a length of broken vine from the fermented grapes that might serve the purpose and approached the kit again, but cooperation seemed very unlikely.

She had wedged herself solidly between two standing splinters of the trunk. What's more, she had locked her jaws onto one of them and wrapped her tail tightly around the other. Embers from the lightning bolt still smoldered under the tree bark and smoke curled up around them. Seventy feet below, Momma barked encouragement, but the kit's brain had tuned everyone out.

Lolly and Poo dangled a loop of vine in front of her nose while Airy explained the plan: The kit should seize the vine with her teeth and hang on. Just that. The pixies would do the rest. But it was like talking to the tree. The kit's wild eyes never blinked.

"We want to help", said Airy in exasperation, "but we'll leave you here if we have to. Try just one thing at a time. Bite the vine at least. Bite down hard! You can hang onto the tree with everything else".

That fetched a reply. The kit wiggled her mouth enough to mumble, *"Never!"*

Okay, then - if that's how she wanted it! Airy broke off a loose splinter and stuffed it under the bark down by the hot coals to catch fire while she had a quiet word with the others, and then a final word with the kit.

"You can see th'smoke, an' smell it", Airy pointed out. "The tree is burning! Th'fire is getting close to your rear end. You'd better think what to do when it suddenly burns you".

With that she fetched out her splinter, now afire, and jabbed the kit in the butt with it. All else had been a waste of time but this worked almost too well. The kit leaped and grabbed the vine in mid-air, but the sudden weight was too much for Lolly and Poo. Airy lent a hand but the kit was too heavy and there was no slowing the descent once in motion. Tumbling downward branch by bruising branch they inevitably reached the bottom. The kit was knocked out but would recover, the Momma was ecstatic, and the other kits immediately began 'purring' and rubbing themselves against Lolly and Poo like friendly kittens.

"Look", exclaimed Momma. "You've already become friends! You simply must stay awhile and play".

"Well, we want to eat breakfast", explained Airy. "We can't stay long".

"Oh, please! Don't go yet. We owe you so much! Let's find some breakfast together. What do you like?"

"We're thinking about acorns this morning".

"Perfect! There might be mushrooms too, after the rain. We'll eat those. I'm raising the girls to be vegetarians".

"That's a surprise. The *stone* foxes eat big rats and anything else that moves!"

The vixen leaned closer, breathing quickly. Whatever she'd been eating certainly wasn't fresh fruit or vegetables. *"Ahhhh! Stone foxes?* You must show me after breakfast! Do they look like me?"

"Just like you, or even uglier. Same bad breath".

The vixen flashed her teeth and changed the subject. "Oh look! See her now, the kit you saved!" The conked-out kit was coming to her senses, getting up and staggering around. Momma nudged the youngster toward Airy. It didn't take much nudging. Very soon she was purring and rubbing against her new friend just like the other kits.

"I'm sure you prefer to fly", said the vixen, "but why not walk with us on such a fine morning? Let's walk together to find breakfast! My girls are so very fond of you!"

"Well..." Airy suddenly noticed that Poo was studying her hand, shaking it. Lolly was too. They had been 'petting' the kits and their hands felt like they had gotten into nettles. Stinging nettles! Ouch!

Seeing the game was up, the vixen lunged, trying to grab both of them in her mouth, while the three kits attacked Airy and knocked her down. Such surprise worked with other prey, but pixies are quicker than other prey and strong for their size. Lolly swung the scrap of vine and Momma got that hard across her nose. She yelped and backed away. Then the kits got smacked too, wherever Lolly could lay it on 'em, allowing Airy to get free. With that, the pixies skedaddled up into the treetops to throw off pursuit and scratch their itches.

———————◦◆◆◆◦———————

The tussle tired them way more than it should have, and they needed a safe place to rest, but the forest canopy and much of the forest itself had changed in the storm. A path of destruction scarred the southern part of the hill from the southwest corner all along the slopes going east. The pine woods had been spared, and of course the huge stone trolls couldn't be hurt anyway, so that's where the pixies went.

They perched atop the young troll's head where Lolly and Poo immediately flopped down exhausted. Their hands and legs - wherever the kits had rubbed against them - itched like crazy, but at least didn't welt up. The worse symptoms were fatigue and drowsiness, especially for those two. They nodded right off, and that's where Atel found them. She listened with growing alarm as Airy scratched her arms feverishly and recounted the experience.

"I'll take my chances with th'stone foxes any day before *this* gang", Airy vowed. "They're tricksters an' liars! And we fell for it".

"They fooled me too", replied the hummingbird in dismay. "The vixen is a *witch*, as I see now. But we'll worry about that later".

"Will Poo and Lolly be okay?"

"I don't know yet. Let's wake them up!"

They didn't wake easily and when they did they were only interested in scratching their itches. Atel prescribed baths as soon as possible, but it took serious coaxing to make them understand the importance – or even stay awake. In desperation, she gave them a hot foot with her mirror, which brought them wide-awake and angry.

"Baths right *NOW!*" she ordered. "You need to wash off the germs, the contagion. So get moving, or I'll give it to you again!"

As nanny or guide, the hummingbird had no peer. She won all the important arguments. She accompanied the pixies and nagged them to stay awake. She nagged them until they washed thoroughly and returned to the trolls where she could keep lookout and they could rest. But the bath did help. Now the pixies sat sullenly and expected an explanation for her rough tactics.

"I won't sugarcoat it", she told them. "I think you're past the worst danger now, but you've had a close call. The vixen is a witch as we have learned, but her kits aren't and never will be. Kits like those usually grow up to be ordinary foxes and that's the end of it. But there is a path to a longer, nastier life for them: They can become *hop-goblins* if they steal life from others. Stealing it from common creatures of the forest isn't enough - but stealing a *pixie's* long life would be strong medicine. Medicine for *them,* poison for *you*".

"From just rubbing on us?" asked Poo.

"Yes, like poison ivy. And you make it worse when you scratch it. Then the poison gets into your system, same as any itch. Get it?"

They got it. But they were tiring again. Airy too, by now. Atel instructed them to take in the sun for the rest of the day - a natural antidote against all *unnaturals*, the logic in this case being that while witches can abide sunshine they don't like it.

"Don't dress up either, for a few days", she reminded them. "But it's fortunate that you *were* dressed. It protected a lot of skin and made a difference. One last question: Since you didn't get any other rashes from this, what's the big welt on Lolly's cheek?"

Lolly was embarrassed, so Poo answered, "A toad kissed her there. She calls it an *icky*".

"A *hickey?*"

"Yeah. Right Lolly?"

Lolly nodded her head, and the dictionaries ought to give her credit for the word. But the toad shall remain anonymous.

When the pixies were asleep Atel set up a spell of concealment on their troll so hunting birds wouldn't find them. It wasn't easy. The troll's life-force was suppressed in the stone, but still present. All she could do was bend the sunlight around him, allowing it to bathe the pixies up top while leaving the troll in the dark. The sleeping pixies, then, were difficult to see with no troll to draw attention. But it would only last until sunset and her best effort wasn't perfect: The tongue, and the arm that Gronk favored could both be seen faintly. That was all she could do. She needed to leave. There were other dangers afoot.

The whirlwind had continued past the hill and swept directly over the sinkhole, uprooting trees and brush. The entrance to the Underground was laid wide open. Anyone could walk in and discover Ishi standing there with the wands at her feet. Atel did not want that someone to be the vixen/witch.

There are very few real witches in the world, and they all belong to the Sisterhood of the Coven. Was this one aware of the stone foxes – her sisters? If so, she could free them this very evening. If not, her fox would soon discover the open cave entrance anyway.

Atel retraced the path of the twister looking for the fox family, but they weren't to be seen. They could be anywhere in the tangle

163

of destruction and never be seen, so she guessed that's where they were. She toured the rest of the hill, noting that the Crow's Roost was still standing, and the top of the hill showed less damage. That was a good bit of luck. The very top of the hill was the only place left with fresh flowers and nectar, without which she must leave on her winter migration.

Speaking of crows, they were everywhere, sightseeing and rubbernecking, bragging about their Hero. The fact that their Roost was left standing, and no one killed (no crows, anyway) was taken as validation of their whole glorious history.

"Did you hear the Storm Crow this morning? Well! What did we tell you?" was a typical remark. To which the hummingbird replied, "Yes, you are so right! Have you seen the foxes today?" But no one had, which confirmed her suspicions. The vixen was aware of her, Atel was now certain, but what else did she know?

The hummingbird had an aversion to guessing games so she turned immediately to the next pressing problem: What could she feed the pixies if they were too weak to find their own food? That was less of a riddle. The answer probably lay at the bottom of the Juggler's bag. He was the Master Chef.

The condition of her patients was stable when she checked around mid-afternoon; that is, they hadn't improved. She went to the Juggler's bag and found it ripped halfway open, flour and spices torn apart and strewn. But an egg had been overlooked in a fold of burlap! She returned to the babes in good spirits.

"Wake up, slowpokes," she chirped. "Climb down if you can't fly. You're going to be treated to a home-cooked meal! Who wants to help?"

Airy managed to roll the egg out where Atel wanted it. That sapped most of her energy, but it was enough. The hummingbird started 'cooking' it immediately while the sunshine was brightest. They would have a hardboiled egg, she explained. The news was met with blank looks.

164

It wasn't as easy as she had hoped. The egg was white, which reflects light, and when she got a hotspot going, the egg wanted to roll. Airy took an interest at that point and propped it up. That helped, and before too long steam arose faintly from the egg.

"Okay, it's done", Atel announced. "Roll it over by the girls and crack it open. Let's see how we did".

Airy peeled some of it and Atel sprinkled salt, as she had seen the trolls do. Hunger overcame fatigue for Airy and Lolly, but Poo remembered that eggs were 'home' to baby birds.

"It must be *snowbirds* then", said Airy. "See? It's all white inside".

"You better eat some", said Lolly. "There's nothing else".

That convinced her and they all ate eagerly for a while, sprinkling more salt occasionally, until they reached the yolk and Poo screamed.

"It's looking at us!"

That sort of phobia requires a long answer or none at all. Atel chose the latter and went off to scout the foxes again.

She still couldn't find them. It was worrisome. The vixen had been everywhere all summer, and now - nowhere. So be it. The fox would look for the pixies, but they were safe atop the troll. These were red foxes, not the tree-climbing gray species. She would stake out the sinkhole and let the fox come to her instead.

In the scoured-out sinkhole little remained to perch on. Only the tall stump of one tree remained standing. It wasn't much cover for a spy, but the hummingbird didn't need much. She nestled into an old woodpecker hole and waited.

Sightseers and gawkers came and went continually. Like an old pond unexpectedly drained, everyone wanted to see what was at the bottom. But the 'sunken treasure' didn't amount to much, just some partially buried junk. That, and the gaping hole that made such a topic of discussion. Crows and others fluttered about the hole, peering into the dark entrance. By now the news must have spread for miles. The place had become a tourist stop and something needed to be done about the wands - soon. But Atel couldn't do it alone and the pixies were in no shape to help.

Then things took a serious turn. The vixen turned up and trotted quickly down into the sinkhole and right up to the hole, frightening the birds away. She took one step into the entrance, caught a whiff of something she didn't like and stopped in her tracks, not daring to go further. She backed off, uttering that involuntary, whiny yelp that canines use when they can't get something they really want.

"That helps!" thought Atel. But it would only help until sunset when the fox would become the witch again. *She* would dare the entrance right away, or during the overnight for sure. But now the vixen turned suddenly and looked directly at the stump, feeling the attention. She couldn't see the hummingbird way back in the hole but felt she was being watched. The vixen never took unnecessary chances. She left at once, in a different direction.

Atel made up her mind quickly. First, she must see Ishi. If that conversation went well, the rat Snitch was next on the list. He would be perfect for the job she had in mind if she could find him. The Arsi had been loose for a few days now and might be anywhere within...well, no telling how far they might have strayed. But Snitch himself might be having second thoughts about leaving home. He had run away from a very privileged position and regular meals.

She waited a little longer until she felt sure the fox was gone, then zipped into the cave entrance, pausing politely to greet the stone foxes.

"Good evening, lovely ladies! May I enter?" ... (no answer) ... "At least *sniff* me. You'll like it. I smell like fresh air!" ... (still no answer) ... "Okay. Don't, then. I'll take it as a 'Yes'".

Atel proceeded past them, confident they were still locked up, and greeted Ishi. To her surprise, the Troll Mother was cordial.

"Hello, pest. Have you come to set me free?"

"Later, maybe. Are you mad at Snitch?"

"What do you *think*!?"

"Ah! But I want you to forgive him. A lot depends on it".

Ishi waited, so Atel went on: "Another witch has turned up. Sent to find out what happened to her sisters here, I'm sure. Her fox has discovered this entrance. She'll come in person tonight and you don't want her playing with the wands, do you? You would lose your doorwards and probably be stuck in their place, hmm? Meanwhile, I've got three pixies to protect from one witch already, so I don't want yours loose too".

"You'll outsmart yourself one day, bird. What else?"

"If I find Snitch, what can I promise him? Bear in mind that I can't use the wands. Can't lift them. But *he* can".

"I'll forgive him if I have to".

"I want your word".

"Okay, I'll swear on my trolls. Why not? I swear at 'em all the time".

Satisfied it was the best she would get, Atel left on her quest. The best possibility was the local dump. Rats and dumps go together like kids and candy. But it didn't smell like candy when she got there. Lots of garbage had off-loaded during the summer.

The place stunk even worse than Atel remembered, but she reminded herself it was this very essence that attracted consumers. She had counted on it and wasn't disappointed. Even now in broad daylight several rats - ordinary rats - were scampering about sampling the freshest entrees. The prize of the day was a bag of spoiled dog food which the rats tore open even as the hummingbird watched.

Three rats worked together at this and were soon rewarded with puppy chow spilling out of a hole. The teamwork was interrupted by a mad scramble at that point but slowed down pretty quickly. There was some problem with the buffet. Atel moved closer to see, then backed away again. So did one of the vermin, but not the other two.

The puppy chow was already being eaten by maggots, and rats do not eat those. There are limits even at their level of the food chain...but, by using finesse a meal could still be sorted out. The important thing was to hurry before the worms spoiled everything. The two rats picked out some nicer bits while Atel struck up conversation with the finicky one.

"Not hungry? I see the others eating".

"You mean *that?* I'd rather et the bag!"

"Oh, pardon me! I don't know much about rats".

"No kidding! What are you doing here anyway?"

"Looking for a friend".

"Well, you can call off the search. He's et by now. Little birds get etten around here".

"Not a bird. He's a rat like you, but he *glows* in the dark". That got everyone's attention.

"Big goon? Eyes like *this?* Ears like *this?*" The finicky rat pantomimed exaggerations. Atel nodded.

"Never seen him!" declared the rat and dived out of sight. So did the others.

A cloud bank grew in the west promising an early sunset. Good! The Arsi might show up sooner. They'd better. Time was running out. The vixen would be very eager to become the witch tonight.

The sun fell behind the clouds and sure enough several cave rats did appear, but not Snitch. They emerged from underneath the garbage heap where the sun never shined. It was already their new home. The Arsi would blend pretty quickly into the common rat population. Their personalities were much the same and all rats prefer the shadows anyway. The new bloodline would just increase the ugliness factor. Atel greeted them.

"We've met before, I believe?"

Their reaction looked like 'yes', but their mouths were too busy to confirm it. They were eating the dog food and not being fussy about the worms, another trait they would contribute to the surface population.

"Where's Snitch? I need him".

No answer. They would have to be bribed and she had nothing to tempt them with. Cave rats are incredibly loyal to their superiors unless there's some reward to be had. Atel gave it up. True sundown arrived with its deeper shadow, and she left to scout the woods. If he was in the area he would certainly show up now.

She spotted him approaching the sinkhole, returning 'home' with some pals as she had hoped, no doubt missing the easy meals they were used to. She waited at the cave entrance and surprised him, flashing him with her mirror.

"Homesick?" she asked. "Sneaking back in?"

"Out-out-out of the way!" he chittered. "Mind your own business!"

"But it *is* my business, Snitch. I've been talking to your Mum, and she has a surprise for you".

Snitch growled, waiting for it.

"She misses you. If you will help Mum with a small errand, all is forgiven. You know how to work the wands. Set her free".

Wow, that was better than expected! Too bad he didn't know it a bit sooner. In the next moment, the fox/witch Irrada stepped into the sinkhole brandishing her silver wand.

"Go!" shouted Atel to the rats and moved to block the spell that would be coming, but Irrada had already cast it over the grounds. Ivy stirred, sprouting new growth where it had been torn apart by the storm. Even as Atel shouted, eager new shoots snaked rapidly toward the cave entrance, twisting around rat legs and rat necks. Snitch scrambled into the cave ahead of it and suddenly popped into Ishi's view. Mum bellowed encouragement. Irrada heard and issued a reinforcing command to the ivy.

Atel partly deflected this one but most of it touched the ivy like a shot of adrenaline. The fastest, freakiest vine caught up to Snitch and tripped him near the stone foxes. He lunged for the wands but fell short and the vine jerked him back. Ishi screamed her displeasure. Outside, Irrada heard and guessed what happened. She laughed and prepared to make a grand entrance. She knew what to expect now. Ha! She would liberate her sisters and do away with the traitor Ishi all in one delicious minute! It was worth having lived an animal's life all summer.

But she didn't want to trip over the stupid rat and look silly. She ordered the ivy to drag Snitch out and clear the way for herself. The vine reversed obediently but snagged and stopped.

"*C'mere, rat!*" came a guttural voice from within. "*I want your bunch back down in Court. Garbage is piling up!*"

It was Gorrah himself. He stomped on the straining vine, squishing it against the rock. Irrada felt that sharply, for the vine was an extension of herself. She screamed and called off the spell. The ivy quickly wilted and began to turn brown. Irrada bolted into the woods and disappeared. Snitches bunch, now free of the vines, stampeded into the cave. Atel followed, worried about Mum, but the Troll King just ignored her and headed back down into the Underworld followed by the rats - all but one.

Snitch had both wands aimed at his Mum. "Move!" he ordered. He had the wrong command again.

"Try 'GO!'" said Atel.

That did it. Snitch skedaddled into the down-passage after the others. Ishi yawned and stretched. So would you if you were stoned for days. She teased her foxes a bit with the wands until their eyeballs bulged, then tweaked their foxy noses and put them back to work with an extra caveat.

"No other witches are allowed in here! Block them OUT!"

That solved Ishi's problem but left the hummingbird to deal with Irrada alone. Unfortunately, witches do carry a grudge and this one knew a great deal about local customs and habits. Atel was anxious to move the pixies somewhere else, some place safer, but when she got back to the trolls they were asleep, and she didn't have the heart to wake them.

In the morning she found a few ripe gooseberries and served them for breakfast. It was better than nothing, but not by much. Then she went scouting for quiet, out-of-the-way hideouts for the pixies. Nothing grabbed her fancy, but the trolls weren't safe anymore. A glance in their direction as she returned proved that much.

The spell of concealment hadn't fooled the early morning crows. There sat the pixies where they had been, talking to Gronk who was perched on the troll's tongue. They were pleading ignorance and Gronk was demanding answers. Other crows jostled for space on the ghostly arm, and still others perched on Red and the Juggler, or circled above. The 'disappearing troll' had now taken over as the most famous object in the neighborhood.

"They're speaking the truth", Atel told Gronk. "I did this. The fox wants these girls, so I hid them. You saw through it, huh?"

"Sure. Crows see everything!" boasted Gronk. "But hey! Neat trick! Now you will disappear some friends of mine, okay? Ho-ho! Just leave butt-feathers!"

"Sorry! Can't do that. Doesn't work on living folks".

171

"Not dead ones either!" Gronk pecked the young troll's tongue to prove the point. "You need new trick".

"Okay, my next trick will be: We're going to perch in your Roost tonight. At the *top* - *with you* - not at the bottom".

Whoa! That brought sudden silence. Then crows all around noisily passed gas, signaling that the request was bad form. At least Atel had put it to Gronk, an important crow, but he reacted like the rest of them. The rude response was followed by a hullaballoo as every crow took wing and went off cawing in different directions. Soon the entire hill was yakking about it.

"The fox has to be deaf not to hear this", grumbled Airy.

"I don't care", replied Atel. "The top of the Roost is out of her reach, if we can get permission".

The notion was very doubtful. Along with Crow Mother and Storm Crow, the Roost itself formed the third part of their Glorious History. *Yaccaw* weren't allowed, unless at the very bottom maybe. The *Caw* were an exclusive race.

"So how do we get permission?"

"We'll ask the Top Crow. Top Crow has the final word on all earthly arguments. That's how the Great Spirit set it up in the Beginning. It still works that way".

"I can't guess where He got *that* idea, unless Top Crow is a lot smarter than the ones we've met so far".

"Just mind your manners when we get there. I'll do the talking".

"I'm with Airy", put in Poo. "They argue every morning, but it's always about little stuff".

"It used to be about BIG stuff. I'll tell you the story while you take in the sun. You need to understand this or there will be more trouble".

Top Crow

In the Beginning, when the earth had been made safe to live in, Great Spirit moved on to new works in the heavens, appointing the crows to settle disputes in His absence. To this purpose He created the Tree of Wisdom - tallest of all trees - for the crows to roost in at night.

"All wisdom rises to the top", He explained to them. "Take a question under advisement each evening. By morning, the highest crow will know the answer and make a Ruling".

The plan worked well with mortal creatures, but crows lacked enough wisdom to resolve arguments among the great primal forces of the planet: Spirits of the Sea, the Land, and the Sky.

"We need to be much higher, way up at the top of the Tree", they told Great Spirit, "But we can't fly that high".

Another Hero was needed, so Great Spirit summoned *Top Crow* from the twilight to go up and settle the Great Disputes. He explained the job and the bird had a question or two.

"So I get to be the Big Boss? Is that the idea?"

"When I'm not here, yes".

"Do I get the last word on everything?"

"Yes, and you'll have the wisdom to support it. That's the plan".

"I like it", said Top Crow. "I'll do it".

"Just so you're aware", warned Great Spirit, "three old arguments are still pending". Then He left.

In the first case, Sea Spirit was still upset that Lands had arisen from the ocean and wanted permission to wipe them out.

"Go for it", ruled Top Crow.

Waves immediately assaulted the beaches, washing them away bit by bit. It would take a while, but Sea Spirit was determined.

"That's the way it should be", said Top Crow. "Who's next?"

Land Spirit appeared next, showing evidence that the Sea had been cheating since the Beginning. He demanded permission to defend himself.

"Go for it", ruled Top Crow.

Volcanoes erupted immediately, building new islands and expanding the continents, but only until the waves could wash them away again.

"That's the way it should be", said Top Crow. "Who's next?"

Sky Spirit was next, unhappy with the weather which had become sustainable and (ugh!) predictable. "My children want to play", she complained, "but the rules are too strict. Let the winds blow where they will!"

"Go for it", ruled Top Crow.

So they did. The Four Winds kicked up and produced the unruly weather that we know today.

"That's the way it should be", said Top Crow.

Great Spirit returned to find earth evolving much faster than expected and went to have a word with Top Crow.

"What did you do?" he asked. "Just give them whatever they wanted?"

"Sure", said Top Crow. "It's 'survival of the fittest' now, and that should take care of everything".

His job finished; Top Crow went back to the twilight to spend his retirement. But today, Ages later, crows still uphold his responsibility. The Great Tree is gone but crows still roost together and debate the problems of the world each morning before breakfast. It's loud because it's important, and when everyone has given their opinion it still falls to the Top Crow to make a ruling.

"Is that true?" asked Airy when the hummingbird finished. "Is there really a Top Crow?"

"Yes. The Top Crow has the loudest voice. He breaks up the Big Quarrel each morning with words of wisdom".

"Does he have any?" laughed Lolly. "What does he say?"

"That it's time for breakfast, usually. The crows are having their breakfast right now. Where does that leave you?"

There was no answer. The pixies were noticing hunger pangs, now the subject was brought up. Atel prodded them some more.

"You seem to be pulling out of your funk. How do you feel?"

In answer, the Three took wing and tested their strength. It already showed signs of the swifter recovery common among creatures in the wild. Okay. Bring on breakfast!

Atel led them to a broken tree with honeycomb spilling out of it. Animals had gotten into the open hive despite the angry bees and a skunk was rooting through combs spilled onto the ground below. Atel asked permission to join him.

"We only want a bit of honey", she promised. "You can have everything else".

The skunk seemed agreeable. He didn't actually answer but shook his head up and down trying to get rid of a honeybee that had found his unprotected nose. His favorite combs were 'everything else', meaning nursery brood cells with juicy wigglers too young to sting. While those treats were available he didn't seem to care about anything else, so the pixies were introduced to honey, the finest food the wildwood has to offer.

"How do you like it?" asked Atel after a while, breaking the silence. The pixies nodded their heads exactly like the skunk (minus the bee). Perfect! Her own appetite was satisfied, and she was anxious to query the skunk for news.

"Pardon me..." she began, but the skunk turned and pointed the wrong end at her. Had he not heard? Atel zipped around to the front and spoke louder.

"Excuse me, but have you seen the foxes?" The skunk stiffened and regarded her out the corner of his eye.

"Did you call me *Butt?*"

"No".

"I heard you! You said, *Excuse me, Butt!*"

"I didn't mean it that way".

"You did! Here, I'll give you some!"

The skunk reversed again, this time raising his tail. Atel beat it. The skunk watched and smiled inside. He wasn't about to waste his ammunition on a tiny bird and didn't have to. A bluff was usually enough to get rid of troublemakers. Speaking of which...he cast a critical glance at the pixies, but they were minding their own business...Good! Keep it that way! He had enough trouble already with a bee that wouldn't leave him alone.

Atel used the time to scout the nearby Crow's Roost which was mostly vacated this time of day. The Roost wasn't just a single tree but a group of them, a grove of White Pines in an otherwise deciduous forest: Stately and taller than the hardwoods around them, but otherwise recalling the noble 'Tree of Wisdom' not at all.

The grove was filthy, actually. Not a place for the squeamish. Last night's droppings - plus those of other nights and other years - decorated the twigs and branches. She flew to the upper levels and found the Top Crow's perch - a very high branch concealed against predatory Great Owls by smaller, overhanging branches. There was no doubt the perch belonged to the Top Crow because it was clean. All poop splatters were below this level.

As luck would have it, there was another clean branch opposite, only slightly lower, that would be perfect for herself and the pixies.

That was the good news. The bad news would reach her in just a few seconds. Back at the honey tree the bee had finally stung the skunk's nose. It hurt, and the skunk let fly in automatic reaction. He totally missed the bee, but the pixies were caught in the periphery of the exhaust: The *perifumery*, we'll call it. They screamed, so the hummingbird knew what happened before she ever got there.

The skunk had waddled off by now and the pixies stood stiff with arms, legs, and wings outstretched, groaning like it was the worst thing in the world. Atel was relieved to see at least they hadn't gotten it in their eyes.

"Come along", she ordered. "It's bath time again, the quicker the better. Skunk spray is an oil, and some will lift off underwater. You'll be fine. It's not like you were going out on dates tonight".

"What is *dates?*" asked Lolly crossly.

"Oh, just talking to boys, laughing at their jokes. Silly stuff like that".

"I will never find my handsome prince after this!"

"You have to clean up anyway. Dump those dresses! Let's go!"

Spring water did help. Faint oil slicks arose from the submerged pixies. But then it washed onto shore and stuck there, fouling the local aura. That's what the fairy boys smelled now, as they came walking by. The pixies quickly ducked under overhanging grasses. Noggin broke the silence with a bad word, as usual with him.

"The spring is cursed!" he declared. "It stinks around here all the time now!"

"Not any worse than last time", argued Boo. "It's just skunk".

"Last time you said 'Wood Nymphs'. You're wrong now, too".

"There's nothing wrong with skunks. Just leave 'em alone!"

Noggin took another whiff and rubbed his nose. "Use the nose on your face, Boo! There's more than skunk in the air".

Boo finally sniffed and scowled. "Smells familiar!"

Nary grinned and jerked a thumb upstream in the direction of the hazelnut bush. The others took notice. They always took notice when Nary made a point. He had the best nose.

"*Pixies* again?" translated Noggin. "Them little stinkers still hangin' around?" Nary nodded.

"Cute little twerps", chuckled Boo. "But stupid. You'd think they would learn".

The boys disappeared as suddenly as they had arrived, but not as quietly. Their laughter floated back on the breeze.

The pixies were nicely dressed and their own aura somewhat improved when they caught up to the hummingbird later, but they weren't too talkative. They did mention the 'stinky' hop-goblins again, but mostly they wanted Atel's opinion of their own stinkiness.

"Fairly decent", she ventured, but she didn't venture too close. "If you want to try something else, scrub with fermented grapes. The alcohol might take away some of the skunk odor".

That had no appeal. Fermented grape odor was another smell they wanted to forget. What they wanted - and didn't know the word for - was *perfume*.

"...Some *nice* smell to cover up *this* smell", is how Lolly put it.

"Oh, a *fragrance!* Well, there are lots of those this time of year: Turning leaves, ripening seeds, frosty mornings, and much more. But none of them will cover up what you have. Sorry! In a few days, maybe. But not yet".

"Not even flowers?"

"I doubt it. There aren't many flowers left anyway. But on a happier note there still is good honeycomb! Are you hungry?"

The pixies looked at her suspiciously, but she was serious. Hunger won the argument, so long as there were no skunks.

"You should also be happy to know I've scouted a nice perch for us in the Crow's Roost", remarked Atel. "Way up by the Top Crow. If we're quiet and polite I think they'll let us stay with them tonight".

"Did you ask permission?" asked Airy.
"Not yet. My plan is, we'll arrive quite late when they're asleep".
"An' sneak in? What happens when th'wake up?"
"We'll have permission from the Top Crow by then. I think".

Of course the Top Crow turned out to be Gronk. Atel knew it and wasn't worried except that he might be too soundly asleep. She spoke a greeting directly into his ear which roused him to a low state of awareness. He could hear, but not quite focus.

"Greetings from *underlings*", said Atel, using the proper crow dialect. "May we perch *down there, BELOW YOUR LEVEL?*" She described the slightly lower branch.

"Go for it", answered Gronk, already nodding off again.

It was that easy. They settled down on the clean branch opposite, which happened to be just above the #2 crow. Atel hadn't counted on him. Worse, the #2 crow had been awakened by the disturbance and now glared up at them.

"That's *my* branch!" he squawked. It wasn't, although he dearly wanted it. Gronk didn't allow #2 to get up that high. But now #2 hopped up to the outer end of the branch and tried to claim it away from the new arrivals, forcing them in toward the trunk. Atel looked to the Top Crow to defend his territory, but Gronk was sound asleep again.

"You heard the Top Crow!" she said firmly. "We have permission".

"Trickery! You got *nothing!*" countered #2. But he spoke more quietly this time, worried about waking Gronk. When the 'trespassers' didn't leave he side-stepped threateningly toward them, then back out, then toward them again, then back, then... and then *he* was plucked off the branch in a squawking burst of feathers by a Great Owl, attracted to movement on the open branch. Gronk wakened just enough to guess what happened, then simply closed his eyes again.

"That's the way it should be", he mumbled.

There was trouble in the morning when the Roost discovered the newcomers, but there's trouble every morning anyway. The quarrel always breaks out. Most are unhappy with the pecking order and there are challenges as lower birds try to move up. But today the Top Crow issued a Ruling that was popular with all.

"Everyone moves up one place!" he decreed. #2 had left a vacancy.

Gronk accepted them surprisingly well, although he didn't care for the lingering skunk odor. He was surprised that the owl hadn't grabbed the pixies too, for that very reason.

"Owl *eats* skunks", he told them. "But maybe Owl doesn't believe his nose? Three little skunks up a tree? Ha-ha! That's just too stupid. But here you are!"

They were allowed to stay the next night too, but by the second morning the pixies were tired of ridicule and went off by themselves to look for 'fragrance'. Almost anything strong enough would be welcome - but being girls they hoped to find something *nice*. And they did.

On the east end of the hill, near the top of the pine woods, flowers still bloomed where the morning sun found them. Several types were in evidence this morning but most spectacular by far were the foxgloves, loaded with their tubular blossoms. That's what drew the pixies as much as the fragrance: The *shape* of the flowers. Atel would have warned them had she known, but she didn't know.

"Look at these", said Poo, who discovered them. "They're like pink mittens!"

Indeed they were. That's what pixies are *supposed* to think when they see them. That's what they were designed for in the Old Days when there were lots of pixies. It's a major reason why there are less pixies now, but more hop-goblins. Witches began it, cultivating flowers in their gardens. They knew how pixies are attracted to flowers. So they raised flowers and crossed different varieties, looking for something to trap pixies. In time they produced *foxgloves*, naming them after their own alter-egos. It was a match made in Witch-Hades. Pixies couldn't resist putting their hands inside them. From there, it was a simple matter of adding a spell to the 'gloves' to grab and not let go! The hop-goblin devilishness works quickly then - when the pixie can't get away.

"Oh, they *are* like mittens", agreed Lolly. "Airy! Come look at this!"

"An' look inside!" marveled Poo. "See? *Fingerprints!* Others have tried them on before us".

But Poo was mistaken. Witches put the 'fingerprints' there as a final touch, to show false proof that it's safe.

Lolly tried a mitten on and was thrilled. The sensation was soft and welcoming. But it didn't lock onto her. Not yet. The plants knew there were more pixies. They were bred to be aware of such things. That's why there are so many 'gloves' on each stalk: To catch all the foolish pixies. They had two of them suckered already. Soon maybe three! Poo tried on a pair of gloves and closed her eyes in bliss.

"They're snug and warm!" she whispered. "It's like they try to fit perfectly".

Lolly put on a pair. "I can feel it too", she sighed. "They snuggle around my fingers! Try it, Airy!"

"No. It's too much like reaching into a knothole. That always gives me the willies".

"Take mine then. These don't bite. I'll try different ones".

So Airy was finally teased into it, and that was all of them. The mittens 'snuggled' around everyone's fingers and suddenly latched on with a frightening grip. It hurt. The pixies struggled and panicked but couldn't pull loose or even break off the flowers. The soft blossoms had become strong, as if the devil had gotten into the plants.

"*Now* what?" said Airy finally, but nobody answered. There was no good answer. None of them could even sit down. All they could do was stand there like little fools and hope someone would come by to help. At least they wouldn't have to wait long. Someone was already trotting through the woods, coming to check her traps. Who else but Momma Fox?

"Well, look who's put on the gloves this morning!" she said with obvious pleasure. This was a breakfast stop for her each morning when she was out hunting. Usually the gloves had trapped a grasshopper or two, sometimes a large moth or even a mouse. But this is what the vixen/witch had planted them for! She couldn't help gloating.

"Times change, but pixies never wise up! Ha! You still fall for the same old tricks". The vixen scratched up the ground at the base of the plants, sniffed it, and backed away.

"I'd rather have foxgloves than a fox nose!" said Poo.

But the fox wasn't even listening. This had turned out much easier than she expected. Now she must decide the pixie's fate before she was quite ready.

She was torn between two final solutions. Her witch, Irrada, was bound by the Coven to find her Sisters and free them. She could likely trade these little fools to Ishi for their release. On the other hand, she could give the pixies over to her three kits to finish what they had begun. Her decision turned on motherly instinct.

"Don't run off!" she teased. "I'll fetch my girls. They'll be so pleased to see their good friends!"

Things got worse before that. An ammonia odor had been released where the fox scratched the ground, which got up into their eyes and made them water. The kits had been using the plants to mark their territory and now as they arrived it was the first thing they checked. The plant with their scent was theirs, and a pixie came with each one. What excitement! The kits ran in circles yipping, then paused breathlessly to see which pixie they had won. Well, bless the black magic! They each got the same pixie as before! That really pleased them. There were scores to settle. But if they expected it to be easy they were wrong.

Kit #1, the one from up in the elm tree, immediately began rubbing her cheek against Airy's leg and got kicked hard in the nose. The others wisely stepped back. Momma arrived then and sized up the situation. It was kits against kickboxers and kit #1 already had a bloody nose. A frontal assault wouldn't do. But their other end wasn't as sensitive. She barked out an order.

"Turn around, ninnies, Use your tails!"

It was like being feather-dusted. The pixies even laughed from the tickling but couldn't do much to stop it, and then it began to sting and sap their strength, slowing down their wings. The blur faded to just a laborious flap and quit. Their legs felt heavy too; the kicks slowed and missed their mark. When the kits moved in and commenced body-rubbing, the pixies found themselves unable to resist and soon fell into unconsciousness.

"We got 'em! We got 'em now, Ma!" barked the kits, and began yelping excitedly again.

"Oooooff!" replied 'Ma', as she was kicked hard in the stomach and sent sprawling. That was Noggin's doing. Nary and Boo grabbed the kits by the scruff of their necks and banged their heads together.

"Don't need any more hop-goblins around here!" bellowed Noggin.

Then things took a nasty turn. In a rage Irrada threw caution to the wind, shedding her fox body and becoming the witch in broad daylight. She brandished her wand with a flourish, holding it high, pausing only a moment to taunt the fairies.

"Hop-goblins we will have!" she cackled. "And no more fairies!"

The silver wand glinted in the sun and attracted onlookers. As she went to aim it, a crow swooped down and snatched the shiny object out of her grasp.

"Cawww! (*This is mine!*)" declared the bird and flew off with the prize.

That ruined the day for Irrada. A witch without a wand is a witch without a chance against three stout fairy boys. She fell back into her alter ego and barked at her kits to get their wits together. In a few moments they all vamoosed.

Boo leaned down to the pixies and stood right back up again. "Well, what next?" he grumbled. "Now they stink like the foxes' outhouse!" Mercifully, the pixies didn't hear that, and they knew no more until evening.

The boys uprooted the foxgloves and took pixies and plants together back to the trolls where they found Atel (who was no stranger) and told her the story. They found it very amusing that a pesky, thieving crow had saved the day.

"We'll turn the pixies over to you then, ma'am", said Noggin. "We didn't think it wise to rip them loose of the flowers. You can worry about that".

"I surely will. Are the pixies aware that you saved them?"

"Dunno. They were overcome by their own smell, I think".

The boys laughed and laid them out on Red's broad back to soak up the sun once more. Then they went on their way, but they had been right to uproot the plants. The beautiful, diabolical things begin immediately to draw out the victim's willpower. This is important with strong prey like pixies who would otherwise tear themselves loose. So some of the pixies' strength had already drained into the green plants - but might flow back as the plants wilted. Only time would tell.

Near dark, the pixies showed signs of wakefulness. They were weak and groggy but aware when the boys returned to make a last check on them. Their eyes got big as memory rushed back. Atel prodded them.

"Are these the *hop-goblins* you've been telling me about?"

The pixies were embarrassed. "Yes *and* no", answered Airy, "if you know what I mean".

"No, I don't. But maybe you've been confusing *hop-goblins* with *handsome princes?* These handsome princes saved you from becoming hop-goblins yourselves. Do you remember that part?"

"Thank you", mumbled Lolly. The others nodded in agreement.

"All's well that ends well!" declared Boo. "And the little stinkers should be fine if they take baths every day!" The boys laughed about that and disappeared into the woods, and this tale does not tell if they meet the 'little stinkers' again; but if they do, it had better not be any time soon.

The pixies ripped their hands loose in a fit of temper and shook their fists after the wise guys. It was all a huge relief to the hummingbird.

"Boo was right about everything", she reminded them. "You are showing recovery, and you certainly need another bath!"

CHAPTER

7

THE WATER WITCH

Irrada's wand had many owners in the following days. The original thief carried it back to the Roost to show it off. Another crow stole it from her, and another from him, and another and another. The last crow just dumped it from a high branch because it made her feet 'tingle', and it tumbled to the ground.

Later in the afternoon the sun found it there and it glinted again, setting off another string of crow-ownership. This time the last crow liked the tingle and brought the wand to Roost in the evening where he owned the prize until moonlight glinted off it in the wee hours. A Great Owl took notice of that and snatched crow and wand together off the branch, but it didn't bring good luck to the owl either. The wand glinted into his eyes every time he flapped his wings and he ended up hitting a branch. Yikes, that was embarrassing! He dropped the crow, and the crow dropped the wand during the confusion.

Next morning, a pack rat saw it glinting in the sunshine. Recognizing value in the shiny object she immediately began to drag the wand back to her midden. She was thrilled! It would be the shiniest object in her collection! But when it glinted again a turkey noticed and wrestled it away from the pack rat, because turkeys, too, are fascinated by shiny objects.

The turkey played with it the rest of the morning, carrying it around and trying to swallow it, until a fox attacked her. She launched into the air with her shiny toy and escaped the fox but accidentally dropped the wand, which fell *splash!* into running water. The fox pursued swiftly because she knew what the shiny object was. She heard it splash, but when she got there it had already washed down the rapids into a deep pool.

That brought her to a standstill. The water was clear, and she could see the wand at the bottom - *her wand!* - but could do nothing about it. Foxes can swim a little, but they do not dive, and without the wand she was unable to become the witch again. She was stuck in her fox body. But the wand was no longer hers anyway. Another creature had already taken possession: Amaam, spirit of the water.

The fox was afraid of her. Many creatures who breathe air are instinctively afraid of the Water Witch, even though we don't know her. We just see the water. But the Witch sees us.

This spring was her home, but so too was the pond down below, and the creek in the next valley, and the moving water under the hill that fed them. She was in all of them. Her domain began wherever raindrops soaked into the ground and didn't end until they flowed into the sea. Another Power ruled there.

She was well aware of the wand, and also the fox that wanted it. That's why she had given it a little nudge, to be sure it ended up in the deep pool. It was shiny, and she liked that too, as a creature out of water might like jewelry. She felt the power of it and was mildly interested. Her own power was superior but in a different way, a more passive way.

The wand was antsy. It itched to be active. Amaam could feel it wanting to do things but was unmoved. So? Let it *want.* All of its secrets would eventually seep into her own mind, and that would be soon enough. For now she was entertained by the fox who so obviously wished to retrieve it, but never would. She would make sure of that. This fox had an ill presence, not native to the natural world.

The thought recalled other unnatural things to mind: The trolls, the troll mother, the witches...oh yes, the *witches.* That's what the fox was! But - *whoa!* She slowed her thought for a while and just luxuriated in the movement of the water. There was no need to get worked up.

The fox left and returned several times during the day to sit and stare at the shiny object deep in the pool, even to paw at the water and yelp at what she could not have. It became distracting and Amaam finally looked to the future, to learn how long she must put up with the annoying creature: Ah! Just one more day. Then the fox/witch would try to dive and drown in the attempt. Afterward, all would be well.

The fox jumped back, then crept ahead again. The surface of the water had changed. She no longer saw the wand or her own reflection, but Amaam's happy vision in the water. Ghastly! She turned tail and prowled the woods in doubt. What was the truth of this? She was a relative newcomer to the hill, ignorant of the pool and its portentous power.

It was quite true what the fox saw - or would be when the time came. In her mind, Amaam could go downstream to the sea and back again and learn many things that would happen while the water flowed. As for the specter on the water, Amaam was Mistress of her Element. She could put up any picture she wanted so long as it was true or would become true. It was her favorite diversion. She loved to tease the *Unnaturals*.

Next day the fox returned and left, and then returned and left again. And returned a third time, having finally convinced herself that the ghastly vision she had glimpsed was merely a reflection of her own fears. After all, it was gone today! That would be due to her regained confidence. How silly she had been! All she need do is remember that she was a Great Witch. As such, she could make her fox do anything.

Regardless, it must be risked. The wand represented her whole future. Without it she would be nothing. All right then! She could see the wand clearly. It hadn't moved since yesterday. She calmed the fox's nerves and dived into the pool almost to the bottom, there to discover in horror that she was no longer steering her 'ship'. Primal fear had seized the fox, who panicked and began taking on water. In a few moments enough water was aboard to hold the 'ship' on the bottom, right next to the shiny wand. Irrada's last thought was to seize the wand in the fox's jaws, but the fox had become unresponsive.

It was a dumb way for a Great Witch to perish, especially being forewarned. The outcome didn't thrill the Water Witch either. For those who don't know, foxes do stink. The Mistress of the pool could really smell it. So later that night a fresh current pushed the offending carcass into the rapids below the pool and gave it a nudge, enough to send it on its way toward the sea. That's where all the smelly stuff should go if Amaam had her way about it, and she usually did. Let that Power deal with it.

Back at the sinkhole, it was some time before Ishi ventured outside the cave. Irrada's presence required some forethought. Ishi would be at risk if they should meet after sunset, that was certain. In daytime it would be a different story. But Irrada had suffered a reversal in the sinkhole and hadn't come back, surely a good omen.

After a week or two Ishi was bored with teasing her stone foxes. It was time to see about her 'boys' upstairs! She finally stepped outside one fine morning and breathed the fresh air. But the fresh smell reminded her of *pixies*.

Her scowl returned and she made her way through the brush to the troll's campsite. It was a mess. Animals had routed everything and dragged stuff around the area. Even the big brew vat had been overturned, she noticed with a twinge. But her boys were fine - plastered with bird droppings, maybe, but a nice rain would fix that. Red, whom she did not count as one of 'her boys', sat on his stump exactly where she had 'stoned' him. Judging by their posture, her boys had obviously been surprised by sunshine.

She stood on top of an overturned kettle to peek up into the young troll's eyes, a trick she had learned over the years. At just the right angle of light she could see the last thing the troll ever saw, a snapshot in time preserved within the eye. The bright sun is always there, of course, but in the periphery she could pick out clues to how it happened. In Laddie's eyes she could see the pixies swimming in the water kettle. She went to The Juggler next and stood on tiptoes. The snapshot was mostly a bright flash but there was something behind the flash, not the big sun. It wasn't hard to guess it was probably the *bird*.

That steamed her, but she had already guessed as much. She glanced over at Red with satisfaction. The last thing that one ever saw was her finger on his nose!

Well, the situation was simple enough and not so bad. She was back where she started. There were still three pixies in the area with wings attached. She didn't know how to capture them again, but that might be remedied shortly. She would have a peek at the water pool and see what it showed.

Ishi often used the pool when in doubt. She was aware of Amaam, though not on speaking terms. The Water Witch didn't share her view of the world but showed her some things just to annoy her. The knowledge usually helped in some way even though it wasn't meant to.

"Good morning!" said Ishi, dabbling a boot in the water to get Amaam's attention. The pool was rough and murky this morning and she didn't really expect any reply, but the breeze calmed a bit and the surface gradually smoothed. A reflection tried to appear of the troll Red sitting on his stump, but the wind kept disturbing the water. A bird or more likely a pixie seemed to flutter in and out of the scene. Finally the reflection surrendered to the wind and was gone. It wasn't much but gave Ishi something to go on. Pixies and trolls...hmmm...She decided to do a bit of eavesdropping.

She searched for a suitable rock near the trolls, but the closest ones had been fouled by animals. Ishi's feminine instincts revolted. She liked dirt, but that wasn't *dirt*. One suitable nose-shaped rock had been spared luckily, or at least washed off when the beer vat overturned. It would have to do. She plopped down and commenced to fold herself inside: Feet and legs first, then working her way up she tucked in her dress, pulled in her arms, and finally ducked her head inside. It was more of a squeeze than usual, and she thought fleetingly about dropping a few pounds, but as the sun warmed the stone the thought went away. She took a nap.

The morning wasn't much older when the pixies arrived for their daily chore. It was fully a week after the incident with the foxes and they were back to normal, if not more so. They had skipped their duty during convalescence and were determined to catch up! Today, they each mooned all three trolls, and it was rowdy enough to awaken Ishi, who peeked out with one eye. She was offended by the goings-on, which she had never witnessed before. But it gave her an idea. She went back to sleep.

When night came she stayed inside her rock, fearing the witch Irrada, whose untimely end she was not yet aware of. It was no great inconvenience to stay put except for missing supper, and there was a bonus tonight: The beer had soaked into the rock and she was beginning to enjoy it. Must be careful, though. She would need a clear head in the morning to judge the weather. She squirmed a bit, trying to get comfortable in the rock, and reminded herself that missing supper wasn't all bad.

Dawn arrived on schedule and brought disappointment for her. It would be a sunny morning, and that would not do for her purpose. She went back to sleep but awoke later, groggy, to pixie revelry. Worse yet, it was still sunny. Not good. She blocked the pixies out of mind, closed her eye and tried to sleep, only to be shaken up minutes later by pixies dancing on her rock. Her peeking eye had given her away, and when she opened it now in surprise she got water in it. What could she do but close it again? She endured their merrymaking and counted the ways she would get even.

Mercifully, pixies also have other things to do so Ishi was finally left in peace. She didn't risk opening her eye again until near nightfall, but her nose detected a change in the weather as evening approached. Not rain maybe, but at least cloudy weather. That was all she needed. Ishi's spirits soared. She rolled out of her rock and made her way back to the sinkhole and the troll caves. Firefly season was over in the outer world, and she needed some.

The pixies took a bath after their morning frivolity. 'Trolling' was great fun but there was simply no way to avoid the bird droppings on the noses. They took baths regularly now, always in the same shallow pool with overhanging grasses. There was a larger pool downstream, a deep pool where they wished to swim, but it was always murky. Today when they flew over after their baths it was strangely clear, revealing a shiny object at the bottom. A familiar object.

"It might be *hers* - the *fox-witch's*", said Poo in hushed tones. The pixies had heard the story, but no one knew where the wand ended up.

As they lingered, the surface of the pool changed, showing now a different picture. A fox appeared and leaped into the water, diving toward the wand. She didn't reach it and didn't come up again. The pixies cheered, recognizing the vixen.

Then the pool changed again, showing the pixies themselves in trouble. The Juggler had them all by the hair, dangling from his big hand - a bad moment from not so long ago.

The pool went murky finally. The pixies relaxed and even laughed at the bad memory. Here was a bundle of news! Life was getting easier fast. Their enemies were dropping like flies: First the trolls, now the fox-witch. Only three orphan kits remained, plus Ishi who couldn't even hide from them inside a rock. All they needed was for the Top Crow to proclaim: "That's the way it should be!"

The hummingbird drew a different conclusion when they related the news.

"That's very interesting", she commented. "But take it with a grain of salt".

"What does that mean?" asked Poo.

Atel smiled. "If you shook salt onto the pool it might show a different picture. The pool is often misleading".

"Well, we saw what we saw", insisted Airy. "It shows things that happened. The Juggler did hold us like that".

"Or he will again one day. Remember, the trolls can be reawakened! But show me the wand".

The pool was still murky when they got there but they searched downstream and found the fox carcass tangled in brush. All foxes look the same after floating for a week, so it was hard to say. But the story added up. Atel believed it. The Water Witch never showed false pictures that she knew of. They were all true, although some had not yet happened. That's where it got tricky. But either way – thanks largely to pixies and their foibles - Irrada was gone to wherever Great Witches finally go.

That still left Ishi and an army of trolls to deal with. Pixies aren't quite up to *that* task. The Three had caused a local uproar, for sure. But the Troll Mother might turn that around whenever it pleased her.

"I wish I knew what Ishi is up to", Atel said mostly to herself. The pixies looked away a little too quickly. Atel stared at them.

"What do you know that I should know?" she asked. She had to ask twice before they answered.

"She was over by the trolls", admitted Poo.

"Inside a *rock*", said Airy. "We saw her eye looking at us".

"And how do you know it was Ishi?"

"Th'rock looked just like her *nose*", answered all three.

"Okay, I believe it. Then what?"

There was no answer, but it wasn't hard to guess from their fidgeting.

"A word to the wise, pixies: She's smarter than you think. Don't tease her! But show me the rock".

The rock was still there but Ishi wasn't in it. She was down in the Underworld, still steaming about the peeping eye incident. Taunted by puny pixies! Ishi had never been so humiliated. She stomped with her tiny steps into the stalactite room and seized her lamp - but blast it! - the lid was ajar, and the fireflies had escaped. She stomped off into the down-passage seeking new ones, her nice day in ruins, while 'upstairs', all was well for a change.

194

Atel went to find her own supper and the pixies fetched acorns back to the trolls again. The thrill of dropping them on Red's skull never got old, but tonight they were hammering them open with rocks because it was getting dark. It attracted an audience. A coyote sauntered into the campsite as if he owned the place and watched for a while, glancing about and testing the breeze occasionally.

He was Top Dog in the area because the wolf pack was away, and it was he who had torn apart the troll's packs and scattered the contents, eating everything that was edible. He stopped regularly now, hoping the trolls had recovered from their trouble, whatever it was. They used to toss him scraps and he missed those! He was hungry.

"Acorns good to eat?" he finally asked.

"Sure", replied Lolly, nibbling at one.

"Let me try".

"Go get your own! Th'woods are full of them".

"Doesn't work for me. I can't eat shells".

"Well, I'm not going to shell any for you! This is my last one anyway".

The coyote looked disappointed but didn't leave. "What are you?" he asked after a little while. "Dragonflies or birds?" The pixies laughed.

"We're fairy folk", replied Airy. *"Pixies"*.

"Pixies", repeated the coyote slowly, as if he'd never heard of it. "Do you nest in trees?"

"You might say that. These *trolls* would say that if they could talk". Airy smacked her rock on Red's noggin for emphasis.

"Trolls", repeated the coyote as if he never heard that word either. "That's news to me, too. What next, I wonder?"

"Oh, gosh! There's lots of oddballs around", replied Poo, ticking them off: "There's Ishi, an' a fox-witch, an' a magic pool where th'stupid fox drowned". She laughed, saying it.

The coyote's mouth twitched. "Someone's bad luck is nothing to laugh about!"

"Well, she had three nasty kits. You can look after *them* if you feel sorry for her!" retorted Airy. "They're as nasty as she was".

The coyote calmed down. "No thanks! I know them".

"Oh, yeah. I guess you're related", said Poo.

The coyote snarled but checked himself. "Do I look like a fox to you?"

"Not exactly, but you haven't told us what you are. What are you?"

"I'm a *wolf!*" said the coyote. "If anyone asks, I'm a *wolf!*"

"Then why would anyone ask? What else could you be?"

The coyote barked impatiently and went off a short distance by himself. Idiotic pixies! He sat down and watched the moon rising in the east. Soon it would be time to howl.

The pixies went to the spring for a drink and discussed the animal. They didn't trust him for being sympathetic to Irrada and they were right not to, but their immediate concern centered around his unpleasant smell. In their young lives the pixies had learned that 'stinkers' usually turned out to be *stinkers!* It helped when he moved off and took his smell with him. They planned to spend the night atop the trolls. It would take the fun away, should he come back. But when they returned he was still off by himself.

When the moon came up the coyote loosened his vocal cords with a few ear-jarring warm-ups. The pixies flew off to the magic pool again to get away from it. The pool showed only the moonrise, but as they talked and ignored it the reflection changed, offering an amusing view of themselves atop the young troll, sleeping and snoring with their mouths open. Of course that would have been during their recovery.

"Wake me up tonight if my mouth falls open!" said Lolly.

"Sleep face down", replied Poo. "I'm not going to watch".

A dark shadow suddenly swept across the picture and erased it, startling them. What was *that*? It was unsettling, but they were determined to camp on the trolls like the victorious fighters that they were.

"If th'wolf stinks the place up, we'll move", said Airy, "but at least wolves can't climb".

He was still there, probably just too lazy to go hunting after a summer of mooching off the trolls. He threw his head back and howled again as soon as they returned but this time his initial howls quickly smoothed into a crooning, pleasing song. A *lullaby*.

That's how it affected the pixies on top of the young troll. They usually talked themselves to sleep but this night they barely finished a sentence. It didn't happen naturally. The coyote meant it to happen. When he was quite sure they were asleep up there he approached their troll and stood up on his hind legs, grasping the statue with his claws - but they weren't claws when they came out. They were *fingers*. Powerful fingers to grip and pull himself up.

A Great Horned Owl watched with interest from the pines as the hairy beast climbed toward the fledglings. She had lost her own babies in the big storm and felt a sudden urge to adopt these and rob the animal! She flew swiftly to the trolls, casting a shadow over the fledglings as she snatched them up neatly and made off to her new nest high in a hollow tree. The fledglings slept through it all.

No sooner was the owl out of sight than the hummingbird appeared looking for the pixies. The coyote creature was standing on the young troll's arm, scarcely believing his reversal of fortune. The hummingbird guessed part of it.

"Good evening, Mongrel", she greeted him. "Or maybe I should say *half*-goblin, or *hop-goblin?*"

The creature retracted his threatening fingers and leaped to the ground, landing on all fours as a coyote should, and backed slowly away. He knew the little bird and feared her sting. Atel laughed at him.

"What did you expect to find up there? Pixies? But they weren't asleep?"

The creature laughed his annoying coyote laugh. He was indeed a hop-goblin: A fusion of different species by witchery, in his case a stolen child raised on wolf's milk. He turned out to be inferior when he grew up and the wolf pack didn't want him, but the witch Irrada found uses for him. He had become very loyal and lately learned of her mortal departure. *Pixies* and *fairies* were to blame, the kits said. Well, he missed his revenge tonight, but the owl would do it for him!

"They were sleeping like babies", he informed Atel with great pleasure. "Someone got there just ahead of me".

"And who was that?"

"Like I would tell? Tough luck, bird. You're too late!"

He loped off in fine spirits. Yes! The owl would surely have killed them by now - or her owlets would!

But his glee was premature. At that moment, the Great Owl was undecided. The 'fledglings' looked dead, but they were breathing noisily with their mouths open. She decided they *were* alive and in need of nourishment. This meant they were still in danger: Their new Mama might kill them with kindness. She went looking for mice, and hunting was good.

Poo got the first one, luckily a dead one. 'Mama' jammed a mouse leg into Poo's mouth and went for more, but when she returned Poo hadn't eaten it yet. Oh, well. She certainly would when she woke up! Mama had raised a dozen clutches in her day and knew what to do with the young ones: Feed them! Stay ahead of the demand (if possible)! She stuffed the tail of the second mouse into Airy's mouth and went for more.

When she returned with a third mouse she frowned at the two slowpoke eaters but went ahead and shoved the new one nose-first in Lolly's yap, who was snoring like the others with her mouth wide open. That's what Mama was looking for: *Open mouths!* Yes, Mama was rounding back into practice quickly. Away she went again, but Lolly's mouse happened to be still alive and squiggly. Lolly awoke, locked mouth-to-mouth with the thing. She jerked away and shrieked. That awoke the others also. They promptly shoved all the mice out the door to the ground far below, just as "Mama' approached.

Please sympathize with the Moms of the world who must endure this behavior. There are different ways to deal with it, but Mama Owl's method was to take the 'fledglings' down to pick up the food again while she watched. So they did this, and you would too if you lived in a nest with a huge hunting owl twenty times your size. But Mama was forgiving when she had got them back in the nest with their food in front of them.

"Eat!" she ordered. "Makes strong talons! Sharp beaks!" With that she left, and so did the pixies a minute later, but Mama would probably understand. There comes a time when all babies must leave the nest and make their way in the world, find their own mice! She had seen it before.

But the pixies went directly to the spring to wash their mouths out. When all the gargling was finished they went on to the magic pool and were rudely treated to a rerun of their mouse-nibbling adventure. Wouldn't you know, that's what was showing when Atel found them.

"My goodness!", she commented. "You certainly aren't finicky eaters anymore, are you? And Lolly, surely you'll find your handsome princes someday! That will be soon enough. You don't have to practice kissing rodents".

The moon clouded over, and the reflection faded out, but it wouldn't be forgotten. Poor Lolly! Of such things, reputations are made.

Atel took them to the Crow's Roost, to their empty branch near Gronk. The Top Crow gave them a sleepy eye and told them to "Go for it". The rest of the night was peaceful.

Ishi reemerged later armed with an energized lamp and made her slow trek to the trolls. The sky was lightly overcast by now. Would the clouds thicken? Her hunch was 'yes', but with that came a new worry. Would the pixies return tomorrow for an encore performance? She wished them the very best of health until morning. If any odd misfortune befell the little darlings overnight she would never forgive herself. She wanted to administer that personally! Then she smelled *hop-goblin*, and the hair stood up behind her neck.

There he was - across the ravine watching her, the nasty thing! And if he was there, where was Irrada? Ishi was well aware of the coyote and his Mistress. She moved closer to the Juggler with her lamp, ready to awaken him if she had to. He would protect her! She couldn't protect herself out here. But now the dratted hop-goblin came trotting in her direction! She readied the lamp as he approached.

"Hold it right there, Mongrel", she ordered, "or I'll sic my boys on you!" The coyote stopped in his tracks, amazed.

"Can you do that?" he asked.

"Yes! Don't come any closer."

"Wow! *Do it!* These are my pals!"

Chance encounters are so pleasant when folks discover common interests. It can lead to a beautiful relationship if there isn't too much treachery in their hearts. That would shake out eventually for these two. But now, as they chatted, they each saw advantages.

Ishi was thrilled with the coyote's story. Everyone cheers when a wicked witch is dead. And to top it, the hop-goblin hated fairy folk as much as she did. He might be useful!

As for the coyote, he was eager to get back on the gravy train. Ishi promised him lots of scraps when the 'boys' were themselves again. She never meant a word of it, but he had enough dog in him to trust his betters. Ishi was the Troll- Mother, he figured, and the trolls were his pals. The deal smelled okay.

With the coyote tamed, Ishi returned her worries to the weather which was still uncertain. But as dawn approached the clouds thickened nicely and she put her plan into motion.

She awoke the Juggler first, holding the lamp to his eyes. He was cool-headed and some sense would be needed when she awakened the others. Trolls often 'come out of it' a little wacky in the attic.

"Good morning, *Sunshine*", she greeted him. "Have a nice nap?"

The Juggler gathered his wits quickly. "Thanks, Mum", he said, and began to lower his arms but Ishi stopped him.

"Wait! Remember exactly how you're standing there, reaching out with your arm! You'll need to fake that later when the pixies show up. Do you remember the pixies?" The Juggler scowled.

"Oh yeah, like it was yesterday! Was it?"

"No. You've missed a few meals. But listen carefully! You'll have a chance to catch the pixies again this morning - *if* they think you're still stoned. If you move, or look different in any way, this won't work".

"I don't get it".

"You don't have to, yet. Just listen! I'm going to wake up the others too, but first I want you to take a good look at them. Remember how they are right *now*, so you can coach them on it later. You gotta look natural when the time comes".

"How long might that be?"

"Not long. Have some self-control".

The Juggler groaned. "I'm stiff and thirsty, Mum! I'd give a lot for a beer right now!"

"Well, forget that. The beer got tipped over and your money's been stolen too. Probably a hummingbird behind the mischief".

As if the Juggler needed another reason to dislike Atel! The gold really was his life's savings. He cursed the 'bird', but Mum had no sympathy.

"Forget her too! Get even with *her* through the *pixies*".

"Fine and dandy. But I'm gonna stretch whether you like it or not! And why wake up Red? Leave him out of it".

"Can't. I need all three of you or the plan won't work. Any other questions?"

"Our eyes, Mum. They'll see our eyes shining. Pixies ain't stupid".

"It'll be daytime. They won't notice.".

The Juggler raised an eyebrow at that, but he knew weather as well as Ishi. The morning would be cloudy. Which still left plenty of other problems, beginning with the young troll.

Laddie woke up wild-eyed and wouldn't listen to anyone. He tramped about the campsite kicking dirt, and then kicked Red in the rump. That hurt and slowed him down, but the Juggler finally had to get in his face and explain a few things.

Red came out of it *mean*. In other words, perfectly normal. He refused to pay attention out of cussedness. When Ishi threatened him again with her finger he finally listened, but time was wasting. The sun wouldn't show today maybe, but dawn was growing behind the clouds. Morning wasn't far off. The pixies could turn up before long and the trolls were nowhere near ready. Ishi looked over her bumbling 'actors' and lowered their odds of pulling it off. Then it got worse.

"I'm thirsty!" declared Red and stomped off to the spring for water. If that wasn't enough, the others followed him. Ishi lowered their odds to about zero and plopped down in frustration.

◆◆◆

Water was surely on their minds, lots of it. Rocks dry out in the sun and their bodies were parched. But superstition drew them more. Like goblins or witches, they have no religion and feel the lack of – *something* - so they're drawn to paganism. And why not? A first-class soothsayer lived nearby.

Okay, let's be honest. Most of the time the Water Witch predicted the *past*. Anyone can do that. It was when she showed things yet to come that she attracted followers. The trolls were willing to sit through a lot of re-runs to get one little peek into the future, and tonight was significant. Reawakening from the stone was a big deal, like a turning point in their lives. The Water Witch must have sensed it. She showed them a glimpse of the past that worked for the future too, as she often did to tease *Unnaturals*. Ha! It was true forward or backward. Let them figure it out!

The trolls saw themselves in their stoned positions waiting in ambush for the pixies, exactly as Mum wanted them - and here come the pixies! They grinned in anticipation, watching. Mum had promised that they would get 'em! But then the picture changed. Now the pixies were perched on their noses, mooning them! They took turns on all three trolls and flew away laughing! What the.....!!!

Of course the trolls didn't know it, but the last scene had been repeated many times while they were stoned. They started to kick dirt into the pool, but the Witch changed the picture. Now they saw themselves playing cards, a favorite pastime. It was a game of poker and they each had excellent hands, obviously, because they held their cards close. A fourth player was in the game, just out of the picture.

The jackpot in the middle was piled high with gold coins and something else, something very interesting: The Juggler's jug with three pixies inside.

Hey! This was more like it. Something special to look forward to! The brutes loitered about the pool, elbowing each other and trying to peek at the cards, but their reflections held them too close. Even when the pool wouldn't let them cheat they still loitered, anticipating some fun.

Then the picture went dark, and the trolls suddenly showed haste like Mum could never get out of them, wading right into the pool like it was a bathtub, splashing water all over the place and slurping it up between splashes. We can guess what the Water Witch thought about that, and Mum wasn't any happier when they returned dripping wet.

Wet trolls on a dry morning? That would certainly tip off any visitors, but Ishi didn't bother to say anything. There was a light breeze and that would gradually help. And now look! The boys were actually trying to get back into their old positions even as she watched. She made up her mind to be proud of them!

They needed coaching, especially the young troll, but when Mum was finally satisfied of their positions they had no problem holding them. Their bodies remembered two weeks of it and locked in. As for Ishi, physical exertion took its toll as always. She needed a break. The beer-soaked rock was still handy, so she folded herself into it and slept. Too deeply! She began to snore.

Something needed to be done about that. The Juggler came out of his stance, gently picked up the rock, and carried it over near the pines where he scooped out a hole several feet deep and buried it, putting the sod back on top. Sorry about that, Mum. But he had a different plan, and Mum wasn't in it. He took up position again and waited.

As it happened, the breeze picked up and dried the trolls off nicely. Around mid-morning the pixies showed up, eager to do their chores. They immediately alighted on the ugly noses and mooned the ugly faces behind them. It was utterly ridiculous, and ridiculously easy for the trolls to grab them.

CHAPTER

8

THE JACKPOT

Roars of triumph split the air. At the distant end of the hill the hummingbird heard and came to investigate. Over by the pines, under three feet of dirt, Ishi awoke to the noise and was shocked to open one eye and get dirt in it. She wouldn't be coming to investigate. A third interested party watched from the knoll across the ravine. The coyote saw his pals awake and happy. He circled closer to the camp. Surely they would toss him something to eat! But he didn't know Red, the newcomer. Red was nobody's pal. When the hop-goblin approached too closely, Red kicked and sent him sprawling.

As for the pixies themselves, they shrieked for help while they could, but only until the Juggler popped them (Yes, again.) into his jug and jammed in the cork. At least the jug was empty this time, but that's all the hope Atel saw when she arrived moments later.

"What are you going to do to them this time?" she demanded.

She was totally ignored. The trolls actually joined hands – even Red - and danced in a circle around the cold campfire, laughing like three-year olds. Well, one of them was three years old and the mood was infectious. Revenge was sweet, and nothing was going to screw it up this time!

"I guess this was your Mum's Idea?" suggested Atel finally. "Stoned trolls don't wake up like geniuses".

That got a reply. The Juggler jerked a thumb toward the pines. "She's right over there. Go ask her!"

Atel went and came back none the wiser. The Juggler enjoyed his little joke immensely.

"Huh? Nothing clever to say? I'm not surprised. Hummingbirds ain't known to be geniuses. Not enough room in their itty-bitty heads".

He laughed. They all just roared, laughing. This time it would be different! No slip-ups! There was no quarreling at all among the trolls now. The whole gang were so polite to each other it was disgusting. But pretty soon they got down to business and the first order of business was to play it safe and haul the pixies off to the sinkhole - into the Underground - just in case the clouds should unexpectedly break up during the day. They would return in the evening to gamble for high stakes and finish the celebration. Atel followed and the Juggler tossed back one last wisecrack as he entered the cave.

"We're playing cards tonight", he called over his shoulder. "Bring some money and we'll deal you in!"

Atel thought about that. *Playing cards tonight? Deal her in?* There was a ring of truth to it. That would be the Juggler itching to know what had become of his money. The game would be poker, naturally. That's what they liked. The Juggler had taught Laddie the game as part of his education, so even the three-year old knew most of the finer points. They played for 'funsies' because the Juggler had long ago won Laddie's few coins away from him. But tonight Red would be in the game so it would be more serious. What stakes might they play for? That was easy: The pixies, naturally.

Atel returned to the campsite looking for more pieces to the puzzle. The game would be played here, she was sure. Probably right on the ground near the fire. The big trolls were surprisingly limber and often sat cross-legged while they played. But what about Ishi? She would be a wild card if she turned up. Atel found herself hoping the Juggler could figure a way to deal Mum out.

Which brought her back to herself being dealt *in*. A hummingbird can't handle cards so she would need an assistant, but she did have a lot of money if she could locate the *trustees*. She laughed at the little joke. Trustees was quite a stretch. But as the train of thought chugged down the tracks in her mind she recited an old saw: 'Grin and bear it, ask a ferret'. Okay, she would! The last time she asked for their help the jokers had been useful, actually showing a serious side she wasn't aware of. Might they again?

They were roamers. She hadn't seen them since they made off with the troll's purse at her request, never even learned where they stashed it. Hopefully, the money was somewhere nearby. But where could the ferrets be?

She knew the burrows they favored this time of year, mostly borrowed ones. They dug their own to raise their litters but abandoned them soon after. By autumn they didn't call anyplace home and in the early mornings were usually out and about, probably hunting in a rabbit warren somewhere. Unfortunately, if their hunt was successful they would have breakfast and take a siesta right there in the warren through the middle of the day. Then she would get just one last chance to find them in the evening. Okay, so be it. She had other work in the meantime. She must arrange for someone to hold the cards and play for her. There was only one possibility.

Hop-goblins are also generally nocturnal, but he was awake when she found him. He bared his teeth in greeting.

"Good hunting!" she said. "I hope you were successful?" Maybe he had found some small prey, maybe not. He looked gaunt as ever.

"Beat it!" growled the coyote. Atel didn't leave.

"I noticed the trolls were a little rough last night. I can help you get close to the fire".

The coyote laughed at that and laid down by a log. It made a good windbreak on a cool morning. His empty stomach didn't keep him warm.

"Your pals are going to play cards tonight. You've seen that before. The Juggler wants me to play with them".
The coyote laughed louder.
"I want you to play my cards. I can't hold them myself, naturally. Just do your best and we'll split the winnings".
The creature sat up on his rear and studied her. He knew poker. He had watched more than a few games and the human part of him caught on right away. But this smelled suspicious.
"What are the stakes?"
"Pixies and gold coins. They have the pixies again and I have their money. If we win you get the gold. Keep it and be rich or trade it for bones with meat on them!"
The coyote licked his lips. It seemed like a sure thing, offering several ways to get back into the troll's good graces.
"Deal?" asked Atel.
Why not? If nothing else there would be a warm fire. "Deal, but I'll wait outside the firelight until it's safe, know what I mean?"

That didn't need explanation. It was a start. Atel flew off in search of the ferrets.

Just inside the sinkhole cave there were other growling bellies. The trolls had missed a lot of meals and felt the lack of them. Now they eyed the little pixies in the jug and fancied eating them to calm the hunger pangs. Laddie was outspoken about it. The pixies could hear every word.

"Why not? We're gonna eat 'em anyway! Why not now?"

"Because the little boss stole our gold", answered the Juggler patiently. "We'll use the pixies for chips and have a poker game. She'll bring the money to get into the game, hoping to win the pixies".

"How? She can't play. She's too small!"

"Don't worry. She'll figure a way".

"You got rocks in yer brain!" scoffed Red, taking Laddie's side. "You ain't woke yet!"

"She stole your purse! Don't you want your money back?"

"No need to gamble for it! We can take the pixies down right now for Gorrah's reward! It's way more than I had in my purse".

"Don't start that again. You know I ain't going down."

"Then gimme my share. I'm going down. I want the redhead, the one that bit me. I wanna turn her in!"

The Juggler shook the pixies out and handed Poo over. Red grabbed her very carefully, but Poo didn't try to bite him this time. She just smiled sweetly as he tramped off.

"Have fun!" called Airy. "Moon old Gorrah for us again!"

"I will!" laughed Poo. "He'll *triple* the reward after this one!"

Red stopped in his tracks and looked at her, then back at the other pixies. The Juggler dangled Airy and Poo in front of his nose.

"What have you scamps been up to since we saw you last?"

That would be a long story, but just their favorite part was enough to alter the trolls' plans. The bounty had surely jumped after their recent audition, probably by a lot. And who knew? Maybe more yet could be negotiated! Red beamed. Even the Juggler looked interested. Red handed Poo back.

"Stuff her back in the jug", he grinned. "I'm gonna see what the reward is first".

"Bring back some beer!" hollered the young troll. "We need beer for the party!"

He left, and the Juggler regarded the pixies almost with respect. "You do get into - and out of - a lot of trouble, don't you?"

"We're charmed", said Airy. "I have a good luck charm".

"What? Something you carry with you?"

"Yes! Set me on your nose and I'll show you".

By late morning Atel decided the ferrets must have settled in somewhere for the day and took her own lunch break. The last flowers of summer were dried up now, but honey still dripped from the bee tree if wind wiggled the tree enough. It was her last source of food, but a good one.

As afternoon wore on she reviewed all the places she had scouted, all the logical hunting spots and trails, and concluded she had been thinking too sensibly. Ferrets do have some of that in them, but it's not their most famous trait. More often, if one knew where a bit of mischief might be found they probably weren't far away. She thought of an abandoned homestead and a salvage yard, but both were quite a distance off. The local dump was closer. That's where she found them, but a heart-wrenching scene awaited her.

Jill stood on her haunches wailing above the prostrate body of her mate, Hob, who had suffered horrible injuries. He was a bloody mess, and it was some time before Jill even spoke coherently.

"One minute he was fine", she finally sobbed. "And the next minute he was like this!"

"I'm so sorry! What happened?"

"Oh, it doesn't matter now. Sob! He's gone".

"I truly am sorry! He was...such a dear".

This was only partly true, but the situation demanded something polite and consoling. This was a terrible blow to her own plans as well, but that must wait. She counted the ferrets as friends in spite of...well, one must let bygones be bygones.

"Oh, he was! He *was* a dear!" wailed Jill. "His last words were, *'Mind the children, Dearest'*. It was just delirium because the children are all grown up and gone, but it was a nice thing to say, wasn't it?" Atel nodded, wishing she could do more. Jill smiled sweetly and went on.

"And then he said, *'Darling, I apologize for the times we argued. I was wrong, and I don't want to take that to my* grave', and then he said---"

"---But you said his *last words* were..."

"Yes, yes. But you know Old Hob! He couldn't stop talking even *after* his last words. So then he said, *'I wish I hadn't died so fat, and now you'll remember me like* this". Here she gave him a critical dig in the ribs which caused a sharp intake of air.

Atel gasped as well. "Listen!" she said. "Did you hear? I don't think he's gone completely! Let me talk to him".

"Oh, go ahead. But it's probably just gas. He was so full of that, you know! Hardly safe to be near him".

Hob's belly was quivering now, and he appeared to be trying to move his lips. Atel hovered close.

"Is there anything we could bring that might comfort you?" she asked. "Water, maybe? Or soft grass?"

Hob struggled mightily to speak but only managed a feeble whisper with his last breath. Atel moved a little closer to catch the words:

"You could bring more ketchup. I love that!"

Both ferrets went into great rolling, hopping belly laughs, bumping into cans and bottles and causing a racket. They had pulled off their little joke. When they calmed down Hob began licking ketchup off himself, which is what he'd been doing when they'd heard Atel calling for them and went into their act. The plastic ketchup jug was lying nearby that Jill had pounced on, squirting the contents all over her mate. So that's ferrets for you if you want a definition. Atel felt silly, embarrassed, and more than a little irritated.

"Forget I even came!" she said. "I'll ask the raccoons to help!" She spun around and left.

"What for?" Hob shouted after her. "Raccoons are nothing but trouble!"

"That's perfect!" Atel called back as she zipped out of sight. "I'm in trouble already!"

She went off quite some distance in a huff and finally perched on a barbed wire fence to let her temper cool down and the ferrets catch up, as she knew they would. Sure enough, as evening fell they came bounding through the tall grass in their humpitty gait, one behind the other, as if they were a two-humped animal. Atel sat quite still, but the ferrets came right up to her in the twilight.

"We decided to help", said Jill. "You mustn't trust raccoons. What's the deal?"

"I'm going to play cards with the trolls. I'll be needing the money".

Down in Gorrah's Court at that moment, Red was bragging, "You want pixies, eh? I've got three of them!"

The King of Trolls regarded him like a cat might watch a mouse. "Yeah? Where?"

"I ain't sayin'. That would be tellin'".

Gorrah laughed. "You want the reward, eh? There it is! It's been setting there forever, but nobody brings me a pixie. I think you're lying anyway".

He gestured to a small stack of gold coins, seven or eight of them. Red's jaw fell in disappointment.

"That's *it?* I thought it was much more!"

"You're a *Biter*", growled Gorrah. "You oughta know we're not made out of money down here!"

"But I'm talkin' *THREE* of 'em, Yer Highness".

"Okay, I'll double it".

Another troll might have given in at that point, but Red had nerve. Not for nothing had they made him a tax collector! He waived away the offer.

"My pixies claim they were right here smarting off to you just the other day, and Mum was a witness", he said with a little grin. As a shakedown bully he couldn't quite hide the grin. "THAT'S the three pixies I'm talkin' about".

Gorrah hauled himself up off his throne and glared down at Red, who was kneeling as required of all petitioners, and no longer grinning. The Treasurer was summoned and wheeled in a big chest heaped with treasure. He added a few coins to the reward at the Boss's direction and divided everything into three smaller stacks. Gorrah leaned forward threateningly but Red barely noticed. He stared at the paltry little stacks and his Biter instincts seized him. His mouth flapped out of habit.

"That's nothing! I'm gonna see what Mum will pay!"

Gorrah broke right through the partition, got Red by the neck and shook him like a rat, which was startling. Red was nearly as huge.

"I WANT 'EM! AND YOU BETTER BRING 'EM*!*"

It was near evening when Red returned from his failed errand in a very foul mood, but at least with a small keg of beer. The beer would soon be missed down below. The Juggler wisely didn't ask a lot of questions, but Laddie did, and it almost started a brawl.

"We're gonna eat 'em after all!" barked Red. "The reward ain't much, so don't ask!" He suspected now it would amount to nothing, after tax. Worse yet, he was out of a job. No way was he going down there again.

"No big deal", said the Juggler, guessing most of it. He uncorked the jug and chuckled at the pixies. "Turns out you're worthless except for snacks! Just thought you'd like to know".

"So are you", replied Poo. "Except for the birds to poop on".

Was that wise? Nope. He shook the jug until the prisoners quieted down.

Atel returned to the troll's camp with the ferrets and laid out the plan. It wasn't complicated if the rules of poker were followed. The purse and loose coins had been stashed in a hollow tree around the hill and were still there, so there should be no problem except distance. The ferrets excused themselves to go hunting and Atel went to the Crow's Roost, hoping someone was awake enough to give a forecast.

Nobody was. It had been a long day for the crows. A Great Owl had been discovered roosting in a neighboring wood and the crows had harassed the owl until nightfall. It was great fun, but very tiring. Now the roles would be reversed until morning and some unlucky crow would have to pay for it. Yes, as the world turns there is always payback. Atel went up and perched on the usual branch. Gronk was sound asleep, but she asked anyway.

"Cloudy tonight, nicer tomorrow", he intoned without even opening his eyes. Then he turned in his sleep and looked straight at her, so she tried again.

"Sunny at sunrise?"

"Yeah, sure. Maybe". That was all. He turned away.

So it's true what they say, thought Atel as she left. Crows can do it even in their sleep. But she wouldn't pay anything for it. She went to her old listening post to begin what would be a long wait.

Across the ravine the hop-goblin waited for the crescent moon to rise behind the clouds. Maybe it would shine through enough to howl at, and he could forget his growling stomach. Arrrgh, he was hungry!

It was well after midnight when troll racket arose in the distance: Arguing noises, cursing, and bumping into things. Obviously, she would have drunken trolls to deal with. That wasn't always bad. Drunken trolls were more predictable. Of course they were more violent too.

The gang had caught three turkey toms which the Juggler now proceeded to clean and pluck while the young troll fetched wood for a fire. Red's chores were limited to sitting down on the stump and guarding his keg of beer. Atel decided to wait where she was. Then the hop-goblin smelled turkey offal and tried to sneak in and snatch the garbage. Red heaved himself up and kicked the creature away. The Juggler didn't like that.

"Hey! Leave him alone! You ain't gonna eat that stuff".

"Can't stand hop-goblins! They *stink*".

"Ahh, loosen up! Grab another mug. We're gonna have fun tonight!"

Red wasn't in a fun mood just yet, but he did have a refill. The beer was extra-good, brewed especially for Gorrah and his crowd down at Court.

They had no matches so it would be flint and tinder to start a fire and Red was called upon to fetch dry grass. The hardest part was lifting his great rear off the stump, which he managed with a grunt; and after he gathered some grass he plopped right back down again, feeling he had now contributed more than his share. After all, it would be a lousy party if he hadn't swiped the keg! He helped himself to yet another mug and made sure the hop-goblin stayed well back.

When the turkeys were roasting on the spit and everyone's interest had refocused on the keg, Atel went to say hello and have a closer look at the pixies in their jug. They appeared very listless.

"I hope you give them a little air from time to time", she scolded. "I remember you saying, 'they're best when they're lively'".

"Don't worry, they're fine", explained the Juggler. "Just a little woozy from knocking around".

"I see. So - what's your schedule for the evening?"

"From here I see a couple hours of drinking straight ahead".

"And then?"

"Supper! You're invited, little boss. We're planning a real social evening".

"I think I'll take a nap".

"Don't oversleep! We're playin' poker after supper. Five-card draw. D'you know the game?"

"Certainly. But I don't normally play, you understand? I can't hold the cards".

"Too bad. We would've given you a chance to win back your brats".

"In that case, I'll ask the hop-goblin to play for me. Do you mind?"

That caught the trolls by surprise. The creature grinned and took a step forward. Red threw a chunk of firewood at him. Laddie kicked Red in the shins for that and the fight was on, until Red realized he was one against two.

"Let's not have an accident!" he protested. "There's no more beer if we spill the keg!"

"It's settled then", ruled the Juggler. "The hop-goblin plays for the bird. Don't oversleep, bird, or you'll miss the game!"

"Not likely around here. But I'm warning you again to let the pixies have some fresh air". It was obvious they needed it.

The Juggler turned a big thumb down. "Nah! We got a new policy. If the cork never comes out, the pixies can't either".

Only the Almighty could change a mind like that, thought Atel, and they'll never meet. She returned to her listening post and heard discouraging noises in the pines. The ferrets were back but Hob wasn't feeling well. She went to see what that was about, with plenty of doubts.

It was a 'tummy-ache' now. Yeah, sure. And there was Jill standing over him again, all concerned. At least she wasn't wailing this time.

"Gas", Jill explained. "Constipation too. He's had trouble recently. Something he ate, I guess". Then she fell to squeaking softly, and that gave Atel misgivings. It was exactly the behavior one would expect if she was telling the truth.

"No matter! I can fetch the coins myself", pledged Jill. "I'll make extra trips. Is that all right? I just can't leave him alone like this for too long".

"What next?" muttered Atel as she returned to her post. Some *good* news, maybe? Something actually going according to plan?

But no. When the turkeys were nicely browned and served up, the hop-goblin managed to sneak a bite out of Red's bird before he did. Red wouldn't stand for it unless the Juggler swapped birds, which wasn't simple either because he'd already had a bite out of his. Then the question of salt came up. There wasn't any. No pepper either. Then it was something else. Atel began to worry about dawn. She wanted the gang to be seriously into gambling by then. But of course the trolls were watching the sky too. Finally the turkeys were eaten, the beer was all drunk, and their fingers licked off properly. A deck of cards came out and the players sat down: Red on his stump and the others cross-legged on the ground. Atel and the hop-goblin took the place across from Red and the Juggler dealt out five cards apiece. The hop-goblin picked up three deuces and a pair of aces, a Full House on the deal! Outstanding! But he held them face-out so the trolls could see them.

"Right! Now we ante", announced the Juggler. He set his jug in the middle. "That's one pixie apiece for us", he told Atel. "Do you have a pixie to ante? No? Then you'll have to buy in". He turned to Red. "What was the going reward for a pixie?"

"Ten gold dollars", lied Red.

"Show us the money", said the Juggler with a smile.

Atel did the arithmetic. The price could be managed, but there were other considerations. How many coins could Jill carry in her mouth? If not ten, would the trolls allow a delayed shuttle service? She excused herself and went to the ferrets, only to find things had gotten worse with them.

Hob was a mess, rolling back and forth in the grass. It was becoming a serious concern. But at least Jill wasn't worried about ten coins.

"That's a mouthful, but I can do it", she insisted, "because *I* can keep my mouth *shut*...." (Here she glanced critically at her mate in spite of his misery) "... which is more than *some* ferrets could ever do!"

"I could if I had to!" Hob groaned. But it only proved her point.

Back at the game, Atel said nothing - didn't even answer questions - until Jill came and spit ten gold coins into the pot. Now there would be a betting round and the hummingbird would go first, being to the left of the dealer. She signaled Jill who went for more coins.

"The bet is ten dollars", announced Atel when Jill returned. Would anyone call? They could see her Full House, which ought to scare them out in an honest game.

They all called. They matched the bet using small sticks and pebbles for IOU's. Atel's protests were met with snickers and guffaws.

"We don't have handy cash", replied the Juggler. "But don't worry. Trolls always pay their gambling debts".

This is technically true. They do pay up between themselves. But tonight they intended to recover their money by kicking Atel out of the game when she couldn't match the last raise. Then they would have a show-of-hands for the pixies.

The game resumed. Next would be the 'draw' where players can throw away some poor cards, hoping to draw better ones. Atel was first again.

"Stand pat", she told the hop-goblin. But he seemed not to hear and discarded everything except one deuce. The trolls roared with laughter. The hop-goblin howled. Atel protested. The game adjourned for a minute while the Juggler had a word with the hop-goblin. After due consideration he allowed Atel to keep her three deuces and throw just the aces.

"After all", he explained generously, "your helper is just learning the game".

Atel still had to draw, and the hop-goblin picked up the last deuce, making *4-of-a-kind* - even better than the Full House! He tried to throw the deuce away again before anyone saw it, but Red swatted his fingers so Atel ended up with it. The hop-goblin showed the four deuces to everyone.

The young troll was next. He had just a king for a high card, nothing else, and couldn't decide how many cards to throw so he called for a potty break. He wandered off supposedly on his errand but went instead to the Water Witch's Pool hoping for a peek at everyone's cards.

She did show him Red's hand, but not the Juggler's. Red held four spades - queen high. Laddie frowned. His lone king was better for now, but if Red drew another spade he was sunk. He decided to throw everything except the king and hope for the best. He hurried back to the game just in time to see Red taking leave for his own potty break.

Of course Red had the same idea, and the Water Witch helpfully gave him a peek at the Juggler's cards. Red smiled. The Juggler had three aces, but if he got his spade on the draw the Juggler could *eat* those aces! *He* would eat the *pixies!* Red felt pretty good about the odds. He hung around an extra minute trying to get a look at Laddie's cards, but the Witch didn't allow it.

The Juggler went next, and the Witch helped him cheat too. He was allowed to see Laddie's cards, but not Red's. Laddie's lone king didn't worry him, but what did Red have? He walked around the pool trying to get a peek until the poker scene suddenly winked out and he saw his own reflection, stone-cold, with a crow perched on his head. He splashed water angrily to get rid of it. Blasted pool! He could imagine the disgusting things that must have happened, he didn't need to see them!

Atel watched and waited politely. The sky was thickly overcast all the way to the eastern horizon with sunrise less than an hour off - if it would occur at all. That was the real question. The 'potty breaks' were no mystery. They meant mostly that the gang was looking beyond her to a 3-handed 'showdown' when she ran out of cash. Red and the Juggler knew when that would be as well as she did. It was their money, and they could count as well as she could.

The Juggler returned and play resumed. Laddie threw four cards and picked up two more kings, making *3-of-a-kind!* Big, big improvement! He tried to keep a straight face but that's not easy for a three-year old.

Red discarded just one and got his spade. The *ace*, no less. An *ace-high flush!* Should easily be the winner. He leaned forward for a better look into the jug. The brats were quiet. Well, he would stir 'em up in a few minutes! He imagined them squirming, trying not to be swallowed. He licked his lips.

The Juggler threw two cards and drew a pair of jacks: *Full House!* Well! Wasn't *that* sweet? A new plan came to mind: When they had busted the bird, he would make a side bet with Red for all the money! Red would go for it. He had a decent hand, the way he was acting.

"Now the real betting starts!" he announced. "What does the little boss bid?"

"Ten dollars", she answered without delay, and signaled Jill, who went for the money.

"I hope you have a lot of it out there", chuckled the Juggler. "You might need all of it".

"Shouldn't", said Atel. "You can see I have four deuces".

"Yeah, but there's no limit on raises".

"Big game, huh? Maybe I'll have to put up an IOU".

The Juggler shook his head. "Nope. Trolls only trust each other for IOU's. You'll have to pay cash".

"Your game, your rules. Until your Mum shows up, anyway".

"Turns out, Mum's not coming tonight. So there won't be any interruptions".

Jill returned with the coins and spit them in with the others. Laddie called and tossed in some gravel for IOU's. So did Red, without even pretending to count. The Juggler called and raised the bid ten dollars. Atel signaled Jill and calculated mentally. At this pace she would go broke in ten minutes. Out the corner of her eye she could see no sign yet of any dawn. But nature was about to slow things down in a different way.

First Laddie, and then by turns all three trolls had to take potty breaks again, this time for real. None of them had actually tended to business earlier and all that beer was beginning to demand

222

attention. It was during this intermission that a faint glimmer appeared in the east. The clouds still covered it well, but they were drifting west. Good!

Maybe the trolls noticed it too, or maybe they just felt better when everyone sat down again, but they were eager to speed up the game. The Juggler barked at Atel.

"Your turn, little boss! I raised it ten dollars".

"I call, but you'll have to give me a little time again". She signaled Jill. At least there was no argument. She would be given the necessary time. But when Jill brought the coins, Laddie and Red both called immediately, and the Juggler raised the bet another ten dollars.

By her calculations there were thirty coins left in the purse and no change yet in the eastern sky. She could only play along. She called and Jill fetched what was needed. Laddie and Red quickly called, and the Juggler raised the bid by twenty dollars with a wink at Red. He might as well have laughed out loud. That would exactly wipe out Atel's bankroll. She had counted it twice before sending it off with the ferrets and was quite sure of the amount. So were Red and the Juggler. They didn't try to hide their glee.

"Call", she said. "But you'll have to allow extra time for extra coins".

"Sure. You haven't spent any, then?"

"No. You'll still have to pay all those taxes".

The Juggler laughed. "That's been forgotten. Red has retired from the job. We're pals now".

"How nice. Then he'll be around to feed the hop-goblin".

They growled at each other, those two. The sounds weren't all that different.

"He likes turkey right off the spit", reminded Atel. She laughed at Red.

A fight was about to break out but at that moment Jill returned.

Hob was with her this time, clearly in anguish but determined to help. Jill spit out ten coins, and Hob nine. That put a smile on the Juggler's face, but Hob sprawled in misery, rolling back and forth near the jackpot.

"End of the game for *you*, little boss!" ruled the Juggler. "If you don't have the money, you're out!"

He turned to Red to offer a side bet but Hob suddenly blurted, "It feels better now, Dearest!"

He laid on his back and everyone watched a bloated hump work downward through his tummy. Jill backed away. The others didn't know any better. The bloat reached bottom and a gold coin suddenly exploded out and cracked the jug, followed by pent-up gasses that overwhelmed the campsite.

"I'm back in the game!" shouted Atel.

The ferrets launched into their wild weasel war dance, leaping and banging into everything. Laddie and the Juggler stood up and backed away. Red grabbed up his big club.

During this commotion, the clouds shifted a little more westward, allowing a sliver of blue sky above the eastern horizon. The sun peeked through, bathing the hill and all the players. The game ended and the trolls lost, by chance ending up in exactly the same poses as before.

There were winners too, and one who thought he was. That would be the hop-goblin who now imagined himself boss of the camp. The idea of taking on crazy ferrets didn't appeal to him but eating helpless pixies did. What did they taste like? It must be sensational the way the big trolls acted! He broke apart the cracked jug and reached in with both hands.

That's when the ferrets sunk their teeth into his haunches and a hot beam of light from Atel's mirror found a tender spot under his tail. The creature reverted to the coyote and ran. But he would be back.

The pixies spilled out onto the ground where the air was beginning to clear, already showing signs of recovery - or maybe that was just from Hob and Jill licking their faces. But recover they did, in time to wave at the departing ferrets.

They were very curious about the poker game and when they could fly again Atel showed them the poker hands, which the stone trolls still held.

"The Juggler would have won with a Full House", she explained.

"And *we* were the jackpot?" asked Airy. The pixies were perching on the trolls again.

"Half of it. He also wanted the money".

"Money is nothing but trouble".

"Some might say that of pixies, too".

"Th'might", laughed Airy, hopping down to the Juggler's nose. "But does it count if th'can't talk?"

THE END